Praise for *The Hatmaker's Heart*

"Fans of Carla Stewart's work won't be disappointed with this Jazz Age tale. With lush sensory details, Stewart brings us deep into this historical setting...Readers will savor the sweet escape."
—Julie Cantrell, *New York Times* bestselling author of *When Mountains Move*

"Carla Stewart captures this time period with amazing accuracy... When choosing 'never-to-be-missed' writers, put Carla Stewart at the top of your list."
—Kim Vogel Sawyer, bestselling author of *What Once Was Lost*

"Deep and delightful! Carla Stewart's beautiful language, intriguing characters, and thought-provoking story are treats to savor. I loved this book!"
—Sarah Sundin, award-winning author of *On Distant Shores*

"Set amidst the glamour of 1920s fashion, Carla Stewart has woven together a classy and sweet tale of love and new beginnings. *The Hatmaker's Heart* is a standout of its kind."
—Joanne Bischof, award-winning author of The Cadence of Grace series

"Fans of the Jazz Age will cheer Nell's journey and treasure this richly rendered taste of the Roaring Twenties."
—Lisa Wingate, national bestselling author of *The Prayer Box*

"*The Hatmaker's Heart* contains love, betrayal, and family secrets—all the elements that delight fans of *Downton Abbey*."
—Kellie Coates Gilbert, author of *Mother of Pearl*

"Bestselling author Carla Stewart employs exquisite detail and charming characters…I cannot wait to read the next one she has in store!"

—Jolina Petersheim, bestselling author of *The Outcast*

"I was swept away by the story…readers will love this wonderful new novel from this very gifted author!"

—Carrie Turansky, author of *The Governess of Highland Hall*

"*The Hatmaker's Heart* draws you back in time and will make you want to bob your hair and don a cloche hat."

—Lynne Gentry, author of The Carthage Chronicles series

"A fascinating journey into the world of couture fashion in the 1920s!"

—Anne Mateer, author of *A Home for My Heart*

Praise for *Sweet Dreams*

"*Sweet Dreams* is an inspiring novel and one that is heartfelt. Readers are sure to savor every page of this wonderful story."

—Michael Morris, author of *A Place Called Wiregrass*

"Carla Stewart is masterful at creating characters you care about— and places that seem so real you feel like you've gone for a visit."

—Judy Christie, author of the Green Series and *Wreath*

"Capturing the angst of the '60s in the struggles of two determined women, *Sweet Dreams* is another outstanding novel from one of the best!"

—Myra Johnson, award-winning author of *Autumn Rains* and *A Horseman's Heart*

"Like the best of Patsy Cline's music, *Sweet Dreams* is a book to be savored and enjoyed. What a funny and touching read!"
—William Torgerson, author of *Love on the Big Screen* and *Horseshoe*

Praise for *Stardust*

"An enjoyable, worthwhile read."
—*RT Book Reviews*

"*Stardust* is told with heart and skill and obvious love for her characters. A gripping storyline that is inspiring and unforgettable."
—Julie L. Cannon, bestselling author of *I'll Be Home for Christmas* and *Twang*

Praise for *Broken Wings*

"While the story is heartbreaking, there is much more to this book...Stewart skillfully entertains and engages the reader with each character's private pain and survival skills."
—*RT Book Reviews*

"With apt descriptions and artful prose, Stewart delves into the vibrant, jazzy 1940s, at the same time creating a true-to-life present."
—Christina Berry, award-winning author of *The Familiar Stranger*

"Carla Stewart writes powerful, beautiful, emotionally evocative stories that touch my heart. *Broken Wings* is no exception. I couldn't put it down."
—Susan May Warren, award-winning, bestselling author of *Nightingale*

Praise for *Chasing Lilacs*

"Coming-of-age stories are a fiction staple, but well-done ones much rarer. This emotionally acute novel is one of the rare ones."

—Publishers Weekly, starred review

"A warm, compelling tale."

—BookPage

The
HATMAKER'S HEART

Heartfelt Fiction from Carla Stewart

Sweet Dreams

Stardust

Broken Wings

Chasing Lilacs

Available from FaithWords wherever books are sold.

The
HATMAKER'S HEART

A Novel

CARLA STEWART

New York • Boston • Nashville

FaithWords

Hachette Book Group

237 Park Avenue

New York, NY 10017

www.faithwords.com

Printed in the United States of America

RRD-C

First Edition: June 2014

10 9 8 7 6 5 4 3 2 1

FaithWords is a division of Hachette Book Group, Inc.
The FaithWords name and logo are trademarks of Hachette Book Group, Inc.

The Hachette Speakers Bureau provides a wide range of authors for speaking events. To find out more, go to www.hachettespeakersbureau.com or call (866) 376-6591.

The publisher is not responsible for websites (or their content) that are not owned by the publisher.

Library of Congress Cataloging-in-Publication Data
Stewart, Carla.
  The hatmaker's heart : a novel / Carla Stewart.
    pages cm. ISBN 978-1-4555-4994-8 (pbk.) —ISBN 978-1-4555-4996-2 (ebook) 1. Hats—Fiction. 2. Millinery—Fiction. I. Title.
  PS3619.T4937H37 2014
  813'.6—dc23
                                        2013047235

For Allison,
who loves a great hat

Acknowledgments

Confession time. Writing about an era that wasn't part of my life experience scared me clear to the bone. However, like leaps of faith often are, once I'd committed to this book, people and events began to intersect my life bringing vision, passion, and an abundance of ideas. I fell in love with the Roaring Twenties—the turbulent, glorious Jazz Age! To God be all glory for seeing me through and confirming once again that all things are possible through him.

Special thanks to Sandra Bishop for her ready inspiration and steady hand on my writing career. I wouldn't dream of navigating these waters without you.

To Christina Boys for helping me find the heart of this story and for your patience when I faltered, thank you. You are phenomenal! Virginia Hensley, you're a gem! Thanks for tending so many details and answering all my questions. JuLee Brand and the cover art team: all I can say is "Wow!" *The Hatmaker's Heart* is lovely beyond words. My gratitude extends to all of the FaithWords team: Harry, Laini, Shanon, Erica, and the editorial, sales, and production staff. It truly does take a village. A special mention to Sarah Reck for sharing your creative soul and enthusiasm. We can split a pizza any time.

This journey wouldn't be possible without my fellow authors

who freely share hugs, inspiration, advice, prayers, and wisdom. Thank you Myra Johnson, Camille Eide, Courtney Walsh, Lisa Wingate, Sarah Sundin, Anne Mateer, Julie Cantrell, Jolina Petersheim, Judy Christie, Shellie Tomlinson, Kim Vogel Sawyer, Lynne Gentry, Missy Buchanan, Joanne Bischoff, Kellie Gilbert, Carrie Turansky, Julie Garmon, Marybeth Whalen, and Kathy Murphy (and all of the Pulpwood Queens!). You enrich my life beyond measure.

For Max, who indulges me with research trips and never grumbles when deadlines and promotion duties come around. You have my thanks, my love, and my heart.

Kids, grands, my dear sisters, and my dad—your support and inspiration are unwavering and so much more than I deserve. Thank you.

Dear, dear readers. My heart is filled with gratitude for you. Thank you for journeying into a different era with me in *The Hatmaker's Heart*. May your own leaps of faith bring joy, courage, and belief in the impossible. I tip my hat to you.

The
HATMAKER'S HEART

New York City

1922

CHAPTER 1

The workroom at Oscar Fields Millinery pulsed with the usual chatter, the gentle hiss of steam at periodic intervals, the ever-present adhesive and sizing fumes that hung in the air like gauze. Nell Marchwold bent over the hat block before her and first tacked the flexible buckram into quarters, then eased in each section, coaxing the foundation fabric into shape. She envisioned the magenta velvet that would be the outer covering, the satin piping that would grace the rolled brim, and a rosette stitched at a jaunty angle for a lovely touch. The question was, would Mr. Fields like it?

She bit her lip in concentration. A wave of the hand could reduce two days' work to nothing. A nod meant the design would be slipped into the work orders on the assembly table and appear on the shelves in the showroom in due time. It wasn't that her boss was fickle—he knew what he liked—but his moods were hard to predict. Two years as a junior apprentice had taught her that.

Sixth Avenue traffic sounds drifted through the open windows, a nip in the September breeze that had changed overnight. The workroom door opened, bringing a gust of air flushing through the window and Nora Remming standing there, her usual bright face the color of paste.

The workroom clatter came to a halt. No hiss from the steamer. No whispers from Nell's fellow workers. On the street below, the trolley clanged as Nora slammed the box she carried on the table. Nora's nostrils pinched as she inhaled; then her cheeks puffed as she let the breath out.

Steiger, the assembly manager, broke the silence. "Nasty mood, Mrs. Remming?"

Nora glared at him. "You don't know the half of it."

He folded reedy arms across his protruding belly and raised his snowy brows. "Care to enlighten us?"

"I've been sacked, that's what. Poof! Just like that Oscar fired me." A collective gasp went up from the workers as the color returned to Nora's cheeks, and she stormed over to the bin that held her personal belongings—shears, measuring tape, pin cushion—and tossed them in the box. "So much for being a principal designer. 'Your hats aren't selling,' he says. 'I can no longer afford to carry dead weight.' Dead weight. That's what he thinks I am because I have original ideas. Clever new styles."

Calvin Gold, Nell's fellow apprentice, sympathetically smiled. "Rats. I thought you were onto something with the crinoline and grosgrain ribbon creation you did. Can't believe those didn't sell."

Nora's lips drew into a straight line. "They might've if Oscar hadn't put them on the back shelf where the lighting is wretched. You've noticed, I'm sure, that he puts his *standard* line in the window. All he wants is the same old garb in a new color. You ask me, it's a miracle he's selling anything at all."

Nell swallowed hard. "I'm so sorry. We're going to m-miss you, Nora. What will you do now?"

"Heaven only knows. Guess I'll have to figure out some way to feed my two boys and pay the light bill." She hefted the box in her arms and marched out the door.

Steiger said, "Guess we won't be throwing her a going-away party. Easy come, easy go."

"Stuff it, Steiger," Hazel, who had a way with making hat brims do exactly what she wanted and didn't take any of Steiger's flack, shot back. "Just goes to show, none of us should get too comfortable."

Steiger smirked, but didn't answer. He wasn't worried about his job. He'd been there since the elder Mr. Fields was alive, and as the senior assemblyman, probably thought his position was free of worry. Nell didn't have that luxury.

She picked up the sketch of the cloche she intended to show Mr. Fields as a promising new design. Her stomach soured. She was anything but comfortable.

A pall fell on the room, which got heavier when Marcella opened the tin of adhesive, sending more fumes in their midst. Nell concentrated on the hat block before her and sighed in relief when one of the workers turned on the rotary fan to dispel the acrid odor.

"Miss Marchwold!" Harjo Pritchard's bark split the air.

Nell flinched, noticing the other workers jerk their heads in her direction, no doubt glad it wasn't them being singled out by Mr. Fields's secretary.

"Yes, Mr. P-Pritchard?"

"Here you are. Mr. Fields said I would find you in the studio, but I find you in here dillydallying. You keep that up and you'll be kicked to the curb before you can whistle six bars of 'Yankee Doodle Dandy.'"

"I wasn't d-dillydallying. I'm doing a p-prototype for a new d-design." Nell pointed to the block and lifted her chin "I was experimenting, not d-dillydallying. Besides, I can't wh-whistle."

"She can't talk, either." The jab came from the middle of the worktable, but when Nell whipped her head in that direction, all heads were down, not even a smirk from the guilty party.

Heat rose in Nell's neck until she was certain her own face was the same shade of magenta as the felt in the center of the table. She didn't always stammer…only when rattled. And the entire morning had thrown her off guard.

Calvin looked up from stitching a lining in a bowler and clenched his jaw, a shadow edging his brow. Nell changed her attention to the stodgy, balding Harjo Pritchard who ignored the remark about her speech. "Experiment or not, Mr. Fields wants you in his office five minutes ago."

"It will be my p-p-pleasure. Anything I should know?"

"It's not your place to question. Just make it snappy and go." He turned and stalked off, waving away the scent of adhesive as if it were a pesky fly.

Steiger scoffed. "Sounds like ol' Fields is on a tear." He eyed Nell like she might be the next one packing her things.

Calvin said, "Don't pay him any mind."

She hung her work smock on a hook and gave him a playful punch on the arm. As she sailed out of the workroom, Calvin hollered, "Break a leg, Nellie March."

Nellie March? Nell shook her head and wondered where he'd come up with that. It was a far cry from the Prunella Marchwold she was born with, her parents having no idea she'd never be able to pronounce *p*'s worth a farthing. She'd shortened it to Nell when she and her mother and baby sister had come from England, thinking it sounded more American. Nell Marchwold. That's how she was known at Oscar Fields Millinery, and she prayed today wasn't her last day here.

Mr. Fields met her at the door, his back erect as he cradled his pocket watch in his palm, its gold chain secured to the vest of his pin-striped suit. "Ah, finally you are here. I hope whatever was keeping you was important."

"I was in the workroom and had to clear my things. Then I stopped in the s-studio for my portfolio." She held it up and smiled.

He waved it away, replaced the watch in his pocket, and pointed to two head mannequins on his desk with cloches she'd designed.

"I'll get right to the point since we don't have much time. These are two of your designs, is that correct?"

"Yes, sir." Two of her hats he'd graciously put near the front of the showroom, not in the rear as he had Nora's crinolines.

"I have a prestigious client coming in, and although I've tried to tell her I can assist her, she insists she wants whoever designed these."

A ripple of relief skated through her. "Is she anyone I know?"

"It's doubtful." He stroked his thin, dark mustache, gathering his thoughts. Or trying to make up his mind. He huffed out a breath. "I guess I have no choice. Mavis can be quite persistent, and I do hope to stay in her good graces."

"M-Mavis?"

"Yes, Mavis Benchley, wife of the president of Benchley and Associates, the architectural firm responsible for half of the new buildings along the Upper East Side. She's quite particular and has two fetching daughters. The hats are for them…an unveiling ceremony of some sort where photographs will be taken. Newspapers will undoubtedly run the story, and Mrs. Benchley wants her daughters portrayed in the most favorable light."

"I would be h-happy to assist them. Will Mrs. Benchley require a h-hat as well?"

"She didn't say, but they are probably already in the consulting salon, and I don't want to keep them waiting. I only hope to high heavens you can keep your wits about you." He cleared his throat.

"Mind your words, too, if you will. I won't have you insulting one of my preferred clients."

A slow burn bubbled up. Just because she stammered didn't mean she was a moron. But a chance to prove herself was definitely better than being fired. She smiled. "I won't disappoint you, s-sir."

He ignored her and started for the door, expecting her to follow. *Just relax and take your time when speaking. Picture the way the words look before pronouncing them.* The words of her former elocutionist, who'd moved to Boston, bounced through her brain as Nell hurried behind Mr. Fields, his stride long and impatient.

The thought of seeing an influential client constricted her throat and made her mouth as dry as if stuffed with balled wool.

A tall, handsome woman in a suit the color of cream tea was waiting when they arrived at the ground floor consulting salon. Nell guessed her to be in her midforties.

"Ah, Mavis, you're looking spectacular today." Mr. Fields clasped her hands in his and kissed her on the cheek, then greeted the two young women who trailed behind her. One was a young likeness of her mother, the other more petite with a swing in her hips as she teetered on spooled heels with button straps, her legs in patterned silk stockings. They reminded Nell oddly of Iris and Mittie, her twin cousins back in Kentucky. Mismatched, yet each striking in her own way.

Mr. Fields introduced Nell as his "talented junior apprentice" and the woman as "my dear friend, Mavis Benchley, and her charming daughters, Claudia and Daphne."

"Nell will be assisting you dears today." He checked his watch and said he was late for an engagement, which drew a raised eyebrow from Mrs. Benchley. He gave Nell a look that said he expected her to live up to his expectations.

Nell waited until Mr. Fields had gone, then took a deep breath. "I'm honored to be of s-service. Won't you have a s-seat?" The girls

immediately sank into the cushions of one of the two brocade dav-
enports. Nell pulled the cord for Bea, the receptionist. "I'll have
some tea brought in, unless you'd p-prefer something else."

"Colas for Claudia and me," Daphne, the more petite of the two
girls, answered and crossed her legs.

Mrs. Benchley eyed Nell, sizing her up, it seemed. "I must say,
when the girls took a notion to the cloches in the showroom, I was
expecting someone with more experience. You look like you just
stepped off the playground."

Nell had heard the schoolgirl remark before. She tried to wear
clothes that made her look older—slim-skirted suits and high-
collared silk blouses—but she feared they only made her look as if
she were playing dress up.

She laughed, more nervous than she would've liked, and said, "I
hear that sometimes, ma'am. I'm twenty-one and have b-been with
Oscar Fields for over two years. I've been studying design m-most
of my life."

Mrs. Benchley made an O with her lips. "Why, you're British,
aren't you? I had no idea Oscar had brought someone from the con-
tinent. That makes a world of difference...if you're any good." She
eyed the other davenport and nodded. "Here, you sit by me. I want
to know all about you. I assume you've studied in Paris."

"No, ma'am, just here with Mr. Fields." Her dream *had* been to
study in Paris, but fate had intervened in a most unexpected way.
Not that she would burden Mrs. Benchley with the details.

"However did you get into such a fine establishment?" Her tone
was no longer accusing, but curious, light.

A warning bell went off in Nell's head. No discussing private lives
with clients. Ever. All conversation was to be directed back to the
customer. But Mrs. Benchley had asked for her qualifications.

"Mr. Fields n-noticed some of the hats I made for women at the
K-Kentucky Derby."

"You came all the way from England to make hats for the derby?"

Nell nodded, not wanting to divulge too much. It wasn't an un-truth. Hat making had preserved her sanity when she, Mama, and Caroline had moved to Kentucky. Kentucky! So far away from the Cotswolds and everyone she loved. She'd made hats for a few of Aunt Sarah's friends and Mama, of course. And she'd been fortunate that one of the hats had been for the wife of the man whose horse won the eighth race on derby day. Mr. Fields had seen the woman in the winner's circle receiving the silver cup and made inquiries. A quirk of fate, but one that had brought her to Mr. Fields.

Nell pulled some sketches from her portfolio, but Mrs. Benchley flicked them away and said to the girls, "I've been telling your father we should go to the Kentucky Derby."

Daphne, legs still crossed, swung her free foot back and forth like a pendulum. "Honestly, Mother, let's do what we came here for." She looked at Nell. "Mother's from North Shore out on Long Island…you know, country estates and all that."

No, Nell didn't know, but it sounded intriguing.

Daphne continued, "She's a pushover for anything to do with horses. She would have us living in the country if she could." She gave a shudder and said, "So, let's hop to it. I'm hoping for some-thing zippy to turn the heads of a few of those attorneys who've taken offices in Daddy's building."

"Z-Z-Zippy?" The word buzzed on Nell's tongue like the sar-saparilla she'd tasted at her first derby. Surprising, but pleasant. "I think we could arrange that. Do you have s-sketches of the dresses you'll be wearing?"

Mrs. Benchley riffled through her handbag as Bea brought a tray with both tea service and chilled Coca-Colas for the girls.

Mrs. Benchley handed Nell an oversized envelope. "Right here. Sketches and fabric swatches. My suit is a Chanel, so something simple but compelling for me in a hat. I prefer brown as black is a bit overdone, I think. I've had Soren Michaels design the girls' dresses, although for the life of me, the irregular hemlines are almost more than I can bear. And so short. Next thing you know they'll be advancing the hems above the knee."

Claudia, who Nell now realized was the younger of the two girls even though she was at least six inches taller than Daphne, cleared her throat. "It's what all the smart girls are wearing, Mother. Mr. Michaels agreed. They're fun loving, like the Brinkley Girls in the comics."

Her mother sighed. "Dresses swept the floor when I was your age, and to show an ankle was considered risqué."

Daphne continued swinging her foot and laughed. "Welcome to the twenties, Mother. So Nell Marchwold—shall we call you Nell or Miss Marchwold?"

"Nell is f-fine."

"Can we try on some hats? There were a couple I had my eye on in the display out front."

"Certainly. Choose any that you like. And I'll have you look at f-fabrics and decorative elements to see how we can coordinate with your dresses."

As Daphne and Claudia tried on the stock hats, giggling and cutting up, Nell noted which ones flattered them the most.

"Oh, look at this! Isn't this just the gnat's whistle?" Daphne donned a red satin cloche with a knot of silver beadwork that was one of Nell's creations. It gave Daphne's heart-shaped face an impish look. She cocked her hip and pretended she was smoking, which brought a frown from Mrs. Benchley.

Claudia, with rich coffee-colored eyes and nicely shaped lips on her slender face, tried on a black velvet cloche that was barely noticeable with her dark hair.

"The sh-shape is nice, but I think more color. Something to draw attention to your eyes." Nell checked the swatches and designs and invited them to move along to the fabric and notions room. Already, ideas swirled in her head. Sparkles and a feather or two for Daphne, and Nell had a rich olive silk velvet in mind for Claudia. She was right. Daphne navigated toward the bin of beads and sequined appliqué pieces like it was the North Star.

They all laughed while Nell jotted notes on an information sheet for each of the girls. "One last thing. I'll need to take some measurements and do a s-sketch of your p-profiles and a view from the front so I can get the p-proper balance."

Daphne's aquamarine eyes danced like sea waves as she posed for the sketch. Soren Michaels had captured the color perfectly in the beaded silk dress he'd designed for her.

The girls asked for the ladies' room, and when they were gone, Mrs. Benchley sighed.

"You've been most helpful, my dear. I'm afraid you've got your work cut out for you with Claudia. She's such a homely girl and upstaged at every turn by Daphne."

"Claudia is l-lovely, ma'am." *And she takes after her mother,* Nell wanted to say. Claudia wasn't homely at all, just an unpolished gem, as Nell's grandmother always said.

Mrs. Benchley waved a glove in Nell's direction. "I only pray that one day she will be." She pulled the glove on and knitted her eyebrows together. "I probably shouldn't mention it, but it was difficult not to notice. Your speech impediment is quite pronounced, isn't it?"

Nell's face flamed. She thought the morning had gone splendidly, and now…Well, now it looked as if it had all been for naught. Mrs. Benchley was going to be difficult to please, and if Nell didn't pass muster, the woman would no doubt let Mr. Fields know. She sucked in a big breath, putting on a casual air.

"Oh, I've l-lived with it my whole l-life. Gu-guess there's no hope for me." Her laugh was thin, squeaky.

Mrs. Benchley gave her a kind look. "Why ever would you say that? My friend's daughter stammered worse than you do, but she went to the most marvelous clinic. Addison Avenue Speech Center. I'll call you this afternoon and give you the number."

"I had an e-el-elo..."

"An elocutionist? They're quite effective in some cases, I'm sure, but I believe you'll find this clinic quite unique."

"Th-thank you. I'm g-grateful."

"Pleasing my daughters is thanks enough. We look forward to seeing your creations. Heaven knows, Oscar could use some fresh ideas. He's a simply adorable man, and so handsome, but surprisingly old-fashioned for someone so young."

It was a matter of perspective, Nell decided. She'd always considered Mr. Fields her elder since he was over thirty. "I'm a-accustomed to old-fashioned where I'm from."

"Kentucky?"

Nell laughed, this time with genuine warmth. "No. At the manor house where I grew up. You know the B-British, we live and breathe tr-tradition." She winced, sorry she'd dropped a personal reference into the conversation.

The girls returned, and as they left, a knot formed in Nell's stomach. The worker at the assembly table was right. She couldn't talk. How foolish to think she would ever succeed in a posh salon—or be the star designer Mr. Fields promised her—when all she could do was stutter. She prayed Mrs. Benchley wouldn't spread the word. She was a society maven and would surely have an influence. Even in New York, people talked, saw each other at galas and charity balls.

And if she complained to Mr. Fields, it could be disastrous. After Nora Remming's experience, anything was possible. Tears of frustration stung Nell's eyes as she gripped the folder of swatches tight in her fingers.

CHAPTER 2

Scents of yeast and garlic and olive oil filled the air as Nell neared her flat. The welcome aromas of the cafés and *ristorantes* of her neighborhood embraced her, her steps lighter when the red-and-green awning of Sal's Diner came into view. Nell was tempted to slip into Sal's back entrance and have a cup of tea with Felice, the owner's wife, before going up to the flat she shared with Jeanette North and Greta Edwards. Felice, though, would be busy serving up manicotti and heaping plates of linguine at this hour. She and Angelo had come from Italy, the *old country*, Felice always said with a faraway look in her eyes. Twenty years and she still missed her homeland.

The prototype cloche had taken longer than Nell intended, but the satisfaction at the finished creation outweighed the ache between her shoulder blades from the long hours at the worktable. If she was going to make it at Oscar Fields and someday make a name for herself, she had to sacrifice, no matter how long the hours. Gone was the illusion that she would be Mr. Fields's next star designer, the promise with which he'd lured her to New York. While it was true she'd learned construction techniques and gotten a grasp of the variety of materials available, it was also clear she was far from moving past the junior apprentice level. She understood that much better now, but it was fun to dream. Patience. And practice. Her twin watchwords.

Nell climbed the stairs to her second-floor flat and turned the key in the door. The Victrola's blaring filled the small sitting room. Jeanette floated by, her eyelids fluttering like she was dancing with some beau, as Billy Murray sang "The Dardanella Blues" on the phonograph record. When the music stopped, Jeanette did a little spin and came face-to-face with Nell.

"Oh! I didn't know you were home. I just talked to Greta, and she'll be here in fifteen minutes. Hey, doll, put your things down and get changed. We're stepping out tonight."

"What on earth? It's Tuesday night. I just got home."

"And I'm over the moon that you're here and can go with us."

"Where? You want to go get something to eat? That new deli over on Houston?"

"Not the deli, but food is involved, among other things."

"What other things?" Nell dropped her portfolio on the nearest chair and sat down to take off her heels and rub a sore spot on her toe.

"Fun things. Maybe some hip bumping and cute fellas, ya know?" Jeanette grabbed a Coca-Cola from the icebox and dug in the drawer for the bottle opener.

"Are you daft? It's after eight o'clock. Where is this place?"

Jeanette poured the cola in a glass and took a long sip. "Over on Broome Street, and I hear it's the berries. Jazzy music and everything." She slumped into a chair. "I could use a little fun after the day I had."

"What happened?"

"I missed the motor bus and had to take the subway. Some bum landed on my lap so I've smelled like a goat all day. And then my prof gave us a quiz I'd forgotten about."

"Don't worry. You've still got worlds of time left this quarter to make it up. But you won't even make it to campus tomorrow if you stay out half the night."

"We won't be out late. Besides, I'm starving. Tonight I'm having lamb shish kebabs and something to lift my spirits." She held up her empty glass in a mock toast before setting it in the kitchen sink. "Come on, help me pick out a dress, one that will swing with the music."

Dancing. That's all Jeanette thought about. Not finishing her education or finding a job. She didn't even seem to care about finding a husband, although Nell was right behind her there. Jeanette went to Columbia University, but before that had attended business school and taken two semesters at NYU. And she was Mr. Fields's niece, which put Nell in the position of having to explain Jeanette's lack of direction to her boss.

Greta had been Jeanette's best friend since grammar school, but her aspirations were to be onstage. In the meantime she worked as a file clerk at a theater on Broadway. Nell was lucky to have them. Luckily they'd been amenable to Nell living with them when Mr. Fields made the arrangements. Otherwise, Nell's mother would have never consented to Nell moving to New York.

Nell sighed. "I know you love dancing."

"Oh, you know it. I'm thinking about wearing the organza with the beads along the neckline. You know, the one you made the cloche for."

"I thought you were saving that for the fraternity dance."

"Piffle. Ernest asked a girl in my anthropology class. What a flat tire he turned out to be."

"I'm going to pass tonight. I met with an important client today and want to start on the sketches tonight." Ernest wasn't the only one who was a flat tire, but Nell wasn't stupid, either. The blind pig joints served illegal liquor. Bathtub gin, the newspapers called it. Sipping wine on holidays wasn't the same as outright breaking the law. The thought of going to the places Jeanette and Greta did sometimes frightened her.

Jeanette stomped off to change clothes and reemerged just as Greta came breezing in.

Greta dropped her bag and gloves on top of Nell's portfolio. "Jeanette, I'm not sure about this place. Ever since we talked, I've been thinking about it. Are you sure tonight's a good night?"

Jeanette threw up her arms. "Not you, too. Nell doesn't want to go, and now you're trying to back out."

"You don't even know what sort of place it is, and I've finally gotten my boss to get me an audition. It's a small speaking part, but I was hoping to read over the lines tonight."

Jeanette's lips flattened. "It's called Lily's Place, as in lily-white reputation. Their lamb shish kebabs have been compared to the ones they serve at the Ritz." She twisted one of her brown curls around her finger. "I hear they play the latest dance tunes, and you could brush up on your steps in case your audition calls for a routine or something."

"It is a musical, but I don't think I'm a candidate for the chorus line."

"You never know." Jeanette turned her back to Nell and pointed to the buttons of her dress. "Do me up, okay?"

While Nell worked the buttons, Greta went to change like Nell knew she would. Jeanette had a way about her that made people want to follow along as if she were a pied piper.

When Jeanette and Greta left, it was like the air had been sucked from the flat. Nell went to the kitchen, which was just a space at the end of the sitting room. She put the kettle on the two-burner gas stove and carved two slices of ciabatta from Sal's and put them in the new electric toaster Jeanette's mother had given them.

While the bread toasted, she grabbed her shoes and went to find her slippers. A tiny hall led to two bedrooms and a bath the size of a matchbox. It wasn't the eighteen-bedroom manor Nell had grown up in or even the sprawling country house of her aunt Sarah and uncle Eli in Kentucky, but she did have her own cozy room. While perched on the edge of the bed putting on her slippers she saw a letter propped against the lamp on her bedside table.

Quentin Bledsoe. Nice. She hadn't heard from him in a while. She tucked the letter under her pillow to read later and pulled out her sketch pad. First things first.

Two hours later, Nell surveyed the sketches for Claudia and Daphne Benchley that fanned across her damask coverlet. For Daphne, a black velvet cloche with a beaded butterfly set slightly off-center. A deep aquamarine color would enhance Daphne's eyes, but Nell would be cautious and make sure the butterfly wasn't so large it overpowered and was too garish. Just the right amount of sparkle to suit Daphne. Nell gathered the ones she'd done for Daphne and stacked them with the butterfly sketch on top.

She spread the ones for Claudia out, rearranged them, tilted her head to get a different angle. The problem with sketches was they were two-dimensional with only the imagination to fill in what would be seen from the back and either side. Oscar Fields had stressed in their many sessions that when considering each angle, time-honored precepts had to be followed. Every view had to be a part of the whole so that the eyes traveled along the lines intended by the milliner who designed the hat. Though Mr. Fields knew what constituted good design, Nell suspected he leaned more toward the traditional styles and wasn't particularly creative. *Old-fashioned*, according to Mrs. Benchley. Until today, he'd never acknowledged Nell as creative, and even at that, he'd done so reluctantly. Still, it was a first step. One she didn't regard lightly.

Nell's eyes returned again and again to one particular sketch that broke the rules of standard design. A cloche, yes, but one with an unusual combination of fabrics and embellishment. Her heart pounded as she wondered if she should dare, but her soul told her she must. Mrs. Benchley's tall, awkward daughter with dark eyes would be transformed when she wore such a creation. Quickly, Nell assembled the Claudia sketches and tucked them all into a clasped portfolio.

She leaned against the headboard and reached for her tea, long grown cold, the toast beside it barely nibbled. She set the cup down and pulled Quentin's letter from beneath her pillow. Quentin had been her best childhood friend from her tiny town of Heathdown in the Cotswolds. Her only friend, really, and the one whose friendship she'd grieved when leaving England. With Quentin it didn't matter that she came from a titled family or that Marchwold Manor employed a dozen servants. To him she was just Prunella, a girl who liked to draw hats and steal kisses from him. Mama had said he was just a passing fancy and her grandmother assured her there would be other boys. They were both wrong. There hadn't been other boyfriends, and Nell still missed the childhood capers, but she had her hats now and a bright career ahead. It was all she wanted and needed.

My dear Prunella,

May this find you happy and in good health. I've finally secured the lease on the flat in Abbey Close that I told you about. Now it will be an easy stroll to the bank each day. I've just returned from Heathdown with a trunk from my parents' attic full of childhood relics and a few odd pieces of china that Mama insisted I would need. Since I take most of my meals out, I can't imagine they will get much use, but even a son of twenty-three heeds his mama.

This evening I stopped at an establishment just around the corner. Plutino's Ristorante. As I bit into the tender ravioli, I wondered if this is one of the dishes you might also be enjoying from Sal's Diner

*that you've told me so much about. If so, I'm green with envy I've
not had the pleasure of eating such fine cuisine before.*

He wrote about the Cotswolds and the golden glow of late summer
on the limestone cottages. He gave news of his four brothers, their
wives, and the eight nieces and nephews who filled two entire rows
of the village church where his father was still the vicar. And then
he told her of the visit with her grandmother.

*Before I left Heathdown, I popped in to see Lady Mira who was
taking her tea in the garden. Her move into the village has been good
for her, but I couldn't help but smile as your grandmother and I sat
amongst the yews. It was in that very garden where we shared our first
kiss. You were all of ten, still sporting braids, and I was a lecherous
old man of twelve. Ah, the days of youth and innocence.*

Nell bit her lip and held the letter to her chest, her heart bruised
afresh with the memory of her grandmother. Of Quentin. Of holding his hand and strolling the cobblestoned streets of Heathdown
with no thoughts of what the future might hold. Tears filled her
eyes, but she brushed them away. This was no time to get weepy
over the past. She had to think about today. And tomorrow. And all
the days that followed. She had a different life now, one that challenged her and had set her on the path to being a real designer. It
wasn't Paris as she'd once dreamed, but Manhattan was closer to her
mother and bursting with opportunity. Now, if only her boss and
the Benchleys liked what she'd done.

CHAPTER 3

Oscar Fields studied the finished hats Nell placed before him. He stroked his chin, his thin mustache twitching ever so slightly, but Nell couldn't read what he was thinking.

He leaned back in his swivel chair. "You've certainly come up with some unique ideas. The aquamarine butterfly is inspired. I can picture Daphne quite vividly, flighty thing that she is." He leaned forward and looked again at the design for Claudia, the furrows deepening in his forehead.

"The proportions are wrong. And the balance. While the silk velvet is elegant, I'm not sure a rose flower on olive green is a wise choice. And the petals are droopy like you pulled them from the bottom of the box. Not fresh nor inspired, I'm afraid."

"I'm g-glad you like the one for Daphne, but..." Nell tried to picture in her head the words she would say, giving her defense of Claudia's design. She was certain this hat would draw attention to Claudia's large eyes, her slender neck, and at the same time minimize her height. Calvin had been skeptical, too, when Nell showed it to him, saying it was her funeral, but he'd come around when she explained.

Mr. Fields drummed his fingers on the shining mahogany of his desk. "But what, Miss Marchwold?"

"I'm not sure what. P-personally, I believe it's my best work to date. I know I don't always explain things p-properly. I apologize. But it would mean a lot to me if you would let Claudia try it and decide for herself."

"This isn't about feeling good about yourself. I am trying to run a successful business. You are but a piece of that, and up until now, your work has been adequate." He looked again at the hat. "I'll make an allowance this time. Just make sure you have something else to show Claudia and Mrs. Benchley should this not meet with their approval. I wouldn't want to disappoint one of my preferred clients."

"Yes, sir. And thank you. You won't r-regret it."

He pushed the molded form with Claudia's hat toward Nell. "If she doesn't like it, we can always put in on the reduced-price shelf."

❦

Nell had all three hats ready and waiting on the consulting salon counter when Mrs. Benchley and her daughters arrived that afternoon. Daphne grabbed the butterfly cloche and put it on at once, her eyes sparkling, her cupid mouth puckered as she tilted her head first one way, then the other, as she looked in the dressing mirror. "It's simply copacetic!"

When Nell shrugged, Claudia giggled. "It's the latest word. She means it's divine." Claudia's long, slim fingers stroked the velvet on the one for her. "May I?"

"Allow me." Nell held her breath as she lifted the hat from the form and placed it on Claudia's dark bob. Nell had chosen the domed crown and the pleated layers of silk velvet for a demure effect. A contrasting band shimmered near the face emphasizing Claudia's mahogany eyes, giving her a youthful glow. The flower added a bit of whimsy. The two wide velvet ribbons that curved downward from the floppy flower brushed Claudia's right shoulder, adding grace and elegance. Mr. Fields had been wrong. It did have just the right balance and proportion. The best part of all, though, was seeing Claudia's eyes widen at her reflection, the tiny quiver in her chin, then her smile, shy at first, growing into radiance.

Mrs. Benchley gasped. "Oh my gracious. It's…why, it's exquisite. However did you do come up with such a stunning idea?" Her mouth hung open like she was seeing her daughter in a new light for the first time.

Daphne hollered from the mirror where she was still admiring herself. "Ya know, it's almost a shame to waste these gorgeous creations on Daddy's little party."

Her mother shot her a stern look. "That'll do, Daphne. You know we all have to make the best presentation possible. You never know who might be there." Mrs. Benchley lifted the brown velvet hat with a modest brim and a small floral cluster for decoration from its resting place and tried it on. "Lovely. Simply lovely."

She grasped both of Nell's hands. "Well done, my dear. I'll have to tell Oscar to guard you with his life. You just never know who might be looking for someone with your talent."

"I'm f-flattered, ma'am, and p-pleased that you like them." Nell turned to see if Claudia was still wearing her hat, and as she did so, Mr. Fields disappeared from the doorway. Heat rose in her face. How long had he been standing there?

"If the fit is all right, I'll get these in boxes for you and give you the t-ticket. Our receptionist will assist you with p-payment."

As the last hat was tucked safely in a cardboard box with the Oscar Fields Millinery design on the side, Mrs. Benchley leaned in and whispered, "Have you made an appointment at the clinic?"

Nell nodded. "At four this afternoon."

"Excellent, my dear." They shook hands, and as the Benchleys left, Daphne turned and gave a fluttery wave. "We'll be sure and send over some photographs when we get all dolled up."

"Thanks. I'd love that. Have a w-wonderful time."

"Please have a seat. The doctor will be with you in a moment." The receptionist was the picture of efficiency, her desk tidy, her gray suit stark. The woman didn't smile, nor did she scowl or try to make Nell feel at ease, but merely pointed to a line of wooden chairs along the wall.

Nell stared at the tips of her shoes until her name was called by a pleasant young woman in a black skirt and white blouse with a ruffled collar.

"Welcome, my love. This way, please. Dr. Underwood will be tripping along soon. I'm Lindy Williams, his assistant." She led Nell into a studio with a window view of a dark brick building. In one corner was a child-sized table with wooden blocks and picture books. "Would you relish some coffee or a cup of tea?"

A catch came in Nell's throat. The Yorkshire rhythm in the assistant's voice was unmistakable, a warm sensation like a glimpse of home after a long journey. "A cup of t-tea would be lovely. With milk p-please."

"Oh, you're British, too." Cornflower-blue eyes crinkled at the corners when Lindy smiled. "Have you been here long?"

"In the S-states almost four years. A tad over two in New York."

"You're a newcomer then. I've been here almost ten. I'm from Thirsk. Do you know it?"

Nell nodded. "My m-mother grew up in Yorkshire, but I was born near Heathdown in my father's family home."

"Heathdown?"

"A tiny v-village. Near Stow-on-the-Wold."

"Oh yes. Lovely country. Welcome, then. I'll run and fetch your tea. Dr. Underwood will be in directly. He's a marvel. You'll see." She hurried off and returned a few minutes later with the tea and a short, round doctor in a white laboratory coat, which he wore over a bright lemon shirt with a black bow tie.

Dr. Terrence Underwood introduced himself and indicated that Nell should take a seat in a large leather chair, which sat at a right angle to his. "Lindy tells me you're from England."

"Originally, yes."

"Tell me a little about yourself, your family."

"My mother, sister, and I moved to K-Kentucky to live with my aunt after my f-father died in the war. Mama has since r-remarried, and Granville adopted my s-sister soon after. I've been here for two years."

"I'm sorry to hear of your loss. That's a lot of changes for a young woman. And New York is quite an adjustment in itself." The doctor had a soothing voice, not probing. He opened a folder that Nell supposed was the information she'd given over the telephone, which included Mrs. Benchley's name as a reference.

Dr. Underwood casually crossed his legs and looked directly at her. "Today, all we'll do is get acquainted with one another. I need to obtain a general history and will do a physical exam to rule out any underlying organic reasons for your stammer. Quite often there are neurological causes, which a few simple tests will determine. From the small amount of speaking we've done so far, I can tell you have difficulty with beginning sounds. It's a common pattern, and we'll work to determine which sounds you struggle with the most. Are you agreeable so far?"

"Y-yes, sir. And thank you for s-seeing me."

"I'm delighted to do so. I individually tailor to each client's needs and have discovered that using exercises and a variety of prompts in an interactive process can give astounding results."

It sounded both vague and full of promise. Nell leaned back and relaxed, sipping her tea as Dr. Underwood wrote in her folder.

They sped through her history. He did a brief physical exam, tapped on her knees and elbows with a small triangular rubber hammer, checked the strength in her grip, and instructed her to walk along a black line painted on the oak flooring. Next, he shone a light in her mouth, had her stick out her tongue and swallow. He had Lindy assist by holding up printed cards with everyday words, which progressed from simple to multisyllabic. On her chart, he made notes, then flipped to the first page where he'd taken her history before speaking.

"You are a milliner's apprentice, correct?"

Nell confirmed that she was.

"As such, you do a good bit of drawing, I presume?"

Another yes.

"Excellent. Fortunately for you, I don't find any abnormalities to indicate a neurological basis for your malady. Can you remember any times you might have fallen or suffered a blow to the head during your childhood?"

"None that I know of, s-sir. I'm su-sure I t-tumbled down the stairs a f-few times when I was s-small, maybe a p-plaster or two on my knees. No head injuries that I'm aware of."

Dr. Underwood leaned back and closed his eyes like he was drawing up the courage to tell her that she was a hopeless case, that he couldn't help her. After a moment, though, he opened his eyes and said, "May I assure you there is no shame in stammering. Many famous people such as Aristotle and Isaac Newton were prone to it. Breathing exercises and desensitization techniques are often of great benefit."

Nell latched onto the possibility as he continued speaking.

"Great strides have been made in the science of human behavior, and I believe you are the perfect candidate for my program. When you return next week, I'll have an easel prepared, and we'll talk about your childhood, what might be the source of your stammering. I'd like you to draw scenes from the prompts I give you. I'm certain we'll find the root of your problem in no time."

It seemed too good to be true. The behavioral issue was something she didn't quite follow, but Dr. Underwood's confidence that he could help her carried her like a feather on a wind current as she clipped along the sidewalk, then darted between oncoming automobiles to cross the street. Just in time, too, as the clang of the approaching trolley rang out. She grabbed the post to board and found an empty spot on the bench. She leaned back and caught her breath. If it were as simple as a childhood trauma, she would be thrilled, but the worst trauma in Nell's life had been leaving Heathdown. She'd been stammering long before that.

CHAPTER 4

"A psycho doc? That's who's going to stop your stuttering?" Jeanette lounged on the settee Gloria Swanson–like with one leg draped over the end. The silent film star had nothing on Jeanette when it came to drama.

Nell cringed. She'd waited until the day after her visit with Dr. Underwood to tell Jeanette and Greta. Jeanette always made such a fuss that she thought dropping it casually into the conversation best.

Greta had said, "Attagirl, Nell!" and went back to drawing red lipstick on her mouth while looking into the compact from her purse. She gave a kissy motion, then snapped the gold case and slipped it in her bag. "If you pick up any hints on how to project your voice, let me know." She put on a wool beret and tucked a strand of blonde hair behind her ear. "I have to dash, my darlings. My destiny awaits."

Greta sailed out the door to attend an acting class her theater manager had recommended. With Greta gone, Jeanette grilled Nell like she'd committed a crime, and Nell told her about the advanced methods of Dr. Underwood. She just hadn't expected Jeanette to be so blunt.

"Don't call him a psycho doc. He's not a psy-psychiatrist. He's a specialist in speech development. There are exercises for me to do."

"But you said he'll have you draw pictures and delve into your childhood. It sounds like that free association nonsense Freud advocates, only with pictures instead of words." Jeanette's foot kept time with the beat of Billy Murray singing on the Victrola. "Hey, here's a song for you." She sat up and moved her shoulders.

Nell threw a pencil at her. "You know I hate that song." Stupid Billy Murray singing "You Tell Her, I Stutter" like it was some joke.

"I didn't say I liked it. I'm simply saying I don't think stuttering is the Mount Everest you make it out to be. Some hills aren't meant to be climbed."

"That's easy for you to say. You're not the one who stutters."

"I'm not sure an analyst is your answer. He'll be probing and asking you if you hate your mother or if your father was cruel and made you eat Brussels sprouts."

"I never should have brought it up."

"Speaking of food, I'm starving."

"We weren't."

"Weren't what?"

"Speaking of food."

"I was, and I'm going to be late to my mother's birthday luncheon if I don't put on some speed. You sure you don't want to come?"

Nell shook her head. She knew she should accept the invitation, but Jeanette's mother made her uncomfortable. Mr. Fields had been married to Mrs. North's sister, Anna, who had been a victim of the Spanish flu epidemic. Mrs. North was nice enough, but her questions always seemed like she was prying. *Who's Oscar dating now? Any juicy gossip?*

Rumors certainly reached Nell's ears that some of the women who came into the salon had other motives than buying hats when they requested a consultation with Mr. Fields. He was, without question, an attractive, eligible man, and his mustache was said to give him verve.

Out of respect for her boss, though, these weren't things Nell would dare mention to Mrs. North. Once Jeanette had left, Nell waited until the noon rush had settled, then went to the back entrance of the diner that led to the Salvatores' quarters. Felice answered Nell's knock on the first rap.

"Ah, *tesoro mio*. Come in." Felice wiped her hands on her apron and pushed a damp curl from her forehead with the back of her hand. "You've come not too late to have a little gnocchi. Angelo make it fresh this morning. He must have been thinking in his head that you were coming."

"Mmmm. Sounds delicious, but just a small bowl. What I really want is ravioli. Does Angelo make that?"

"Ach! Are you coming down with the fever? You ask always for gnocchi." Felice lay a plump hand that smelled of garlic and basil on Nell's forehead.

Nell laughed. "No fever. A friend recommended ravioli so I want to try it."

"This friend, she comes here?"

"Not a she—it's a boy. A man. And no, he hasn't come here, but I know he'd love to."

Felice looked unconvinced and disappeared through the swinging doors that went to the kitchen. As she returned with the ravioli and the gnocchi, a boisterous group came in the diner asking if it was too late for lunch. Felice greeted them like they were long-lost relatives and scurried off, leaving Nell to her thoughts that were an ocean away.

Dr. Underwood wore a tangerine-colored shirt with a deep turquoise bow tie when Nell arrived for her next session. Nell wondered if his wife picked out his clothes or if the bright colors were meant to appeal to the children he treated. They did match his affirming personality, but Nell was wary, unsettled.

After only a moment of small talk, Dr. Underwood said, "Let's get started. You mentioned that you moved to America when your father died. Today I want you to think about your father and draw anything that comes to mind about him. What was his physique, his mannerisms? Was he jovial or stern? What was your relationship like?"

"I-I...my f-father...he was nice, w-wonderful, in fact. And I can assure you, he n-never made me eat Brussels sprouts, and even if he had, I like them."

"Miss Marchwold...what an unusual thing to say."

Nell balled her fingers into a fist, her nails biting into her flesh. "I'm sorry. I didn't mean to blurt that out. It's j-just that my r-roommate said you would ask questions like that."

"Like what?"

"About my childhood, whether I l-loved my p-parents. Psy-psycho..."

"Psychoanalysis? Is that what you meant?"

Nell nodded, heat rising in her cheeks.

"While behavioral principles are at the core of my program, I assure you, I have no intention of doing such a thing. As I explained to you, I will be merely prompting you to draw scenes from your life in an attempt to bring your emotions to the surface. I didn't mean to alarm you."

He closed his eyes the way he had on the first visit like there were pictures inside his head that would give him inspiration. His voice was mellow when he opened them and continued.

"Disregard what I said. For today, I'm not giving you a prompt.

Simply draw whatever comes to your mind. Would you prefer to work at the easel or a desk?"

"The d-desk, please."

"Very well. I'll have Lindy bring you some tea."

When Lindy slipped in quietly and set the tray with a pot of tea on the desk, Nell had already sketched the outline of her first drawing. Not of her papa, so if Jeanette asked, Nell could assure her Dr. Underwood wasn't interested in the nonsense of Freud.

Nell drew her grandmother—Lady Mira she was called—dowager countess of Marchwold. Her hand moved quickly, making long strokes of her grandmother's dressing gown as she reclined on a chaise by the window. She filled in the details of the room, the ornate furniture, the marble fireplace, and the rolling green fields beyond the glass. Seated on a nearby stool, Nell drew an image of her younger self, plaited hair, watercolors resting on a nearby table, and a sketchbook propped up on her knees.

"Observe everything, my sweet Prunella," her grandmother often said. "The sky. The earth. The changing seasons. But most of all, study people. Watch the tilt of the head, the way the chin juts up when a person would like to disagree. Inhale the sweet breath of a baby and the sour fumes of a man who likes tinned sardines, and you will learn about life."

Observation by listening was in a category all its own. The cadence of boots on polished oak floors. The tone of the voice. The inflection. What people say to make themselves look more important than they are.

Grandmama would deliver these jewels, then resume her gaze at the world outside her window. Even then, observing and listening had suited Nell, for the more she took in the world through her eyes and ears, the less she had to speak.

Memories of Grandmama flitted through Nell's thoughts. Her velvet cheeks. The tears that carried sadness at the loss of Nell's father and then her grandfather. The day they left to come to America, Grandmama had cradled her cheeks in doe-soft hands and smiled. In that moment, Nell felt her grandmother's belief in her as fully as if she'd taken out a page in the *London Times*.

Nell had never veered from the promise she made to herself that day, that no matter where she went or what she did, her quest would be to make her grandmother proud.

Lost in thought, Nell didn't hear Dr. Underwood enter the room, and when he spoke, she jumped. "Sorry, didn't mean to startle you." He raised his eyebrows and looked at her picture.

"I didn't f-finish." She pointed to the reclining figure. "This is my grandmother in England." A catch came in her throat. "She's always b-believed in me."

"And you miss her, is that it?"

"V-very much." Nell took a deep breath.

"It's a positive sign that you've had people in your life who've encouraged and inspired you. I think you'll find our sessions most insightful in helping you overcome your speech difficulties." He handed Nell a packet. "Inside you will find the exercises you are to practice each day. Read them aloud a dozen or more times. They've been specifically ordered with your difficulties in mind. You may speak the words or sing them, but the main goal is repetition and completing a phrase without faltering."

He showed her the door. What Dr. Underwood expected was a miracle. Nell wished for one, too, but like the miracle it would take to ever see her grandmother again, she didn't hold out a great deal of hope. With heavy steps, she stepped from the Addison Avenue office building onto a crowded street and waited for the trolley.

CHAPTER 5

Nell removed her scarf and hung it on the coatrack inside the design studio she shared with Calvin Gold and Ed Percy. And until two weeks ago, Nora Remming. Situated at the opposite end of the corridor from the boisterous second-floor workroom, the studio offered respite and quiet so Nell and the other designers could concentrate and create. And it was here where Nell first sat in rapt attention as Mr. Fields talked of the elements of design; the principles of composition; and giving a hat contrast, balance, and rhythm. Nell had taken copious notes in a journal and studied them at night. It was six months before she was given a drafting table and set free to make her own designs.

Now, her table stood next to Calvin's, with Percy's spot and Nora's former one on the opposite wall. Nell thought it was to distinguish the senior designers from the apprentices, but in truth, Percy seemed to like keeping to himself and had a high productivity level with the arrangement. He had a keen eye for color and could sketch like the wind. When Nell had asked him about it, he said it came from experience, something Nell was miles short on.

Now he sat hunched over a sketch, not even looking up to say good morning. As Nell took the pins from her brimmed hat, she caught a glimpse of Calvin strutting around with his thumbs hooked in his armpits like he was a chicken.

"You must have had a fun time over the weekend. Want to tell me her name?"

"You know I'm just lousy with women swarming around me waiting for a date."

"Perhaps you need to let them know you're available."

"Easy for you to say, Miss Talk of the Town." He picked up a folded newspaper and held it behind his back.

"Are you mad? I lead a quiet and very boring life." Nell shook her head. Except for going to church with Felice on Sunday morning, Nell had spent the entire weekend practicing the lists Dr. Underwood had given her. She'd been an utter failure and had even driven Jeanette and Greta from the flat just to get away from her.

Mr. Mister misses his mistress.

Polly Parrot picked a peanut from the parlor floor.

Fudd Phillips found a feather floating by the ferry.

"Not anymore, you won't. Guess you haven't seen yesterday's newspaper?"

"No, I haven't. Is that what you're hiding behind your back?"

"Give me a kiss and I'll show you."

"Calvin Gold, stop this instant. If I did want to kiss you...and I don't...I wouldn't do it because you b-bribed me." Embarrassed, she glanced at Percy. He was old enough to be their father, but he seemed to have no interest whatsoever in their conversation.

"Hey, you can't knock a fella for trying," Calvin said as he shoved the paper at her, folded so that a photograph peered up at her.

Claudia and Daphne Benchley. Wearing the hats Nell had made. "Oh. Oh, goodness. Aren't they g-g-gor—"

"Yeah, gorgeous would be about right. Read what it says."

Daphne and Claudia Benchley, daughters of New York's most sought-after architect, Porter Benchley, lit up Saturday's dedication ceremony of the newly opened Stottlemeir Club.

The Beaux-Arts Classicism–inspired building will house not only the exclusive club, but also offices, shops, and restaurants. Porter Benchley and his associates were on hand to receive the plaque presented by Mayor John Hylan, but all eyes were on Benchley's daughters, who some in the crowd described as ravishing.

The girls, clad in ensembles from Soren Michaels House of Design and Oscar Fields Millinery, had young men asking for introductions and debutante hopefuls scrambling to get the numbers of the girls' designers.

Nell knew her mouth was hanging open, but she couldn't seem to close it. She read the short piece again and looked at the top to see what section had covered the story.

Calvin said, "Yes, the front of the society section. I'm surprised a hoard of people haven't stormed the shop downstairs. Chances are we'll be out of Nellie March hats by the end of the day."

"Don't say that!"

"What? That business will be picking up?"

"No. The Nellie March part. I was fortunate, that's all. Fortunate that Mr. Fields trusted me with his pet Mrs. Benchley. And if you had read more carefully, my name's not even mentioned."

"Guess I missed that."

"Besides, you had three requests last week."

"Yeah, from old maids and senile octogenarians."

"Rich old maids. Don't f-forget that."

"I wouldn't dare." He reached for the paper, but Nell hugged it to her chest. Yes, she knew her place; Mr. Fields was always clear about that. But this. This! She'd been right about Claudia's hat, the one Mr. Fields had sniffed at.

A shiver raced across her shoulders. It was most likely overplay by an eager reporter.

Nell shoved the paper back at Calvin. "*Vanity is fleeting, a sounding gong.* That's what my grandmother always says when the *Tatler* reports an occasion. Nothing to get all in a dither about."

"Not to dispute your wise grandmother, but I wouldn't bet my last nickel on it. Someone with your talent and integrity will go places." Calvin tossed the paper on Nell's desk.

Scarcely an hour later, Harjo popped his head in the studio. "Mr. Fields's office. Now." He left without saying whether she and Calvin were to both go or just one of them.

Calvin told her to go ahead, it was her party.

"No. You come, too. It might not even be about the newspaper article."

"Are you loony? Of course that's what it's about, but I'll go and hold your hand."

Nell glared at him. "You needn't bother. I'm perfectly able to talk to Mr. Fields alone."

Calvin held up his hands, palms facing her, signaling a truce. "I'm going—not to hold your hand—but because I don't want to miss out on the fun."

Nell fished in her handbag and pulled out a lipstick and compact to freshen up the pink on her mouth and powder her nose. She checked her hair in the mirror. The part was straight and no locks had come loose from the chignon at her nape, so she snapped the compact shut and offered her arm to Calvin.

When Harjo opened the door for Nell and Calvin to enter, Mrs. Benchley's throaty laugh bubbled out.

"Oh, there's our darling hatmaker." Mrs. Benchley swooped over and planted ample hands on Nell's shoulders, giving a soft squeeze. She gave a brushing glance at Calvin. "And who might you be?"

"Calvin Gold. Nellie March and I share a studio."

All eyes turned to Calvin, but it was Mrs. Benchley who said, "Nellie March? Nellie…oh, you mean Miss Marchwold. What a sly and witty man you are, giving her a pet name."

Nell knew her face had turned as bright as the lipstick she'd applied only moments before. "Calvin is such a t-tease." She inhaled deeply to steady her voice. "It's lovely to see you again. How was the dedication?"

"Splendid. Simply splendid. Have you seen the article in the newspaper?"

"I did. Just this morning."

The phone on the credenza rang, and Harjo jumped quickly to answer it. He handed the base and receiver to Mr. Fields.

"Yes, certainly, that would work just fine. Two o'clock." Mr. Fields returned the receiver to the cradle and nodded to Nell. "Mrs. Benchley has come to thank us for the hats we designed for their gala evening."

Nell thought perhaps she should curtsy to Mrs. Benchley, but that would be overly gratuitous. She merely said, "The p-privilege was mine."

Mrs. Benchley waved away the comment. "I was telling Oscar I gave your name to no less than a dozen people at the unveiling and could have easily supplied it to more, but one has to be careful, you know, not to encourage the wrong sort of clientele."

Mr. Fields rose and spoke to Mrs. Benchley. "Forgive me. Can I offer you a drink? Some coffee perhaps? Or a glass of sherry?"

"Heavens, no. I can only stay a moment, but I wanted to tell all of you that Soren Michaels just called with the most marvelous idea. He would like to collaborate with Nell—or is it Nellie?—and do a small show at the Stottlemeir Club. Now that it's fully opened and christened, it's the ideal opportunity."

The phone rang again. After a brief conversation, Mr. Fields told the caller three o'clock would be fine. Mrs. Benchley's friends already?

Mr. Fields cleared his throat. "A collaboration, you say? Perhaps at some time in the future, I would take it under consideration."

"Time is of the essence, Oscar. A single mention of your salon is one thing, but having it associated with an event would be pure gold. People will be clamoring for Nell's designs."

"For Oscar Fields's designs, you mean. I would never give all the work to a lone millinery designer. Miss Marchwold could contribute, of course, but having the entire responsibility would undoubtedly put her under pressure to perform and might very well send the entire operation spiraling into disaster."

Mrs. Benchley put her palms on the desk and leaned over, meeting Mr. Fields eye to eye. "Soren specifically asked for Nell. It's an opportunity, Oscar. For the salon. For both of you." She straightened and tilted her head toward Nell. "Nellie March. That's quite catchy, isn't it?"

Mr. Fields mumbled something unintelligible and then in a calm voice said, "What you're suggesting is that I give Miss Marchwold an exclusive. Next thing, you'll be saying I should give her her own label."

"Why, Oscar, I didn't say that at all, but it's a brilliant idea. Inspired, no less." She looked at her diamond-encrusted wristwatch. "Oh, dear. I'm afraid I have another engagement, but I do believe you're onto something, you clever man. Nellie March. Can you just imagine?"

Mr. Fields clamped his lips, his mustache twitching. "No, I can't. I have no intention of giving a label to a junior apprentice. And certainly not one of the female variety. It would go against everything this company stands for, the years my father toiled in building a respectable business."

Nell almost chuckled at Mrs. Benchley's clever manipulation of Mr. Fields, but the "female variety" remark grated. Seeing her mother, Evangeline Marchwold, struggle to find her place in Kentucky with no competence or experience had taught Nell that women could and *should* equip themselves with education and skills to make it in the world.

Mrs. Benchley pulled on her gloves and smiled sweetly at Mr. Fields. "You do have an impeccable reputation, but a girl of Nell's talent will be quite in demand." She extended a hand to Mr. Fields. "I understand Murdoch's is looking for a new designer." She let that morsel hang in the air, then said, "Good day, Oscar."

She gave Nell a quick hug, then looked at Calvin. "What sort of designs do you do?"

Calvin chuckled. "Oh, mostly things for mature women who prefer plums and cherries on their hats instead of beads and baubles."

Mrs. Benchley threw back her head and laughed. "We may need to talk, my son."

The telephone rang as she was leaving, so Nell asked if there was anything else Mr. Fields wanted to discuss.

Mr. Fields shook his head. "Not at the moment, but you have appointments at two and three o'clock this afternoon in the consulting salon."

"Thank you, s-sir. I'll be there."

Harjo stood with the telephone extended toward Mr. Fields, who grumbled and clamped his fingers around the base, then spoke into the mouthpiece. "Mr. Fields speaking. How may I assist you?"

As Nell and Calvin stepped into the hall, Nell heard Mr. Fields say, "Yes, Mr. Michaels. My club or yours?"

CHAPTER 6

Mr. Fields didn't mention Soren Michaels until Thursday. As Nell came from the consulting salon with yet another new client, Mr. Fields stepped from the showroom and fell in stride with her.

"I trust you've had a good day."

"Why y-yes, I have. Thanks for asking. Two of Daphne Benchley's f-friends want hats for a s-sorority dance."

"I'm glad to hear it. Could we have a word, please?"

Nell stopped, unsure if he meant to speak to her in the hall or his office.

"Not here. I'll catch the elevator with you and come to the studio where we can speak privately."

In the studio, Nell switched on the light and produced a stack of new orders and the accompanying sketches she assumed Mr. Fields would want to see.

He sat in the tall chair at her slanted work desk and surveyed each one, making only a comment or two about the choice of materials or suggesting minor changes. Nell made mental notes, pleased that her boss found her work passable.

"This one." Mr. Fields tapped his finger not on the design, but the work order with the client's name—Bette Andover. "I had a call from her after she'd seen you. While she had no quarrel with your ideas, she did mention your…your difficulty in speaking."

Nell swallowed hard. Mrs. Andover was the one who'd been difficult, interrupting and finishing every word and sentence Nell stumbled over.

Nell nodded. "She was in a h-hurry and got impatient with me. She did seem p-pleased with my suggestions and that I could have her hat done by n-next week."

"Don't bother. She canceled, said she was taking her business to Murdoch's."

"That's t-too bad. I looked forward to making her hat."

"You didn't hear what I said. Murdoch's. That's where she's going." His voice was a low growl, and it dawned on Nell the implication. Murdoch and Mr. Fields were rivals. Enemies even, if the workroom babble was true.

Nell gulped and nodded, words clogging her throat. Sometimes the best response was silence.

"This is exactly what concerns me about you, Nell. You have a bit of talent, still raw, not yet refined, but pushing you in the limelight might not be in your best interests."

"Most of the c-clients have been quite g-gracious."

He picked up a colored pencil and tapped it on the desk. "I did promise your mother I would watch out for you." Mr. Fields's manner was guarded. Hesitant. "The collaboration with Michaels would be beneficial to the firm, and I can't keep you sequestered forever. Mavis has seen to that. I'm going forward with Michaels, but it's your neck that's on the line."

An audible catch came in Nell's throat as she caught her breath. "That's w-wonderful. When? Is he coming here? Today?"

"Not so fast. That's what I'm talking about. You need to remain calm…and businesslike."

"Yes, sir. I understand." She stopped herself. "I'm honored."

"He'll be here Monday morning. You might want to brush up on your speech and put together a few of your best designs before he arrives." He rose from the chair and stepped to her, his fingers reaching to her chin. He tilted her head so their eyes met. "Don't disappoint me."

"I w-won't, Mr. Fields."

His hand fell to her shoulder as he brushed her aside and left.

A tiny spider of uncertainty crawled up her spine. Had she received a compliment or a warning? Either way, it was a test. One in which she had to excel.

Soren Michaels. Yes! She closed her eyes and did a spin around the room the way Jeanette always did when the Victrola was playing. When Nell stopped and opened her eyes, Calvin was leaning in the doorway with his arms crossed, smiling.

"Let me guess. You've been promoted from junior apprentice to belle of the ball."

"I wouldn't say that."

"Something good must have happened."

"Yes. And no. I was fired by Mrs. Andover, but Soren Michaels has asked to work with me on creating ensembles."

"Shucks. Guess I'll never get a chance with you if Soren's moving into my territory."

"Calvin Gold. I've told you I'm not interested in anything but designing hats."

"Yeah, I know. And you're saving your heart for some dandy in England who hasn't even bothered to come across the ocean and visit you."

"Quentin? We were childhood friends, that's all. And Quentin can't afford to come even if he wanted to."

"You ask me, he can't afford not to." Calvin went to his desk and pulled out a sketch he'd started that morning. He gave it a quick look, then balled up the paper and threw it in the wastebasket.

Nell bit her lip. "Bad day?"

"I've had better. And I'm not sore at you. Just frustrated. All my ideas stink, and all I'm doing is proving my dad was right. I'll never make it as a designer."

"Maybe you just need some new inspiration."

"And I suppose you have that in a bottle in your desk?"

"No, but you need to get out, do something fun."

His dark eyes grew wider. "You're asking me out? For a date?"

"No. I already have a date this weekend."

"And who's the lucky fella?"

"Two of them, actually. The twin lions at the New York Public Library. I want to spend some time in the stacks looking at bead designs—inspiration for working with Soren Michaels."

"You had me going there for a sec."

"You got me off track. What I wanted to say is that Jeanette and Greta—my roommates—have been after me to go to a dance club. You could go with us, and we could see what people are wearing, get ideas."

"Which sounds like another way to help you with your work with Michaels, but what good would it do me? I don't even dance."

"I don't, either. Just a waltz or two, not what they do at Lily's Place, I'm sure."

"Lily's Place? Over on Broome?"

She nodded.

"I've heard of it. You're on. When are we going?"

"Not this weekend, like I said, so I'll let you know." She curved her lips into a kittenish smile. "You and Jeanette just might get along fine."

"Dancing, you mean?"

"Maybe. Or inspiration of the romantic sort."

"Get out! You're my inspiration in that department, Nellie March."

"And that's another thing. Stop calling me that. I don't want Mr. Fields to think I'm pushy. I'd rather impress him by doing a good job with Mr. Michaels."

Calvin picked up his pencil and doodled on his sketch pad. "Spoilsport."

❧

Dr. Underwood held Nell's latest drawing at arm's length for their end-of-session chat. He adjusted his bow tie, black with pink dots today, and scrutinized the drawing through narrowed eyes.

"Very nice. You've quite an artistic flair. This is your mother?"

"Yes, sir. In the r-rose garden at our home in England." He'd prompted Nell to think of a time of change in her life.

"Was there a reason she was wearing black? Her gardening dress, perhaps, or was this during her mourning period following your father's death?"

"The d-dress is actually d-dark gray, the one she often wore when tending the roses."

"I see. And the shadows, the boiling clouds, the field in the background? Those were black, too?"

Nell glanced at her work. From a distance it *was* dark with only a few splotches of red for the roses her mama was tending. She could see now they were the only bright things on the paper and looked almost like drops of blood. And the layout of the garden was wrong. How had that happened?

Nell shuddered. She supposed Dr. Underwood would assign some theory of anger or fear of death to the drawing. It hadn't been her intention, but she now realized that both had simmered under the surface as she'd drawn. It had been a gloomy day with storm clouds gathering. Her mother wanted to finish pruning the roses so Nell offered to push Caroline in the pram. Her baby sister had horrible colic and had worn the nurserymaid to a frazzle so they'd brought her outside.

Nell explained it all to Dr. Underwood.

"Yes, I see." He set the drawing aside.

"You s-see what?" Maybe she did have some psychological disorder, but she didn't see that drawing pictures was helping with her stammering, although she still had an odd sensation when looking at this one. From the angle she'd used, the garden shed wasn't visible, but she'd drawn one in on the upper right side of the page. Maybe her memory of home was fading.

"I see that you're a perceptive young woman with a keen eye for detail. The introduction of a younger sibling into the family would certainly be a life-changing experience." He stroked his chin. "Interesting that you omitted yourself and the infant from the drawing."

"It wasn't that at all!" Nell's pulse hitched up a notch. Caroline's arrival after the death of her father had brought a spark of joy to the manor that the war had robbed from them. The doctor had come to the wrong conclusion. Dead wrong.

"Perhaps next week we can explore this further. Finding the root of one's problem is often like peeling the layers of an onion. And the process can be painful, but necessary, to get to the heart of the matter." He opened her folder and handed her a new packet of word exercises.

Nell thought it odd that he didn't ask her to give a verbal recital of the ones from the week before, but there were many things she didn't understand about her therapy. She took the list and rose from her chair, uncertain she would even return.

As the trolley lumbered along and cars whizzed by on either side, Nell's thoughts were on that long ago day of her drawing.

While she'd rocked Caroline's pram back and forth soothing her, the constable had come up the drive, delivering the news that her grandfather, the Earl of Marchwold, had been hit by a lorry and died instantly. The sudden loss of her kind and gentle grandfather had brought not only fresh grief upon them all, but it was also the event that sealed her destiny.

Five months later, Nell, her mother, and Caroline had boarded a ship at Liverpool and sailed, leaving all former things behind.

CHAPTER 7

Even though Soren Michaels had a touch of silver at his temples, he didn't look a day over thirty. He breezed into the consultation room, and after the minimum of small talk, he pulled his designs from a leather tube case and tacked them to the cork wall for Nell and Mr. Fields to survey. Nervous energy radiated from him as his piercing blue eyes darted from the sketches and back to Nell and Mr. Fields, judging their reactions.

"I call this one Persimmon Enchantment. The bodice will be a rich but muted shade of burnished orange lace with intricate beading at the waist that will be repeated in the band at the hem."

Nell and Mr. Fields both nodded as Mr. Michaels proceeded to the next dress, a dark brown drop waist made of crinkly georgette with a wide satin band where the bodice and skirt met.

The designs were detailed and stunning to look at, much like Mr. Michaels himself with his sleek dark hair parted slightly off-center. He oozed with confidence, bordering on arrogance. A gifted designer to be sure—an up-and-coming star in the world of couture— but Nell wasn't altogether sure she liked him. She knew she could learn from him, though, and concentrated on the designs, mentally choosing millinery styles and fabrics that would bring out the best features of each gown.

He concluded with a cocktail dress with netting that flared from the back waist in a half peplum, which he called Pink Froth. He made a half bow and said, "For your pleasure. What do you think?"

"You do b-beautiful work, Mr. Michaels. I can see why Claudia and Daphne are so fond of you."

Mr. Fields stroked his mustache. "An interesting mix. Slanted more toward younger women than I had hoped."

"Ah, do you not find that all women want to be thought of as eternally youthful? I strive to establish the illusion and yet make each of my designs in such a way that they disguise the minute flaws of a woman's figure." He pointed to a deep green gown with seed pearls circling the neckline. "You'll notice the ruching at the waist here. The gentle tucks at the midriff are for the curvy woman who would desire to minimize a minor flaw. And yet quite suitable for someone young like Nell here."

Mr. Fields shrugged and gave an almost imperceptible nod of agreement, then pulled a sheaf of papers from his briefcase. "Sorry to rush, but I've had Pritchard, my secretary, work up some figures, what we're willing to invest in this trial venture. Since this is your first formal show and experimental at best, you may find the figures lower than you expected. Not to mention that we will be in a bit of a bind while Nell is pulled from her routine duties to work with you."

Soren Michaels gave a cursory glance at the papers Mr. Fields handed him. "I'm sure we can work out the details. The Stottlemeir Club has been quite generous in their arrangements, and the world is holding its breath to learn more about you and your creative designs. When Mrs. Benchley suggested the name for the hat line, I was quite taken with it. The time Nell takes will return to you tenfold, I can assure you."

Mr. Fields scoffed. "That remains to be seen. And to be clear, the hats will carry the same label as always. The name Oscar Fields means something. Nellie March does not."

Mr. Michaels held up his hand. "You're aware, I'm sure, that milliners are finding dedicated lines quite popular with their customers. Murdoch's has their Mother Goose line for children, and Benton's in Boston has the delightful Nantucket line for fashionable young women."

Mr. Fields sniffed. "Unless this show is a smashing success and there's some reason besides 'Everyone else is doing it,' we'll not be jumping on the bandwagon. Miss Marchwold has proven she can please a handful of clients, not the countless men and women who have come through these doors for more than thirty years."

Mr. Michaels narrowed his eyes ever so slightly. "Very well. Time will tell."

Mr. Fields nodded. "Indeed."

As Mr. Fields neared the exit, Nell said in a cheery tone, "The designs will be s-stunning, you'll see."

When Mr. Fields had gone, Mr. Michaels said, "Mavis told me to expect Fields to be starchy. She didn't mention skeptical and tight-fisted."

"He m-means well. And this is a new v-venture for all of us, Mr. Michaels." She couldn't believe how easily she came to her boss's defense, but he was giving her an opportunity. One where she meant to excel.

He pulled the designs from the corkboard, rolled them up, and told her he would have duplicates sent to her by the following morning. "And please, I'd prefer that you call me Soren."

"Soren, it is."

By Friday, Nell had a dozen rough sketches for her meeting with Soren. Lovely hats with enough traditional air about them that she was sure even Mr. Fields would approve.

Soren looked them over, and after a cursory glance, he tossed them aside. "Mundane. Not quite the flair I had expected from you."

"These are pr-pr-pre—"

"Preliminary. Is that what you're trying to say? My philosophy is to go for the daring right out off the top. If you want to make it in this cutthroat business, you have to stand head and shoulders above the rest. Fresh. Original. Not boring." He handed her a sheet of paper with a list. "These are my final selections for the show. Eight ensembles, and I've included two extras for good measure. Two weeks should be adequate time for you to come up with dazzling, agree?"

She nodded, miffed somewhat that he hadn't given her any direction one way or the other about his expectations. Mind reading wasn't a skill she possessed. Fresh? Original? She thought she'd done that.

"I'll be by on Monday morning to see what I hope will be designs more inspiring than these." He ripped the parchments in two and handed them back, then spun around and left.

Nell's face flamed. What nerve. All her work ripped in half. Perhaps she should tell Mr. Fields the collaboration wasn't a good idea.

Her stomach knotted. Giving up now would only prove that her boss was right and would likely lead him to say she didn't have what it took. He would never give her another chance.

Soren Michaels wouldn't be the first obstinate person she encountered in the fashion world. She looked at the tattered pages. Soren was right. They were mundane.

Dazzling he wanted. Dazzling she would give him.

CHAPTER 8

Dust motes danced in the sunrays bathing the tiny kitchen table in Nell's flat with natural light. She'd been at work since dawn on Saturday after working until well past midnight making new sketches. After a few false starts, she took a new direction and went for the more dramatic. Basic shapes but delicate beadwork and sparkle. More intricate patterns and unusual fabric choices. Her hours at the library poring over fashion books paid off.

She refreshed her tea and surveyed her work so far. A good beginning. She doodled on one of the discarded sketches, writing Nellie March in a fancy script, then block letters. It was silly, she knew, to even dream that someday she'd have her own line. She scratched out the block letters.

Jeanette ambled by and peeked over her shoulder. "Nellie March?" She squinted her eyes and leaned over closer.

"Oh, I see! Nell Marchwold. Nellie March. A stage name, like Greta wanting to be called Greta Leona."

"Something like that. I didn't know Greta wanted a stage name."

"Are you two talking about me?" Greta strolled into the kitchen, her silk robe hanging open, her hair matted to the sides of her head like a golden retriever in need of grooming.

Jeanette said, "Morning, sunshine. Have fun last night or is that subject off-limits?"

Greta got a bowl from the corner shelf and Post Toasties from the cupboard. "Complete bust. The director who promised he'd give me an audition in his new drama never showed. I wore silk stockings and everything to make a good impression."

"That stinks. Guess we're both pathetic. I got my anthropology midterm back. C minus." Jeanette thumbed toward Nell. "Get this. Nell's thought of a keen stage name for herself. Nellie March."

"It's not a stage name. And Calvin Gold's the one who thought of it."

Greta spooned in a mouthful of cereal. "Nellie March. Catchy."

"That's what Mrs. Benchley said. She and Calvin think I'll get my own label after the show with Soren Michaels."

Jeanette snorted. "Shows how much they know. Trust me, Uncle Oscar would never in a million years let you have your own label."

"He hasn't actually said he would, but he did promise when he hired me that he'd make me a top designer. It never hurts to dream, does it?"

"Oh, I'm sure he's promised to take you to the moon and back, too. Anything to make sure his little company keeps selling hats, and he keeps getting credit." Jeanette flicked a curl from her forehead.

"H-how…wh-why are you saying this?"

Jeanette and Greta exchanged a look that Nell didn't understand.

Greta said, "What Jeanette is trying to say is that Mr. Fields is stringing you along, making grand promises when what he's really interested in is what you're willing to do for him." She tilted her head and gave a coy smile.

Nell shook her head. "That's terrible. I would never…and you shouldn't, either." What was even more terrible was the realization that Greta might have already done just that in her desperation to land a part. "You…you didn't?"

Greta grimaced. "No, but I was this close." She held her thumb and forefinger up to where they were almost touching, but not quite. "If the creep would've shown up last night..."

"I'm glad for you that he didn't. You'll make it. You need a lucky break, that's all."

Greta picked up her bowl and slurped the milk from it. "You make your own breaks, that's what everyone says." She put her bowl in the sink and said she was going to take a bubble bath and soak away her sorrow.

"Greta's right. You think you've got this swell deal going with Uncle Oscar."

"I didn't say I had anything going *with* him."

"Same as." Jeanette offered Nell a hand and pulled her to her feet. "Let me tell you a little story about your dear Oscar."

Nell's stomach did a funny dance. Jeanette was serious. Or seriously trying to make something out of nothing.

Jeanette sat Nell down on the love seat. "Here's the truth, my innocent dove. Oscar Fields is out to get whatever he can from whomever he can. Aunt Anna would have been the first in line to tell you that."

"I thought she was happily married to Mr. Fields."

"At first, yes. I was pretty young then and didn't know anything except that Aunt Anna made the most darling bonnets for me and my cousins. She was an apprentice like you, but under Oscar's father. From what I've heard Oscar was only eighteen when his dad died and he inherited the business. He knew next-to-nothing about design, but Anna did. Oscar courted her and said if she'd marry him, he'd make her the principal milliner, give her a line of hats, and make her a star. Ha! All he wanted was her talent."

Nell inhaled through her nose, the familiarity of it nibbling away at her. Jeanette's words were nearly identical to Mr. Fields's promises to her in Kentucky. Without the marriage thrown in.

After securing an introduction to Nell at the Kentucky Derby, Mr. Fields had quizzed her about her experience and arranged to meet her the next day at her rented shop on Bardstown Road. Her mother, skeptical and protective, accompanied her. Mr. Fields had been flattering and oozing with charm, examining her workmanship and her designs.

"You're the kind of designer who could go places in New York, and I would consider it an honor if you would come to Oscar Fields Millinery." Nell would have left with him that day if her mother hadn't stepped in and said that suitable arrangements would have to be made first.

Nell was pleased at her mother's interest, but she got the impression that, once Mr. Fields had presented a plan and spoke privately with her mother, Evangeline Marchwold was glad to hand her daughter off. She was already working with Granville Larson, a botany professor, and Nell suspected her mother was in love with him. Shuffling Nell off to New York would ease any hurt Nell might feel that her father was being replaced. Indeed, six months later, her mother and Granville had married. Unfortunately, the lavish praise from Mr. Fields stopped long before that. In two years, Nell could count on one hand the number of times her boss had given her a compliment. The "going places" now seemed as remote as Jupiter.

"It's not the same thing. He's not *after* me, not trying to get fresh or anything."

"But he's not giving you proper credit, is he?"

"Not yet, but maybe he's just waiting to see if things go well with Soren."

"I wouldn't count on it. Marrying Anna for her talent was just the beginning. He started spending more time at his club, and Anna suspected he might be having an affair. She began to feel trapped, unable to advance her career and stuck in a crummy marriage."

Something was off. If there were bad feelings between Mr. Fields and Jeanette's family, then it made no sense for Jeanette to have agreed to let Nell room with her.

When she asked about it, Jeanette jumped up and put a phonograph record on the Victrola. "I had my reasons."

"And?"

"I needed help. You know we don't have much, Mother and me. And Dad…well, you know."

Jeanette seldom talked about her dad, but Nell knew Mr. North had been injured in the war and suffered from nerve damage and breathing problems. Nell didn't want to embarrass her roommate by prying. "You don't have to tell me."

"It's all right. You asked. The truth is I didn't want you to live with us even though Uncle Oscar offered to pay my part of the lease if I agreed. I thought you'd be some pathetic little thing—whiny or demanding or flighty—but I really needed the money."

"It sounds like you're trying to get rid of me."

"No, gracious no. Greta and I love having you here. We just didn't expect to like you is all. And you make spiffy hats. No one's done that for me since Aunt Anna died."

"It's nice to be appreciated." She scrunched her nose. "And to be your personal milliner."

"Thing is, you're good. And you have an inner strength. Integrity, I guess. You deserve to get your own label, but it's going to be tough with Oscar. Anything I can do?"

"Say a prayer that I get everything done on time."

If Soren didn't like her designs, then it was all moot anyway.

On Monday, Nell met Soren in the salon at ten o'clock. He kissed her on the cheek like they were longtime friends, then asked to see the sketches. Nell's stomach was a swarm of nerves, her palms sweaty, when she handed them over.

Soren narrowed his eyes and examined each one without a word. His expression was unreadable, but when he'd finished, a wide smile graced his face, his eyes like star sapphires.

"Stunning. Mesmerizing. Perfect!" He tapped on one of the sketches. "The most unusual pattern of beading I've ever seen. Fit for royalty."

"Thank you. And thanks for the nudge. I've wanted to do more experimenting, but..."

"Yes, I know. Fields is stodgy, which isn't uncommon in the fashion industry. His way appeals to the masses and pays the bills. He'll give you a little leeway to see if what you design catches on. If it does, he'll want to keep a close eye on you so you remain loyal to him."

"Why wouldn't I? He's giving me a chance."

"Take it from me. When you're young, it's easy to confuse your dreams with vanity and get ahead of yourself. I learned that the hard way."

Nell waited, but he didn't elaborate. "And if my designs don't catch on?"

"You'll be looking for another job."

Like Nora Remming.

It felt like a warning of some sort, that failure was possible. And in a strange way, an echo of what Jeanette and Greta had said. Were they all telling her not to get her hopes up? Or did they think she wasn't capable of success? Maybe getting her own label wasn't imminent, but it was certainly worth going after.

That afternoon Nell tacked the sketches for both the dresses and the hats on the workroom wall so Hazel and Marcella, the other assembly workers who'd volunteered to help with the beadwork, could get a feel for the projects.

Nell retreated to her usual corner, back against the wall, as she crafted new foundations, added the outer fabrics, and supervised both of her helpers. Steiger had been snippier than ever since she'd gotten the show with Soren. The word was he was miffed that he was wrong about her getting fired. She couldn't let Steiger get the best of her. Nor Percy who'd been decidedly cool since she'd gotten the project. Besides, there was really no time with the runway show coming up so soon, and she wanted everything to be perfect.

When the evening arrived, Nell felt ready. When she arrived at the Stottlemeir Club, she found Soren pacing and fretful, not oozing confidence like he normally did.

"Stage fright," he told her. "The house is packed."

Nell peeked around the curtain. Servers in black tails and starchy shirts weaved through the crowd—yes, swarms of people. Potential customers, but finicky critics as well if they didn't like what they saw. In the wings, Soren fussed over the mannequins—"models" they were called in America—tucking a lock of dark hair behind one's ear, running around with a rouge pot and adding more color to cheekbones, cooing that they were going to be simply marvelous.

When the girls were lined up and the president of the club had given the welcome, Soren gripped Nell's hand. "You run on, darling, and sit with Oscar so you can gauge people's reaction. I can handle the script."

She wished him luck, thankful that with her stammer, she wasn't called on to help with introducing the ensembles. Nell slipped into the chair between Mr. Fields and Calvin, took a deep breath, and noticed that Mrs. Benchley and her daughters shared their table. Cozy, like a family. Candles flickered on each of the tables, the effect that of a kaleidoscope with the reflections of the silver place settings and lovely rose centerpieces. Nell's mother would've approved, crazy as she was over roses.

Calvin took her trembling hand and gave it a squeeze. "Nice dress."

It was a nice dress—one of Soren's "extra" designs. The buttercup silk moved with her, and the headpiece she'd designed for it made her feel elegant with its headband of pearls and a center medallion with emerald, topaz, and peridot stones. She wore it across her forehead and let her blonde hair tumble to her shoulders.

Mr. Fields leaned over and whispered, "I hope this isn't much ado about nothing."

Nell did a hesitant thumbs-up at the edge of the table and turned her attention to the introduction of Soren Michaels.

The staging area had twinkly lights like stars on the black curtain at the back and swags of greenery with hurricane lamps before the footlights. The girl modeling Persimmon Enchantment stepped out and struck a pose.

"Our first selection is a rich silk gown with contrasting velvet cording and a waist treatment of decorative embroidery accented with cerulean beadwork. The banded hemline echoes the waist. A dress fit for royalty, but it will be appreciated by the charming hostess or guest at a late autumn dinner party." Soren's voice was as enchanting as the auburn-haired mannequin who pivoted onstage as he spoke. A photographer with his black box atop a tripod was stationed at the side of the stage and captured the moment.

Soren continued, "Topping off the ensemble is a silk velvet cloche with metallic beading and an appliquéd design that complements the gown." Applause exploded as the mannequin glided down the carpeted aisle between the tables and exited through the rear entry. When the murmur died down, Soren introduced the next ensemble in the collection. Mr. Fields's face was wooden as he reached for his glass and took a sip. Mrs. Benchley, though, leaned across Mr. Fields and gave Nell a glowing smile.

The fifth dress of the evening was a merlot gown that shimmered as if it were a second skin on the pert blonde woman modeling it. When she turned and gave a coquettish look over her shoulder, spontaneous applause broke out. The crowd loved it, and as Soren completed the description of the bejeweled hat that completed the ensemble, Mr. Fields draped his arm casually behind Nell, his thumb idly running up and down the back of her bare arm. She stiffened but kept her eyes on the stage.

Soren saved his favorite for last. The mannequin's straight dark hair swung just above her shoulders as she entered and posed. "Midnight Masquerade is our final gown of the evening. Whether dancing with your sweetheart or being the life of the party as you welcome in the New Year, this chiffon chemise features an overblouse with smoky glass bugle beads. The fluid swing of the rhinestone-studded strips of the skirt will guarantee every eye is on you as you dance the night away."

Stepping onto the runway, the mannequin put enough swagger in her walk so the strips of the skirt swayed, alive in the glow of the hurricane lamps.

Soren's mellow voice hitched up a notch. "The ensemble is completed with spool-heeled shoes with a trio of straps secured with jeweled buttons and a delicate mesh skullcap with rhinestones and a band of bugle beads in the same smoky glass as the evening dress."

At the final turn, the brunette's eyelids fluttered and she kicked back one heel, flirting with the crowd. The audience rose to its feet in thunderous applause.

Soren allowed the room to settle before his final remarks.

"It is with utmost pleasure that I thank you, the members of the Stottlemeir Club, for your rapturous attention. And a special nod to my friend Oscar of Oscar Fields Millinery—" He made a wide gesture toward Mr. Fields.

Oscar stood and bowed to the crowd. "Thank you, Mr. Michaels, for a grand show, and my gratitude to all of you who came; I'm delighted at your response and look forward to serving you with all your millinery needs."

As more clapping rippled through the crowd, Mrs. Benchley leaned over and swatted Mr. Fields on the arm. "I would think you would at least have mentioned our sweet Nell. I was so hoping that you might make a noble gesture and introduce her and the Nellie March line."

Nell held her breath. Yes, she'd wished for that, too, but an old nursery rhyme ran singsong through her head. *If wishes were horses, beggars would ride.*

Mr. Fields frowned. "That was never part of the deal. If anyone should get credit, it would be you, dear Mavis. You're the genius behind this. And only time will tell if it brings any business our way."

Wishing for her own label was useless. And Mr. Fields was right. Only time would tell. Calvin leaned in and whispered, "For the record, I think you're the bee's knees. And your hats weren't half-bad, either. Now if you could just sprinkle some of that magic dust on me, we'd both be set."

CHAPTER 9

Calvin insisted on escorting Nell home, and when the cab pulled up to her address, Nell said, "Sal's lights are still on. You want to see if we can get a cup of tea?"

"It's tempting, but the folks in your neighborhood don't take too kindly to serving people like me."

Nell whipped her head toward his. "Because you're Jewish? That's ridiculous. Sal and Felice would welcome anyone who was a friend of mine."

"Tea sounds nice. Why not live dangerously?"

The door clanged when they entered. Chairs had already been stacked on the tables, and Felice pulled a rag mop around the floor like a dancing partner. Her head shot up when she saw them.

"Thank goodness, you're here. I've worried five years off my life waiting for you. First, you don't come home after work; then you stay out late." Her eyes widened when she took a good look at Calvin. "Well, who do we have here?"

Nell gave Felice a hug. "I have someone for you to meet. This is Calvin Gold, the one from work I've told you about."

Felice eyed him up and down. "Happy to meet you."

Calvin tipped his fedora. "Nice to make your acquaintance. I've heard nice things about you and the diner."

Felice nodded. "And a gentleman, too, I see. I hate to bring the bad news..." She pulled a wheat-colored envelope from the pocket of her apron and thrust it into Nell's hands.

The Western Union emblem on the outside was unmistakable. The air inside the diner thinned. Nell squinted to read the type through the envelope to see who it was from, hoping it wasn't something dreadful. Wires they received from England, where telephoning was out of the question, were only to announce important events like births and deaths. Her stomach went queasy.

"Thank you, Felice."

"Aren't you going to open it? Here, step over here where the light is better. I'll bring you and your friend a cuppa tea with a dash of Angelo's secret ingredient, just in case there's no good news."

"That would be lovely. But no secret ingredient, okay?" Although a shot of brandy from Angelo's hiding place might be just what she needed, there's no telling what it would do to her on an empty stomach. Nell set her handbag on the nearest table while Felice hovered next to her, her breath a warm garlic fog. Nell scanned the message, afraid to breathe herself, but then she clapped her hand over her mouth to stop the shriek.

"What? I pray it's not bad news. I've had a terrible feeling—"

"No. Not bad news at all. It's from Aunt Sarah. Mittie. Iris. They're coming, and they'll be here t-tomorrow! Isn't that wonderful?"

Felice leaned on her mop and did the sign of the cross. "Thank heavens. Your aunt, yes? I remember. Stick of a thing, like you. And her girls, twins, no? *Bella* and full of the spice."

Nell gave Felice another hug. "I'll bring them to see you."

"Angelo will make gnocchi just for you. And bring this nice young man with you."

"Yes. Gnocchi. Th-thank you."

After their tea and saying good night to Felice, Nell thought of inviting Calvin up to the flat, but she didn't think encouraging him was a good idea. In the next instant, he saved her from the awkward moment. "It's a nice evening for a walk, so I'll catch the subway. Guess the dancing tomorrow night is out."

"I'd forgotten all about that, but no harm in you going with my roommates. You said you wanted to live dangerously."

"Give me a call." He kissed her on the cheek. "Guess if I can't dance with you, I'll have to make do with someone else."

"You'll be fine with Jeanette and Greta. More than fine."

⚬⚬⚬

People elbowed and shoved as they rushed through the mammoth, clattering expanse of Grand Central Terminal. Nell arrived early so she could station herself on the west side of the giant clock on the main concourse. It had been the agreed-upon meeting place for the previous visits from Aunt Sarah and her cousins. And the place Oscar Fields had first met her when she arrived in New York.

The same nervous anticipation filled her stomach, as it had on that day two years ago. She'd been both terrified and giddy from the possibilities that lay before her. When she'd emerged from the train and asked for directions to the giant clock, she clung to the promise that Mr. Fields had hinted at—that she would be a principal designer within months.

Now, with people brushing past at an alarming click, and the hiss and clatter of the trains, the glow of that promise had dimmed. Or maybe she'd matured with the reality that to make a name for herself might take longer than she first thought. Perhaps even years.

Nell spotted Mittie first and waved. Her cousin waved back and loped toward her. At eighteen, Mittie was still all legs and arms with a wild mane of dark hair like the saddlebred horses her daddy, Eli Humphreys, raised in Kentucky. Aunt Sarah and Iris, Mittie's twin who bore no resemblance to her sister, had to run to keep up with Mittie, but soon enough they were in each other's arms, everyone talking at once.

Then Aunt Sarah put both hands on Nell's shoulders and held her at arm's length. "Oh, sugar, you just get more gorgeous every time I see you. Look at you, so cosmopolitan with that darling cloche—" She turned to Iris. "—This is what I was telling you I saw in *Vogue*." She turned back to Nell and kissed her on the cheek.

"That's from your mama. She came to the station to send us off and sends her love and a package that's somewhere in all this mess." A porter stood by with a cart piled with luggage. "Come on, girls, let's not keep the gentleman waiting forever and a day."

Thirty years in America had erased all but a hint of her aunt's Yorkshire accent, replaced with that akin to warm honey on a hot biscuit. Southern, they called it in the States. To Nell, it was the sound of ice tinkling in glasses of sweet tea, the chirp of crickets as dusk settled on the rolling meadows of Kentucky.

Nell held Aunt Sarah's hand and guided her toward the cabstand, and it wasn't until they were crowded together in the yellow taxi that Nell was finally able to ask what brought them to New York.

Mittie unlatched the back window, shoved it open, and waved away the smoke of Aunt Sarah's cigarette. "Sorry. Mother might have given up some of her vices, but not her Chesterfields."

Aunt Sarah sniffed and waved the cigarette in its silver holder through the air. "It's quite fashionable, you know, and besides, I feel I must support the local tobacco-growing economy."

Mittie tucked a strand of dark hair behind her ear. "Yeah, the way you supported the local bookies." She quirked her mouth into a fake grin.

Aunt Sarah's gambling debacle had nearly ruined Uncle Eli two years earlier. On the same weekend as the Kentucky Derby when Nell had met Oscar Fields, her aunt nearly lost their entire fortune placing bets with an acquaintance, who turned out to be nothing but a gangster. Nell suspected Mittie's remark was a lingering grudge because her favorite horse had been sold to recoup some of Aunt Sarah's losses.

Iris sighed. "Leave it alone, Mittie. We came to shop and have fun."

Aunt Sarah took a long draw on the cigarette and said, "To answer your question, Nell, we simply had to get away. Our upstairs plumbing sprung a leak and ruined half of the Persian rugs, not to mention the water spots on the hickory floors. A week of workers banging and carting things in and out would drive anyone mad. Besides, with Iris being a debutante this season, this was the perfect opportunity to buy her a few gowns for the upcoming balls."

Iris but not Mittie? Pretty, popular Iris. Mittie, the wild one who defied taming. It was no secret that Mittie would rather jump off Louisville's K & I Bridge into the depths of the Ohio River than go through *the season*. She was much happier dressed in jodhpurs and riding boots letting the wind blow through her hair as she exercised her daddy's champion show horses.

Aunt Sarah had made reservations at the Algonquin Hotel in Midtown. Once they were in the suite and the porter had been tipped, Aunt Sarah collapsed on the davenport in the sitting room.

"You know I never sleep a wink in those Pullman cars, and I've developed the most dreadful headache. Why don't you girls do the town without me? Maybe you can catch a Rudolph Valentino moving picture this evening."

Iris said, "Mother, are you sure? I don't want you to miss out."

Aunt Sarah nodded. "Don't worry, sugar. I'll order something from room service and retire early."

Nell said, "Actually, my roommates and I had tentative plans, but we'd love for Mittie and Iris to come, too."

Aunt Sarah put her feet up and lit a cigarette. "There you go, sweet peas. You don't need me for a wet blanket." She pulled a handful of bills from her handbag and handed them to Iris. "Have fun."

Smoke hung like thin clouds in the air at Lily's Place. A jazz combo played "The Four O'Clock Blues" as Nell and Iris sipped ginger ale through straws. They'd arrived at eight, lucky to get a table near the dance floor.

The day had been a whirlwind. When they left Aunt Sarah at the hotel, Nell had taken her cousins to Sal's for the gnocchi Felice had promised. Afterward, Jeanette and Greta joined them for a shopping spree to get sequins, feathers, and elastic for headbands that Jeanette insisted *all* the girls were wearing. Her roommates were thrilled over Iris and Mittie joining them and opened their closets to them. Somehow they'd come up with five outfits that didn't require too many alterations. When they put on the headbands Nell whipped together, they all giggled like schoolgirls.

Calvin was waiting outside when they arrived and let out a low whistle when Nell introduced him to her roommates and cousins. "Bet there's not another fella in Manhattan who has a date with five gorgeous dolls."

Jeanette stepped forward and hooked her arm in Calvin's and batted her eyes. "You've got that right. What I want to know is why Nell kept a handsome fella like you from us all this time."

From the light coming through the front window of Lily's Place, Nell could see Calvin blush. He was sort of cute, with his dark hair and black eyes. He was more like the brother she never had, nothing more, and even if she were interested, she shuddered at what Mr. Fields might think of two employees fraternizing.

Once they were inside, Calvin took turns dancing with Mittie,

Greta, and Jeanette. When Nell teased him about saying he couldn't dance, he told her he'd been to his share of bar mitzvahs. He tried to drag Nell out on the floor, but she told him she'd rather just sit with Iris and catch up on news from home. Which wasn't entirely a lie. That afternoon Iris had confided in her that her parents were concerned about Mittie because she was so unfocused and couldn't decide what to do with her life. But rather than talk about Mittie, who went off dancing with first one dapper fellow, then another, Nell and Iris talked about fashion, and Nell admitted she'd really come to the club to get ideas and see what girls were wearing.

"Like that girl over there in the navy drop waist. You'd look cute in that."

Iris made a face. "You don't think it's too low-cut?"

"Not if it had a sheer georgette overlay on the top. And a real hat, a cloche maybe with soft folds and a beaded flower in gold to give it an elegant look."

Iris nodded toward a girl at the bar. "That rose color is divine."

"L-look at her profile, those high cheekbones. I'd love to do a hat for her."

"I'd like to pack you up and take you home with us. You could help me with my wardrobe. I'm a fright at putting things to-gether. I haven't really said anything, but this debutante thing was all Mother's idea. She wanted Mittie to go through it, too, but you know Mittie—she wanted none of it. The truth is, Mother met Daddy when she did her season in London, so she thinks it's a shoo-in for me to find a husband."

"Is that what you want? To get married?"

"Not when I'm eighteen. Look at you, you're independent and have a career. I'd like to go to college first. Mother says the only rea-son to do that is to find a husband, and then you never know what you'll end up with. At least the gentlemen who come to the debu-tante functions are from *proper families*. Mother's words, not mine."

A guy with his necktie askew staggered by their table, then stopped and turned around to look at them. He blinked his eyes and lifted his glass. "Am I seeing double or are you two twins?"

Iris and Nell looked at each other. They were both replicas of Aunt Sarah and their Yorkshire kin. Their mothers had always joked that someone must have switched Mittie and Nell at birth even though they'd been born three years apart. And on different continents.

Iris winked at Nell and flashed the wobbly intruder a smile. "Actually, I'm a twin, but she's not."

"Huh?" The guy squinted and took another drink. "I'm not sure what they're putting in the lemonade in this joint, but..." He shook his head and wandered off.

Iris and Nell were still laughing when the band called for an intermission. Calvin and Jeanette returned to the table, out of breath but glowing. Calvin took the seat between Nell and Jeanette and asked what was so funny.

"Family joke," Nell and Iris said in unison.

Greta sashayed up, swinging her hips and holding hands with one of her dance partners. "Hey there, I want everyone to meet Spike." She giggled and looked starry-eyed at the newcomer before returning her attention to them. "You aren't going to believe this—" She paused for dramatic effect. "Spike's in my Thursday evening acting group, and you should hear him do Romeo." Greta had an adoring Juliet look on her face and asked if Spike could join them.

Calvin held out his hand, "Good to meet you, pal. Pull up a chair."

Nell looked around for Mittie and spotted her talking to a girl wearing a creamy ivory cloche with a serpentine braid on one side. Odd, it looked like one of Nell's cloches from the portfolio she'd been working on before the show with Soren. Mr. Fields hadn't seen it yet, so she knew it wasn't from their assembly line. Maybe she wasn't as original as she thought. She'd have to toss that idea in the rubbish bin.

"Isn't that right, Nell?" Calvin nudged her.

"Uh…wh–what? I d–didn't hear you."

"I was telling Jeanette about the runway show and how the crowd loved your creations. It's just a matter of time until Nellie March becomes a reality."

Nell winced. "It's really too early to tell."

Jeanette twirled her rope of pearls and winked at Nell. "Uncle Oscar's not known for keeping his promises."

Calvin stopped a waiter going past with a tray of soft drinks. "Any chance you'd bring us a round of those?"

The waiter said they were welcome to the ones on the tray as long as it was only ginger ale they were after. Calvin fished some wadded bills from his pocket and tossed them on the tray. When the drinks had been passed around, Calvin lifted his glass. "To new friends and old. And Nellie March."

A general hubbub went around the table as Calvin explained how he'd come up with the name and that Mrs. Benchley jumped on it like a loose five-dollar bill on the sidewalk. He tried to make it sound like it didn't matter that Nell was getting the attention and not him, but Nell knew it did. It mattered to her, too. Calvin was as good at basic design as she was; he just hadn't found his groove yet. Sort of like Jeanette. But at the same time, it irritated her that Calvin assumed she'd get the nod for the label. The fizz in her stomach wasn't from the ginger ale.

Nell looked around again for Mittie and was relieved to see her jostling through the crowd toward the table.

When she arrived, Iris hissed, "Where have you been?"

Mittie scowled. "Where do you think I've been? Right here. Dancing. And having a swell time, I might add. Matter of fact, I thought that was the point of coming here." She gave a little wave to everyone around the table. "Iris and I can tell all our friends in Kentucky we've been to a speakeasy. Now if we could just figure out how to get a hold of some of that bathtub gin the newspapers crow about, our evening would be complete."

Iris gave her sister a disapproving look and said, "This was fun, but the truth is, we've had a long day. If you don't mind, Nell, maybe you can help us get a taxi back to the hotel. I don't want Mother to worry."

Mittie gave her sister a pouty look and Jeanette protested, "The night is still young. Just starting, actually. Stay a while longer." Nell understood her real meaning. *If you all leave, Calvin might go with you.* Which is exactly what he did, saying he wanted to be a reliable escort. He pecked Jeanette and Greta on their cheeks and said he'd had a grand time.

As they made their way to the exit, the band resumed playing. The lilting melody from a muted saxophone drifted through the haze. Nell nudged Calvin and leaned in so he could hear her. "Maybe you should stay and dance with Jeanette."

He shook his head. "She's swell, but it's not her I'm interested in." He meshed his fingers with hers, the heat from dancing still pulsing in his touch.

Nell squeezed his hand, wishing they could be more than friends, but somehow her heart wasn't in it.

Mittie glared at Iris when her sister held the door for them to exit. "You don't have to be such a killjoy. Things were just getting fun."

Outdoors, a cool evening breeze brushed their faces. Nell said, "It is getting late, but I'm glad you got to come."

Mittie laughed and draped her arms around a street lamp and leaned back, her hair floating in the breeze. "Me, too, sweet cousin. Me, too."

Nell shuddered while Calvin called, "Taxi!"

CHAPTER 10

When Nell arrived on Monday morning, a ceramic vase with a bouquet of red roses was at her place, and a cup of coffee, still steaming, sat on Calvin's empty desk. She sniffed the roses, no doubt from Soren. Mr. Fields didn't seem like the gift and flowers type. As she reached for the card tied to one of the stems, Calvin came in the door carrying a tea service.

"For you, my lady. Just the way you like it."

A small cream pitcher, a china cup, and a pot already steeping the tea.

"How did you know I missed my tea this morning?"

"Just a lucky guess."

"Mr. Fields wanted me here by eight sharp, and I couldn't dare be late." She bit her lip, the unopened card still in her hands and Calvin flashing her a curious, crooked grin.

"You gotta keep the boss happy. So what do you think?"

"About what?"

"The flowers?"

"They're b-beautiful." Slowly it came to her. The look on his face. The tea. They weren't from Soren or Mr. Fields at all. She pulled the card from the tiny envelope and read:

Congratulations, Nellie March!
Yours, Calvin

Tears sprang to her eyes, and when she dared to look at Calvin, he still had the same shy grin and looked as if he were holding his breath.

She stood on tiptoe and kissed him on the cheek. "Thank you, Calvin. How did you know they're my favorite?"

"I didn't. Not for sure. But you're always talking about your mother and her roses...well, I thought maybe you would like them."

"I love them. But you didn't have to."

"I'd have brought you flowers a lot sooner if I'd known that's what it took to get a kiss."

Nell's face grew hot. If ever she needed the right words, now was the time. Her tongue felt as leaden as the knot in her stomach.

"Thank you for the flowers, but please, could we just stop this talk about Nellie March? If I keep expecting it, Mr. Fields might balk and never give me a label. You know I want it in the worst way, but I want to be deserving and ready for it." It was the best she could come up with.

Calvin, bless him, stepped aside. "Better drink your tea before it gets cold." He went to his desk, pulled out a fresh sketch pad, and picked up his coffee mug. He had a nice profile, a muscular jaw that was clean-shaven. His Adam's apple bobbled as he swallowed his coffee.

"You're very nice, you know."

He made a soft snort. "That's what my mother says."

"Well, she's right." Nell poured cream into her cup and filled it with tea. When she took a sip, warmth like a soft throw washed over her. She liked Calvin, but it was wrong to lead him on, and she wished within her depths that she could at least feel a spark of something. If only he and Jeanette had hit it off.

An hour later, Mr. Fields called her into his office, pointed to a chair for her to sit, and asked about her weekend. But his tone implied he wasn't interested in the answer.

"My aunt and cousins from Kentucky made a surprise visit, so it was nice. And you?"

"I've had better. Seems we have a little problem. No, make that a big problem." He measured his words, the dark look lingering on his face.

Nell twirled a strand of hair that had escaped the chignon at her nape, wary of his tone. "Oh?"

"I just talked to Michaels on the phone. He's livid, says his phone hasn't stopped ringing. Apparently Daphne Benchley was shopping on Saturday and saw several gowns from the show in the House of Price display window. Phillip Price, his biggest rival. Daphne called him immediately, of course, but now he's blaming me *and* you for letting the designs come into unscrupulous hands."

Nell's breath caught, the gravity of his words hitting her like a brick. "Me? Why?"

"Michaels works solo, only has two dressmakers who he trusts implicitly. I've assured him you used the standard precautions for safekeeping of the designs, but it gives me pause. Did you show the drawings to anyone? Take them from the office?"

Nell's throat closed off, a sick feeling washing over her. "I...uh...well..."

"Speak up. Think. Who saw the designs?"

"I took them into the w-workroom so Hazel and Marcella c-could see them. They wouldn't do anything. You gave me p-permission to include them for the work. The beads and such. Otherwise, I would never have f-finished in time."

"What about Gold? Did Calvin see them?"

"Of course. We share a s-studio."

"I don't trust him."

"Calvin didn't steal them." Could he have? He did make a number of comments about the designs, but Nell tried to remember if he'd seemed partial to any of them. And he kept going on about the Nellie March label. Was it some kind of a cruel joke since none of his designs captured their boss's eye? No. Calvin wouldn't do something like that.

"I did sh-show them to Calvin, and Percy was there…uh, I think he was. I don't r-remember."

"Here I thought my biggest problem was to keep you from making a fool of yourself with your blamed speech defect, and now you've gone and breached our reputation. Ruined it."

"I d-didn't. I would n-never."

Harjo Pritchard stuck his head in the door. "Excuse me, could I have a word, please?"

Mr. Fields's jaw twitched. "You're excused, Miss Marchwold."

Nell hurried out as fear coiled in her stomach. She stopped in the stairwell to collect herself. She was finished at Oscar Fields Millinery. Mama would no doubt let her return home to Kentucky and mop up her tears, which now streamed down her cheeks, but she was a failure. Pure and simple. And embarrassed. But careless? How? Confusion churned with worry in the pit of her stomach. How had the designs been compromised?

She sat on the last step and put her head between her hands, going over the past two weeks. Taking the tube of designs to the workroom each day, showing them to Hazel and Marcella. Discussing them. The gnawing in her belly grew worse. She'd tacked them up on the cork the way she often did. Had she left them unattended?

She knew the answer. More than once, she'd gone to the notions room for supplies. At least a couple of times, she'd gone to appointments in the consultation room. Someone…anyone could have slipped a design or two from the tube and *borrowed* them.

On legs of lead, she went to the studio, but just outside the door, she took a breath and plastered a smile on her face. She wouldn't breathe a word to Calvin. Not yet, but in her heart, she knew she'd committed the unforgivable crime of the fashion world.

Thankfully, the studio was empty. She slumped into her chair. *Think. Do something.* Her mind was blank. She picked up her appointment diary to see if she had anything scheduled. Missing a meeting with a client would only add to her list of transgressions. Her morning was free. She pulled out a sketch pad and drew a few lines, but all she saw was Soren's face, the way his eyes flashed when he ripped her designs. He was capable of ruining her, but was it her fault?

She paced around the studio, Nora's empty table next to Percy's taunting her. Where was Percy? Calvin? Was Mr. Fields interrogating them? Calvin, she could imagine. Not Percy. He and Mr. Fields were chummy. She glanced at Percy's desk, the shelves above it tidy with his pencils, his supplies, a grainy picture of his grandchildren. A solid citizen.

Moving on, she went to the window and stared at the traffic below. Cars, like minnows, streamed in both directions. *House of Price.* That's where Daphne saw the alleged replicas. She'd seen it from the trolley on her way to Dr. Underwood's.

She grabbed her handbag and headed out the door, and after zigzagging between cars, she made it to the trolley stop. A woman with a shopping bag elbowed her. "Watch it!"

"Beg your pardon, miss. I didn't see you." No sign of the trolley. Just as Nell thought of hailing a cab, the familiar clang rang in the distance. Once aboard, she wished she had called a cab. It would have been faster than the trolley, which crept along at its usual lazy pace. Uncertainty skittered through her mind. Was this a waste of time?

Her steps slowed as she approached the House of Price, but one look at the window display, and Nell's heart plummeted. Two of Soren's designs hung on mannequin forms, and worse, one was his favorite—the black beaded dress with the swingy strips for a skirt. She braced herself and entered the store.

A plumpish clerk with a space between her two front teeth greeted her and asked how she could be of service.

Nell willed herself to be confident and not stammer. "The black dress in the window caught my eye. May I see it, please?"

The clerk lumbered over to a rack and pulled out a dress of the same style. Nell held it up and tilted her head as if to get a better look, but all the while inspecting it. The seams were sloppy, and whoever made it skimped on the bugle beads, which didn't have the exact pattern as Soren's design. A fair replica that looked good from a distance, but was decidedly poor quality up close.

"It's lovely. And so unique, but it's not exactly what I had in mind. Could I possibly make an appointment with Mr. Price and see if he can design something for me?"

The woman pinched her lips and drew up her shoulders. "Mr. Price only does custom orders for preferred customers. Have you been in before?"

Nell shook her head.

"Perhaps you'd find something else that would be more to your liking. We specialize in the latest couture and offer a range of styles."

"I'll just have a stroll around then." *Latest couture.* Right. Stolen from under the noses of other designers.

Nell feigned interest and ambled over to the hat display and nearly gasped before she caught herself. The velvet cloche she'd been working on the day Nora was fired graced the center of the display. Same magenta color, but again, not the best imitation, the rosette cheap, the lining a low grade of satin. Someone in the work-room had to be responsible.

Her neck prickled. She clearly remembered stowing her things when Harjo came in. She'd dashed off, then later remembered, she'd left the sketch on the worktable. Right in front of Calvin.

Nell pivoted suddenly and came face-to-face with the shop clerk. An odd feeling shrouded her—like she should be able to place the woman. "Beg your pardon. Say, I didn't catch your name."

"Mrs. Morris. Nadine Morris."

"Nadine, it was lovely to meet you. I'd relish trying on a couple of dresses, but I'm meeting someone for lunch. Perhaps later."

"And your name, miss?"

But Nell was already halfway to the door and more than ready to be gone. Not only Soren's designs, but hers as well. Someone was very cheeky. She just didn't know who.

❧

By Wednesday, when she met Aunt Sarah and the girls for a farewell dinner, nothing had changed. Nell had been busy with new requests, all friends of Mrs. Benchley from the Stottlemeir Club. The dreaded moment when Mr. Fields would call her back into his office and fire her hadn't come. When she ventured into the workroom, she saw *traitor* written on every face. And mostly, her heart ached for fear that Calvin was, in fact, the guilty party. Avoiding him was impossible, but she invented excuses to run off and not exchange their normal banter. During her lunch breaks, she wandered amid the shops in the garment district, looking for other imitation dresses in shop windows, scrutinizing hat displays to see if one of hers was there. A feeling in her bones told her the cloche with serpentine braid she'd seen at Lily's Place had been lifted from her portfolio as well. But her noontime searches turned up nothing new.

Aunt Sarah looked up from the menu in the dining room at the Algonquin Hotel. "I've heard that some of the *Vanity Fair* writers frequent here at lunch. Not that I would know them in person, mind you, but it does have quite a literary feel, doesn't it? I suppose now that you're moving up in the fashion business, Nell, you'll be moving in the finer circles and might happen upon them."

Nell shook her head. "I d–doubt it. The show wasn't as successful as I first thought." It was vague without going into the details.

"You look weary. Is everything all right?"

"Fine. And I'm happy to see you all again. Tell me, have you had a good trip?"

After they ordered, her aunt and cousins chattered about the shops they'd visited, the clothes they'd ordered, and going to the New Amsterdam Theatre to see the Ziegfeld Follies.

The waiter served their meal and asked if there was anything else. Aunt Sarah waved him away and leaned in. "Enough about us. Tell me, I've had such hopes that things would materialize with you and the young man in your office. What was his name?"

"Calvin Gold." Mittie drummed her fingers on the table and gave her mother an impatient look. "He's not Nell's type. We told you that."

Aunt Sarah nodded. "Yes, sweetie. But that wasn't who I was referring to. It wouldn't be all that unusual for an apprentice to catch the eye of her boss. And if I remember correctly, he's quite dashing."

Nell nearly choked on her sip of water. "Mr. Fields? Oh, goodness, I'm not in the least bit interested. He's much older for one thing, and my career is first." Aunt Sarah's idea was preposterous, although her mother had made similar remarks, had asked if Mr. Fields had taken her out socially, letting her hopes dangle over the telephone wires.

"But, darling, surely you've thought of your prospects." She patted Nell's hand. "Perhaps when you come to Louisville for Iris's Christmas ball, you'll catch the eye of some nice young man."

"Mmmm." It was easier to go along than be the pebble in Aunt Sarah's shoe, and it was difficult to explain how working with Soren had ignited such passion in her. And it wasn't romance.

"It's going to be simply marvelous. Two days after Christmas during that lull before New Year's. We've hired a band and..."

Everyone had their obsessions—even Aunt Sarah. Nell just hoped she still had a job by Christmas.

While her aunt stopped for a breath, Iris clapped her hands together. "I bet that Nellie March thing catches on, and you'll be swamped with orders. Isn't that the cutest name?"

Nell shrugged. "No label. It was silly to get my hopes up."

Aunt Sarah said that was nonsense and then changed direction and told her about her latest project with the Louisville Women's League. When the waiter served their dessert and Aunt Sarah took the last bite of cheesecake, she licked her lips and said, "Delicious. Not that I would put it up against the buttermilk pie the Ladies Aid serves at our church, but quite satisfactory. As I was saying, you need to come up to our suite so I can give you your mother's package."

Nell had forgotten her mother sent something and was cheered at the prospect. She hoped it was a new scarf or a packet of rose petals for the bath. Something she could use and not another recipe book to catch dust and clutter their already-cramped kitchen.

Nell folded her napkin. "I'm ready whenever you are."

Wrapped in brown paper, the package was rectangular, thinner than a book. Inside the brown paper was a layer of newspaper. An envelope with her mother's handwriting protruded between the overlapping edges. Nell opened the note first.

Dearest Nell,

Your grandmother shipped this along with some other things that didn't fit her new surroundings in Heathdown. I've saved them for you but am letting Caroline play with the miniature china tea set. As I recall, you didn't care much for it. You can have a look-see when you come for Christmas. For now, though, I thought you'd like to have this.

Must get this ready for your Aunt Sarah. She's in a frightful rush as always.

With much love,
Mama

With trembling fingers, Nell removed the paper. Her breath caught in her throat. The embroidery that hung in Grandmama's bedchamber above her writing desk. Nell hugged it to her chest, her eyes burning.

"Well, darling, are you going to keep us in suspense forever?" Aunt Sarah puffed on her cigarette, sending out a wisp of smoke.

Nell held the framed handiwork at arm's length to take it in, then turned it for her aunt to see. "It's a s-sampler Grandmama made the year before she married my grandfather." She traced the words from Proverbs 31: *Strength and honor are her clothing; and she shall rejoice in time to come.* The stitching was still perfect; the figure of a woman to one side dressed in a blue dress with a hoopskirt and wearing a spoon bonnet that had been fashionable in the last century.

Aunt Sarah said, "That's lovely…and thoughtful. Not that I take much stock in ancient history. It was a happy day indeed when Eli swept me off my feet and carried me off to Kentucky. I've not missed the cold misery I left behind for even a moment."

Nell shuddered and whispered, "I miss everything about it."

"Even with your big exciting life in New York?"

"New York is swell. So was Kentucky. But they're not the same. They're not home."

"Home is what you make of it, that's what I've always told the girls. Of course, it's nicer if you have a man of means to share it with." She ground out her cigarette in the ashtray and narrowed her eyes. "Your mother would sleep better at night knowing you were at least *looking* for a husband."

She knew now what poor Iris was up against. "Someday, if the right person comes along, I'd love to marry." She flashed a grin. "After I'm famous, of course!" Then, unbidden, Quentin Bledsoe's familiar grin flashed through her head. She added, "I've only had one beau, and that was a long time ago."

Her aunt's eyes widened. "That vicar's son from the village. Oh, sugar. I thought you'd be over that long before now. Trust me, every one of us has had that first sip of forbidden nectar. Like Mittie and the farrier's son."

"Mother!" Mittie stood in the doorway. "I think you're the one that's been dipping in the forbidden nectar. What'd you do, persuade the waiter to doctor your coffee with a shot of bourbon?"

"Mittie, I do not drink. You know that. Besides, it's illegal. I'm merely trying to pass along some of the hard-earned wisdom I've gained over the years. You girls know I love you more than my Victoria sterling, but even it needs polishing now and then."

Some things never changed, Nell decided. Aunt Sarah's insistence on marrying them all off. Her own mother's love for roses. And it wasn't even like she was still in love with Quentin. It was ages ago. Grandmama's gift had merely stirred up old memories.

Nell picked up her handbag and Grandmama's framed stitchery. "It's getting late, and you have an early train, so I should be going." She went to her aunt, leaned over, and kissed her cheek. "I love you just the way you are. Thank you for coming. Give Mama and Caroline hugs and kisses from me, all right?"

After their final good-byes, Nell decided on a taxi to take her home, and as it pulled away from the curb, Nell looked back at the ornate but stately Algonquin, the glow in the bay windows, the doorman at his post. She craned her neck to see the fifth floor where her aunt Sarah, Iris, and Mittie were preparing for the train ride home.

She missed them already, but Christmas wasn't that far away.

Strength and honor are her clothing.

Nell gazed at Grandmama's sampler and huffed out a breath. She was hopelessly without honor if she couldn't clear her name, the shame of her carelessness with Soren's drawings. And she hadn't been strong, either, in finding out who was responsible.

The flat was quiet, her roommates already retired for the night, but sleep eluded Nell. Calvin had said she had integrity the day he showed her the pictures in the newspaper. Did she? And if Calvin said that, did it mean he was also a man of integrity? That he recognized it in her because he possessed it?

It was wrong to suspect Calvin without at least talking to him. She couldn't believe she hadn't gone straight to him when Mr. Fields accused her. She slipped to the floor and on her knees asked God to guide her, to give her strength, and say the right things to Calvin. She had to trust someone or she would never regain her honor.

CHAPTER 11

Calvin sat hunched over his drawing table and nodded to Nell. No *How do you do?* No crooked smile. She couldn't blame him. She practically ignored him all week, afraid he was responsible for the stolen designs.

Nell hung up her coat and offered a cheery hello, then looked around to see if they were alone. "Something new you're working on?"

"Trying to."

"I'm sorry to interrupt, but I've been wanting to talk to you. Could you spare a minute?"

"Anything for you, Nellie M—" He made a face. "Sorry. I know you don't like that. What's on your mind?"

She told him about Mr. Fields and Soren, the designs showing up at House of Price.

"I heard. Any theories about what happened?"

"No, but I intend to find out." She told him about going to the shop and trying to make an appointment, about finding not only Soren's dresses, but her cloche design as well.

"It was odd, though. A Mrs. Morris waited on me—Nadine, I think. She seemed familiar, like I'd seen her before. I don't think she's a client here, and it's probably just that I've passed her on the street or seen her in the library, but it was rather unnerving."

Calvin cupped his chin in his hand and frowned. "Nadine? You sure that was the name?"

"Nearly certain. Have you had a client with that name?"

"No, but..." He glanced over his shoulder and then at the door. "Percy's daughter is named Nadine. He's mentioned her. A week or two ago he said something about one of Nadine's kids being sick." He pointed to Percy's desk. "The man's crazy about those grandkids."

Nausea welled up. The woman had looked familiar because it was like looking at the feminine version of Percy. Even the narrow gap between the front teeth.

Nell pressed her fingers to her mouth. "Percy? Do you think?" While it was true he was a loner, he'd always been pleasant enough. In the past he'd even ask about her work now and then, pointing out minor details that would help her designs—a wider brim, more crown height. But he hadn't done so in a while. Not since her designs had started to become popular. And she didn't remember him offering any advice about the velvet cloche like the one at the House of Price.

"I don't know what to think. It's eerie sometimes—remember when we first came and he showed us how to draw according to what a client described? He could whip out a design in nothing flat."

"He is fast. Not too detail oriented, though." Like the simple bead design on the copycat dress that lacked the intricacy of Soren's creation. "Do you think it's enough to mention to Mr. Fields?"

"It's your job on the line." Calvin raised his eyebrows. "You want me to come along?"

"Not this time."

Nell retrieved her portfolio. She'd use it as a pretense to talk with her boss. With a prayer in her heart, she ran up the steps to the third-floor offices and asked Harjo if Mr. Fields was in.

"Last time I checked." He nodded her in.

Mr. Fields squinted when she asked to have a word. "Come to throw yourself at my mercy?"

Words clogged Nell's throat. She swallowed and gave a thin laugh. "If that would h-help. If what I've uncovered about the c-copied d-designs turns out to be wrong."

"What? Have you added sleuthing to your list of invaluable skills? Seems to me you should be applying yourself to the honorable clients who've requested your services."

"I have been doing that. P-please, hear me out."

She laid bare her suspicions and her conversation with Calvin, the woman's resemblance to Percy. She only stammered a few times, but enough that she knew her recent speech progress had been temporary.

Mr. Fields's look was that of stone, his eyes narrowed. "Pure fantasy, I'm certain. And I'm appalled that you would accuse my top designer, the one whose opinion I value highly."

"I didn't say he wasn't a good d-designer. Only that I think it b-bears looking into."

"You've made your case. Now, skeedaddle. See if you can't find something productive to do and quit wasting my time."

"Yes, sir. And th-thank you."

Her legs were as limp as linguine as she found her way out and scuttled past Harjo without a word. *Please, let him believe me. Or at least do his own inquiries.*

All she could do was trust that her prayers were heard.

❧

Nell crossed her legs, jiggling the top one as she waited for Dr. Underwood. She reached for her tea, furnished as always by Lindy Williams, but it had already grown cold. It wasn't like

Dr. Underwood to keep her waiting, and just when Nell had given up on his coming, Lindy popped back in.

"So sorry for the wait. Dr. Underwood should be here in just a tick." She perched on the arm of Dr. Underwood's chair. "Have you had a good week?"

Lindy meant well, trying to engage her in conversation, but Nell evaded the question. An entire day had passed without a word from Mr. Fields, although Nell had little time to dwell on it with her numerous consultations. The design work would keep her busy all weekend and the upcoming Thanksgiving holiday as well. Lindy smiled, waiting for an answer.

"Not too bad. I'm curious, though. Do you observe Thanksgiving? I find it peculiar since it's not one of our English traditions."

"It did seem strange at first, but my husband's family makes it quite the frolic with the bird and all. And I get an extra two days off to be with my wee ones."

"I didn't realize you had children."

"Two little cherubs. My mum lives in the flat next door and watches after them. Like I said, it will be a merry time." Lindy glanced at the clock. "I'll run on now and check on Dr. Underwood."

Moments later, Dr. Underwood came in, and without ado, he asked how she was.

"My stammering is better, at least when I'm with friends."

"You've always related well to your peers then?"

"I'm not sure. I wasn't around that many growing up. I had a g-governess at the manor, so the only time I was with other children was at the village church."

"Ah, yes. Makes sense. Did you have a best friend?"

"Not when I was younger. I spent a lot of time with Jane Alistair, the lady's maid to my grandmother. She's the one who first taught me about hats."

"So you always lived in a predominantly adult world. Interesting, I'd like to explore this area. Perhaps you could draw a church picnic or a Sunday school class."

Nell sighed. It was a waste of time. Her drawings of her grandmother, one of her father on his Royal Navy ship, and the garden had done nothing but stir up longing for her family and England. And yet, Dr. Underwood's current suggestion had unearthed a scorching memory.

It took longer than usual to do the sketch, and when she'd finished, Dr. Underwood studied it for a moment and pointed to a figure in the corner. "Is this you?"

Nell smiled. "It is. And now that you pointed it out, I know I always choose to sit in an obscure place, my b-back to the wall."

"Any particular reason?"

"It's what I've always done, a way to observe p-people and stay on the f-fringe."

"I prefer that myself, so I'm not being critical, just clarifying. But I did notice that you're faltering again. Perhaps an old wound. Think it over and we'll talk about it after Thanksgiving." He tucked the sketch in her folder and wished her a happy holiday.

On the trolley, Nell stared at the throng out the window. Dusk had come quickly, and with it a chill wind. Through the blur of glass, she thought of the picture she'd drawn and of that day long ago.

A light snow had fallen overnight, the temperature sinking as the day wore on. As she ran to the carriage house, ten-year-old Prunella's breath came out in puffs like the ones from her papa's pipe. Freddy held the door for her to get in the back of Grandfather's car for her weekly confirmation class. The minute Freddy pulled to a stop in front of St. John's Church, Prunella jumped from the Rolls-Royce and ducked her head into the wind. She hated arriving in the car and the jabs from the children who had to walk from school to attend the class.

Prunella the Princess.

What's the matter, your legs broken so you have your chauffeur drive you to catechism school?

If she answered, they ridiculed her stammer. If she remained silent, they taunted, *Cat got your tongue?*

The transept was frigid that day, but it was a relief to get in from the wind, and an even bigger relief that she'd made it without an encounter. She took her spot on the far end of the back row, the stone bench like ice through her woolen dress. Her stomach twisted when Wiggins, the teaching elder, entered, eyeing her with a frown. He turned his back and coughed into his fist, a loud rattle deep in his chest.

With her attention on Wiggins, she didn't see the others come in. Simone Honeycutt slipped next to her. Prunella's stomach wrung itself into a knot. Anyone but Simone. She quirked her mouth into a smile, determined not to let Simone, with her innocent violet eyes and hair that fell to her shoulders in ringlets, unsettle her.

Wiggins recovered from the spasm and led them in the opening exercise. He cleared his throat and looked straight at her. "Prunella, please stand and recite this week's assignment."

The Ten Commandments. She knew them backward and forward, but when his eyes pierced hers, she froze.

Relax, you half-wit. You can do this. She let her jaw go slack and tried not to think about the words lodged in her throat. She rose on jellied legs, biting her lip until the taste of blood filled her mouth. "Thou shalt h-have no other g-g-g..." She stared at her feet, and in her side vision she saw Simone Honeycutt stick a finger in her mouth like she was gagging.

Prunella looked straight ahead and started over. "Thou shalt have no other ga-ga-gags…g-g-gods before me." Laughter echoed from the walls of the transept. Cold. Hollow.

The only one not laughing was Wiggins. Instead his eyes looked as if they were going to pop right out of their sockets. His chest heaved and he leaned over coughing until his face turned the color of beets. He spit great globs of phlegm into a handkerchief, pearl drops of sweat on his brow. His hands clenched the lectern in a death grip.

Prunella held her breath. *Please, Lord, don't let him die in front of us.*

Stubs Pogue nudged Simone with a pencil and whispered loud enough for everyone to hear, "Pruneface is so stupid she even made Wiggins gag."

Her face flamed as she lowered her head. Then a voice came through the fog, a whisper in her head. Grandmama's voice. "You've nothing to be ashamed of. When you make a mistake, lift your chin and go on. Be strong."

She gritted her teeth and lifted her chin. "May I start over p-please?"

Wiggins took off his glasses, his eyes two slits with mushy bags beneath them. In a raspy voice he said he was too ill to continue. He scooped up his satchel and left, crouching in his coat so the collar met his ears.

Prunella gathered her things, unsure what she should do. Freddy wouldn't be back for another hour, and it was too bitter cold to walk to the manor. Maybe the vicar could help her.

Whilst she was trying to ease past Simone, Stubs put out his foot. "You have to give the code word to get by."

"Ex-ex-excuse me, p-please."

"Nope, that's not it. Try again, liver lips."

Simone snickered. "Don't be cruel, Stubs. The princess can't help it that her tongue is tied in knots."

"I'm not a p-princess." Prunella backed up and cut around the end to go the other way and came up against Jacob Rayburn, who smelled of onions and sheep manure. He was the oldest in the class. And the biggest. Prunella shuddered. He yanked one of her braids and grabbed her leather knapsack.

He hollered over his shoulder, "Hey mates, a game of Pickle in the Middle?" He tossed the bag underhand to Stubs. When Prunella lunged at Stubs, he swung it around by the straps and sailed it over to Herb Swenton who then hurled it back to Jacob.

Simone raised her arms to catch the bag, and when she did, the flap came undone, sending Prunella's papers flying through the air.

Herb grabbed the bag and hollered, "Hey, Bledsoe, wanna have some fun? Catch."

Prunella's head snapped up. *Quentin? What is he doing here?* She looked at him with pleading eyes. He was the vicar's son. Surely he wouldn't torment her, too. He narrowed his eyes, the bag clutched in his hands, and looked at the papers strewn across the floor and benches of the transept. "Prunella?"

Understanding crossed Quentin's face, giving Prunella hope that he would put a stop to the nonsense. Although her hopes were slim considering that even though Quentin was older, he was small for his age. So thin that Mama once said the breeze from a door slamming would bowl him over.

Jacob jeered, "Throw the bag, Quentin. You're slowing down the game."

Quentin shook his head. "Game's over." He extended the bag toward Prunella, but Herb lunged sideways into Quentin, knocking him down. Simone's shriek echoed from the stone walls. Quentin jumped to his feet and took a swing at Herb, who ducked and punched Quentin in the stomach. Jacob came from the other side and shoved Quentin against the wall. "You got no right coming in here when it's not your class and messing with the game."

Quentin thrashed his arms. "You got no right to—"

Jacob's fist slammed into Quentin's nose. "That's for interrupting and taking up for stupid."

Prunella covered her face with her hands to stop the scream that rose in her throat. When Quentin didn't answer, she spread her fingers and chanced a look. Blood poured from Quentin's nose, splattered on the front of his jacket, dripping onto the cold stone floor.

Hot tears stung Prunella's eyes, her insides a boiling cauldron. But her feet wouldn't move, her tongue stuck to the roof of her mouth.

Jacob growled, "I oughta slam you with another one. Just let that be a lesson to you." He grabbed his coat and looked at the others. "What are you waiting for? Let's get out of here before his old man shows up."

The transept emptied, the shuffling of feet the only sounds. All except Quentin who held a handkerchief to his nose and walked between the benches, gathering Prunella's papers with his free hand. He stuffed them in her knapsack and handed it to her without a word.

"Thank you, Qu-Qu-Quentin. And I'm s-sorry."

He shook his head. "It was nothing."

❧

It had been more than ten years, but it felt like yesterday. Quentin said it was nothing. But it was the beginning. He'd stayed with her the remaining time until Freddy picked her up. Nell gave Quentin her hankie, and when the bleeding stopped, he asked what happened and clenched his fists when she told him of her embarrassment.

"I'll report it to my father, see if he can straighten it out."

Nell had shaken her head and told him it wouldn't matter, they would find ways to get back at her.

"Not when I'm around." A sheepish grin creased Quentin's freckled face, already growing lopsided with swelling. Nell licked her finger and reached up to wipe away a smear of dried blood.

The beginning of a friendship and had she remained in England, perhaps much more.

CHAPTER 12

On Friday morning, Nell found a notice on the studio door to report at once to the workroom. The entire design and production staff were assembled with Mr. Fields standing at the head of the table. He cleared his throat when she entered. "So glad you could join us, Miss Marchwold."

His vinegar tone compounded the feeling that he'd meant to dismiss her in front of the entire staff. She offered a wan smile and took the remaining seat next to Hazel.

"Now that we're all present, I will be brief. As you've no doubt heard, some of the designs for our recent show at the Stottlemeir Club fell into unscrupulous hands. I've my own theories about how that transpired"—Mr. Fields pinned Nell with a sharp look—"and am grieved that our salon has been humiliated, our integrity brought into question."

For being brief, Mr. Fields was taking a long time to fire her. Perhaps he wanted her to suffer the same agony he no doubt had. Nell shifted in her seat, ready to hear the news.

Mr. Fields continued, "Careless behavior and compromising trusted designs is cause for dismissal. Not just here, but in any reputable salon." Mr. Fields let the gravity of that settle. "We have, however, found our culprit and discharged him immediately. Ed Percy is no longer an employee of Oscar Fields Millinery. And should any of you ponder such an idea in the future, you will be met with a similar fate. Now, get back to work. We have a lot of new orders to fill." He strode erect from the workroom without even a glance in Nell's direction.

She felt as wrung out as a dishrag, and when the usual hubbub started around the table, Nell rose and went silently to the studio to start her day. Her prayers were heard. And answered.

At noon, Calvin caught up with her in the consulting salon as she finished with her last client of the morning. "Glad all that's done with. Want some lunch to celebrate?"

"Sure, what did you have in mind?"

"How about clam chowder? There's this little place I know—"

"Perfect. I'm starving."

They laughed and talked like they hadn't in weeks, but she reminded Calvin that it wasn't really a celebration—she *was* to blame for not taking proper security measures.

"Snakes like Percy will always find a way. At least it's behind you."

But it wasn't. She still needed to make amends to Soren. She called as soon as she got back to the salon and apologized.

Soren was quiet on the other end. "It nearly made me cry when I went by and saw the gowns. Shoddy. Disgraceful. And that weasel Price will be laughing every time his cash register rings."

"I wish there was something I could do to make it up to you."

"You've probably suffered enough from Oscar's wrath. Remember what I told you—it's a cutthroat business. You can never exercise too much caution."

"Thank you. I'll remember that."

Thanksgiving was a quiet day. Jeanette and Greta had both gone to family dinners, and since Nell hadn't grown up with the custom of Thanksgiving, she was content to spend the day sketching at the kitchen table.

By three that afternoon, her neck ached and she needed fresh air, but just as she donned her jacket, the telephone rang.

The operator said, "Long distance for Nell Marchwold."

"Speaking." Clicks sounded through the earpiece, then her mother's voice on the other end.

"Mama! I'm so glad you called when you did. I was just on my way out the door. How are you? And Caroline…did Aunt Sarah give the hugs she promised?"

"Yes, she did. And we're fine. All of us." She said her newest rose cultivar was chosen for a trial at the university where Granville, Nell's stepfather, taught and that Caroline was doing well in school. "You just won't believe how she's grown. She's already lost two of her front teeth and working hard for her first piano recital. She can hardly wait to show off for you."

"Oh, that's lovely…I can hardly wait myself."

"How's the hat making?"

"Busy. Since the runway show I have quite a few of my own clients now, and several are asking for special holiday hats. We've also lost a principal designer so it makes more work for the rest of us."

"I hope it won't interfere with your trip home."

"It shouldn't, although it may only be for a few days."

"We're yearning to see you, and it would be a shame to miss Iris's party. And you never know what eligible young men will be there."

"You sound like Aunt Sarah. You know my dream is to make hats, and I've worked hard to get to this point."

"Yes, you have, dear. I just don't want you to miss out on love, either."

"Someday, Mama."

"One minute," the crisp voice of the operator cut in.

"Are you still there?"

"Yes. I have to go now. I love you."

"And we love you." An audible sigh came from the other end. "The telephone is such a poor substitute for visiting in person. Pray tell, where are you off to?"

The line clicked, cutting off the call. To the silence on the other end, Nell whispered, "Just out for a walk, Mama." She put the earpiece in the cradle and dropped to the settee. Her mama missed her. She blinked back the tears that threatened. Another whole month before she would see them. It seemed an eternity.

On Saturday afternoon Nell curled up on the settee with a hat and an array of beads she was stitching into detailed curlicues. Jeanette turned on the Victrola, but instead of dancing around the room, working on her fox-trot steps, she slumped into a chair. She'd been in somewhat of a mood since Thanksgiving, saying only that everything was fine. Nell suspected it wasn't.

"Want to talk about what's bothering you?"

"You wouldn't understand."

"Try me." She let the cloche she was working on rest in her lap.

Jeanette twirled a strand of hair and chewed on the end of it. "My dad's sick. Dying, if you ask me."

Nell sucked in a breath. "No. What happened?"

"Nothing new. Just weak lungs from the war. Mustard gas is what Mother says. Stupid man smokes likes a coal train, saying if he's going to die anyway, he might as well go out doing something he enjoys."

"I'm sorry."

"When I was little, he'd bring me jelly beans from work and take me for carriage rides in Central Park on Sundays. Now he sits at the kitchen table and stares out the window and smokes."

Nell wanted to tell Jeanette that at least she still had a dad, that she would give anything if her own dad hadn't been on a boat that the Germans sank into the North Sea. Her father would still be alive, and she'd still be at Marchwold Manor, going to endless hunt parties and doing charity work. She might have even married Quentin unless her parents had decided she should do a season in London to find a suitable husband. She shuddered.

Jeanette said, "You look like you're a million miles away."

"Sometimes it feels like it. I was just thinking that I wouldn't be in New York living with you and Greta if my dad had survived the war."

"And I don't even want to think what life would be like without you. Who would make my hats?" She laughed and sat upright. "Truth is, I can't do anything about my dad. Pray and hope for the best, Mother says."

"Your mother's right."

Jeanette frowned. "I'd rather kick some sense into him." She stalked off and closed the door to her room, leaving Nell to her own thoughts and a puddle of beads on her lap.

The next day she went to early Mass with Felice, the day cold and dreary. At the conclusion of the service, she told Felice she wanted to light a candle and say a prayer. Felice linked her rough, calloused fingers in Nell's and walked quietly beside her to the side of the sanctuary. Nell dropped two coins in a box, lit a candle for Jeanette's dad and another in memory of her own dad, then knelt to pray. A calm came over her, the air heavy with the smell of candle wax. When she rose, her cheeks were damp with tears.

By Monday, Nell was anxious to get back to the salon and show Mr. Fields her latest designs. Harjo wasn't at his secretary post, but her boss's door was ajar so Nell gave a brief rap and looked around the corner.

"Busy?"

"Of course I'm busy. And where's Harjo?"

"He must have stepped out. May I have a word, p-please?"

"Since you're already here, I suppose. You're early today, aren't you?" He leaned forward. "You have some hats, I see. Couldn't this wait? I've not even had coffee."

"I have an eight thirty appointment."

"As you wish."

She opened the hatbox and presented her latest cloches. "Some things I t-took home over the weekend."

"Such dedication." The sarcasm wasn't lost on Nell, but he did add, "I trust you had a happy Thanksgiving."

"Quite good, thank you. And you?"

"Of course. The club always puts on quite a feast."

A trickle of sympathy went through Nell. She'd not once considered what Mr. Fields had done for Thanksgiving. No parents. And his wife deceased. She wondered why he'd never sought someone else. Perhaps he preferred it that way.

He stroked his mustache. "I'm glad you stopped in, actually. We have a busy month ahead." He opened his diary and asked her to do the same. She penciled in the new appointments as he dictated. Several were for New Year's Eve occasions, which she would have to scramble to get done early.

He leaned back. "I've been thinking we need to improve your image. You're seeing more clients and will remain an apprentice, of course, but there are occasions where it would be beneficial for you to be seen in public, an image of the forward-thinking Oscar Fields Millinery. A new hairstyle for starters. Your bun or whatever you call that wadded-up hair is too severe. And you need something softer for your day wear and an evening gown or two. I'll have dresses sent over."

"Goodness. That's very kind."

"Image. That's what it's all about. Which brings me to another point. Your unfortunate speech defect. When we're out, I can't have you mumbling like you have marbles in your mouth."

A modern version of Stubs Pogue and Jacob Rayburn from catechism class popped in her head. While Mr. Fields wasn't as cruel as they were, his words still cut.

Concentrate. Look the person you're speaking to in the eye.

"I understand. I'll see if Dr. Underwood can see me more often or try something new."

"Perhaps fish a miracle out of his bag of tricks." He looked at his appointment diary. "We need six new designs by next Tuesday for a women's luncheon. You'll be accompanying me. The ones here look promising, so four more by Friday. I've put Hazel and Marcella back on assembly, but I'm sure you can manage." He snapped his diary shut and bid her good day.

She hurried out, hatboxes in tow. In the stairwell she stopped to catch her breath. He had both ridiculed her and complimented her within the same breath. Should she be furious or flattered? And the way he mentioned her stammer prickled as always. At least he was giving her opportunities to prove herself and providing some new wardrobe choices. She didn't have money like her aunt to splurge every time there was a new moon. It was generous, and for that, gratitude nestled in the hard corner of her heart with his name on it. She made a mental note to take coffee the next time she barged into her boss's office first thing on a Monday morning.

❧

The day of the women's luncheon, Mr. Fields offered his arm. "You look fetching today. Is that one of the new outfits I had sent over from Saks?"

She took his arm, happily surprised at his chipper mood. "Yes, they're all lovely. Thank you." She did feel posh in the aquamarine dress with French lace at the neckline and the new coat, a nubby wool with a fox collar. She knew they were expensive, but she felt elegant and confident, ready for the lunch at the Forty-Second Street Ladies Club, where a group of society wives were hosting a fashion day. Other designers of haute couture and millinery would be there. It was an honor for the salon. And for Nell.

When they were settled in the cab and Mr. Fields had given the driver the address, she thanked him again for his generosity.

"Image, my dear. This is an influential crowd, so it's best to project your best. And let me do the talking. You're charming to look at, but I don't want to put off anyone with your babbling. I'm hoping this event will bring in enough customers to carry us into the New Year."

"Certainly." She knew her place. Look pretty and smile. Let the boss do the talking.

The club ballroom was spacious with Roman columns wrapped in evergreen boughs for Christmas. A harpist sat in one wing, the strains of "Good King Wenceslas" wafting through the chatter. Elegant gowns hung on molded mannequins and hats displayed on stands at eye level were meant to allow the women to walk around, chat, and take notes. Nell and Mr. Fields were guests at the luncheon and available, of course, to talk about the salon and set up consultations.

Nell spotted her hats in the display and a group of women admiring the one with a sequined starburst.

Schmooze. That's what Calvin had told her to do. It would be easier if Mr. Fields gave her some space, but he'd made it clear she was to remain at his side.

He whispered instructions in her ear and discreetly pointed out some of the women. "An ambassador's wife. The cousin of Mayor Hylan. The wives from Eccles's law firm. Pay no account to them— they're faithful to Murdoch's. Let me do the talking."

Mr. Fields's knowledge of who was who was impressive, and Nell felt as if her face would freeze into the wide smile she'd put on for the occasion. She wasn't even sure why Mr. Fields wanted her to come along. *Image.* That's what he'd told her. She smiled some more.

She didn't see Soren until they were nearly ready to go. Mr. Fields was engaged in a conversation as Nell stood dutifully by his side.

Soren swept across the room. "Well, don't you look simply stunning?" Soren clasped her hands in both of his and leaned in to give her a kiss on the cheek. It was a gesture she'd seen him do many times and knew it wasn't personal.

"Good to s-see you, Soren. Did you have a good r-response?"

"Quite excellent, actually. And I might've sent a few potential customers your way."

"Mr. Fields will ap-ap-appreciate it. And me, too."

He winked and said, "Connections, darling. It's always about connections." He waved at a well-dressed woman passing by. "Gotta run. It was marvvy to see you again." He disappeared into a sea of women as Nell turned her attention back to Mr. Fields.

He leaned in and said, "Aren't you the coy one? Too bad you missed the opportunity to meet the woman who is coming in next week to engage us for her daughter's wedding." He cocked his head toward a woman who'd moved into another circle.

"I'm s-sorry. It was nice to see Soren. He looks well, doesn't he?"

"I didn't notice, and you interrupted me before I finished. The wedding is the day after New Year's, but I assured her it was no problem. I'm sure you won't mind missing your holiday trip to

Kentucky this year for such an important engagement." He nodded at a woman with silver hair and gripped Nell's elbow, steering her toward the exit.

"I've already made p-plans. My mother is ex-expecting me."

"I'm sure she will understand that success comes with sacrifice on occasion." He pushed open the door where an icy wind bit into Nell's cheeks.

CHAPTER 13

Nell was certain Mr. Fields would change his mind about her going to Kentucky for Christmas if she worked longer hours and was caught up, had the headpieces made for the wedding ahead of time. One look in her appointment diary told her it was possible if she didn't eat or sleep for the next three weeks. Yes, her career was important—the very air she breathed—but her family was, too. Still, she'd promised her grandmother and herself that she would strive to succeed.

Her family couldn't always be first, but the thought of Christmas without them soured her mood. Something Calvin picked up on right away the next morning.

"What's the matter? Didn't the ladies like your hats yesterday?"

"They liked them fine. I'll be seeing a bride next week about her wedding."

"Guess that means another raise for you?"

"Don't be silly. I get the usual review the same as you at the end of the year. And if I don't meet our boss's expectations . . ."

"It's for sure I won't."

"Guess we're both a little hedgehoggy today."

"What's that supposed to mean?"

"You're acting p-prickly...like a hedgehog."

"I don't even know what a hedgehog is. Some sort of British swine?"

Nell burst out laughing. "It's a cute little animal covered with soft spines. They curl up in a ball and bristle when they sense danger."

"You're dangerous all right. Making up stories about mythical animals and getting all the plum assignments."

"They're not mythical. They're completely harmless, and you know I have no control over who asks to have appointments. For your information, I have to work over Christmas. No trip to Kentucky. No fa-la-la-la-la." Nell stomped off to her desk, grabbed her sketchbook, and left. The only difference between Calvin and a hedgehog was that a hedgehog was cute.

Nell was too busy to worry about her spat with Calvin. Work called. A whirlwind of appointments, ordering special bridal fabrics, and taking trips to the library to look up design elements for the Russian-themed wedding the bride had chosen. She picked up every fashion magazine at the newsstand that might have a bridal idea. Nell's heart raced with each new discovery and client who left glowing with one of her hats. Inner beauty. She strived to bring that out, and the more she worked, the greater the satisfaction. She wasn't sure this was what success felt like, but it did carry her along in the weeks before Christmas.

In brief snatches of spare time, she made hats for her roommates, her cousins, and Felice. She made a tiny red velvet cloche for her sister, Caroline, and sent it with the other gifts she'd gotten her family for Christmas. Her mother had been disappointed at the news that Nell wouldn't be home for the holidays, but to her credit, she didn't chide her for being selfish.

Even with her frantic schedule, she kept seeing Dr. Underwood. Oscar expected her to conquer her stammer, and she doubled her efforts at practicing. Dr. Underwood wore a red shirt with a green and white polka-dotted bow tie one day, green shirt with a gold lamé bow tie another. And it was a joy to see Lindy Williams with her cheerful cups of tea and Yorkshire accent that for a few minutes, twice a week, massaged the homesick corner of Nell's heart.

When Dr. Underwood mentioned that Nell looked tired, she agreed, telling him briefly about work and being blue about not getting to go home for Christmas.

He smiled and told her to take a deep breath and let her shoulders relax.

When she'd done so, he said, "I think for today, we'll try to keep it light, my gift to you. I want you to think of your earliest memory, a happy time. A pair of new shoes, perhaps, or flying a kite. Even if it's just a fragment, try to capture that day."

"The train. I remember riding the train and watching the sheep from the window."

"Excellent. Now, while you're relaxed, I'd like you to go to the drawing table and sketch that day. Anything at all that comes to mind."

She had the sensation of floating toward the desk. With a charcoal pencil she drew the window of the train on one edge of the paper and tried to recall where they were going. Greystone Hall. That was it. To see her mother's parents. Her grandparents on the Payne side. For her birthday. Her mother kept talking about her birthday and that Gramma Jo was making her a cake.

Nell relaxed her arm and drew, keeping her eyes unfocused so that whatever landed on the paper was from her child's eye and not her grown-up ones. Her breaths grew rapid and more shallow as the hairs on the back of her neck stood at attention. *Breathe in and out.* She ran her tongue over her teeth, which felt gritty. She wanted a sip of tea, but it was across the room. She swallowed trying to relieve her dry mouth. It was distracting her from the drawing, and when her throat felt scratchy, too, she laid down the pencil and pushed the sketch pad aside.

She went back to the armchair and sipped the lukewarm tea and waited for Dr. Underwood. He went to the desk and picked up her drawing, holding it at a distance as he always did. He joined her with the paper in hand.

"An interesting choice, using only the charcoal pencil. Less detail than your other drawings."

"I was thirsty, and it b-broke my concentration. Or perhaps I'm just weary."

"Understandable. At any rate, it looks like it might have been a birthday you recalled, is that correct?"

She nodded. "There was a cake, and I remember my mother telling me to blow out the candles."

"You've a cake here with four candles, so I would surmise you were four."

"Something like that." She squinted her eyes to look at the drawing. The cake looked like it was floating, and there were no people in the picture. She'd drawn the facade of a castle, which she thought was a reasonable likeness of Greystone Hall. She had a vague memory of seeing it in pictures, and what she'd drawn was certainly imposing, whether it was accurate or not.

"It's quite an impressive house you've drawn. Were your grandparents titled perhaps?"

"Not anything special. Landed gentry. My mother's brother, Spencer Payne, inherited the house and now has the title of earl."

"Interesting." He leafed through her folder. "You've mentioned your grandmother. I take it she no longer lives in this house then?"

"No, this was where my mother's p-parents lived. When Mama married, she and Daddy moved to Marchwold Manor with his p-parents...where I grew up. This is Greystone Hall, my mother's childhood home. Oddly enough, my two grandmothers were friends growing up in Yorkshire." Her stomach clenched. Another memory pushed at the one with the birthday candles. "Gramma Jo d-died while we were there."

Focus. Picture the words. The sessions were meant to help her speech, not bring on the stammer.

"An illness?"

She took a deep breath. "No, an accident. She fell down the steps of the root cellar. Mama wouldn't allow me near it, said the steps were steep and uneven. Or at least that's what I r-remember."

"I had hoped this would stir up a happy time, and I don't want to dampen your feeling further, but how did you respond to your grandmother's death?"

Nell shrugged. "I'm not sure I was old enough to g-grasp the finality, only that people were sad."

"Perhaps now that you've drawn the picture, something will come to you. It often does. It's like we have to give our thoughts a nudge. Is there anything else you'd like to talk about before you go?"

When she shook her head, he closed the file to indicate the end of the session. "The office will be closed until after the New Year. I'll see you in January."

She left, her steps sluggish as she went to catch the trolley. The memory bothered her, but she didn't know why, and the session hadn't had the effect Dr. Underwood intended. Maybe she could shake the gloomy feeling if she did something silly and lighthearted.

Nell went to FAO Schwarz toy store and found a straw-stuffed hedgehog with the Steiff label in the ear and bought it for Calvin. She tied a ribbon around its neck and set it on his worktable while he was seeing a client. There was a spring in her step when she went to her afternoon appointments.

Calvin gave her a sidelong look when she returned to the studio after her last consultation. "Rubbing it in, are you?" Calvin ran the back of his fingers along the soft fur of the hedgehog.

"Just a friendly gesture. I almost bought one for my little sister, but I'd already sent her package."

"Now I fall in the category of children?" His tone was light, a sparkle in his eyes that had been missing. "I didn't get you a gift. Christmas isn't high on the list of Jewish holidays."

"I know, but this wasn't for Christmas." She held out her hand. "Friends?"

"Yeah." He shook her hand. "And just so you know, I wasn't sore at you."

"If not me, then whom?"

"When I finally got up the nerve to show Mr. Fields the children's line I've been working on, he turned me down flat. Said children don't carry pocketbooks. So I'm back to fedoras and *bubbehs*." When he saw her questioning look, he said, "Grandmothers. Granny hats."

"You do have a gift with the dear ladies."

He groaned and picked up the hedgehog. "Thanks anyway. Gotta run. And if I don't see you again, cheers!"

"Merry Christmas."

❦

Candles flickered in St. Mark's Church in-the-Bowery as organ music played softly in the background. Nell slipped into a pew in the church that was the American version of her village church in Heathdown. The hushed tones in the nave enveloped her, her attention focused as the minister gave the lesson and reading from Luke. As Nell joined the throng of strangers in singing "The Holly and the Ivy," she was transported back to her childhood, the excitement that mounted as Christmas Eve ushered in the season. She wished she'd appreciated it more then. A thought of Quentin interrupted, and she wondered if he might be worshipping at Westminster or another chapel closer to his new flat.

A light snow fell as she left St. Mark's and joined the queue for a taxicab. While she waited, she thought of the horse-drawn landau rides with her grandfather from the manor to the village church. Zilla, the cook, always had a steaming pot of cocoa and a plate with shortbread and tiny mince pies waiting on their return. Nell didn't even have cocoa in her flat, and even if she had, she would be useless at making it the way Zilla did.

Christmas morning dawned cold and dreary. Not a snowflake or blanket of white anywhere when Nell looked out the window and put on the kettle. Christmas. Alone.

Both Jeanette and Greta had gone the day before to spend Christmas Eve and morning with their families. For Jeanette, Nell knew it might be a bittersweet day if her dad wasn't doing well. While having her milk tea, Nell eyed the gifts she'd received in the post. A good-sized box from her mother, a slightly smaller one from her grandmother.

She opened the package from her mother first—a satin box with dried rose petals and spices, the scent like a warm embrace from her mother. Nell blinked to ward off tears. She picked up a package with uneven corners, obviously wrapped by Caroline. Inside the box were layers of cotton wool and nestled deep inside was a crystal hedgehog. Nell burst out laughing. In her hand, the little creature was quite weighty, heavy enough to serve as a paperweight, but it was exquisite with tiny spines that sparkled in the light and fine metal pins for whiskers. A silk scarf from Aunt Sarah and a pair of leather gloves lined in lamb's wool from her mother and stepfather, Granville, completed the gifts from Kentucky.

Nell leaned her head against the back of the chair and told herself she wouldn't cry, that this was the life she'd chosen, and by tomorrow she'd be putting the finishing touches on the hats for the wedding.

Just get through today.

She saved her grandmother's package for last. As she removed the outer wrapping, she hummed "What Child Is This" in her normal off-key manner. Inside the packing box were three smaller ones cushioned with crumpled newspaper. She shook them to see if she could guess what they were. She opened a thin rectangular box first, hoping it was Scottish shortbread, and it was. Her mouth watered, and she was tempted to sample them, but she was going to eat with Felice and her family. A woolen scarf and leather journal were next. And finally, a square tin of her favorite cream toffees made in the Cotswolds. Now her mouth watered *and* her stomach growled.

A note was attached to the toffees on which her grandmother scrawled, "Quentin brought these by when he came to visit his parents. He remembered that you were fond of them." Nell bit her lip. Quentin. Always thoughtful.

As she gathered her gifts, the bits of packing, and the boxes to take to her room, a knock came on the door.

"Ricky! Oh g-gracious, is it time to come down for d-dinner already?"

Felice's soon-to-be-thirteen-year-old son flashed his dark eyes. "Mama says, *Soup's on*, that everyone is here." His teeth were overly large for his mouth, but he had a cute smile. He looked at her with a curious expression. "Is that what you're wearing?"

Nell's hand went to her chest. She was still in her dressing gown, having fiddled away the entire morning in a fit of melancholy. "Goodness, no. That would give your family something to talk about now, wouldn't it?" She told him she'd be down in five minutes.

It was more like ten, with her hair tucked up in a red woolen cloche and a green velvet dress with simple lines that she'd worn the last two Christmases.

"Oh, Nell!" Felice bustled over to her and kissed her on both cheeks. "My family, we all come to the diner for Christmas so we can have the, what you say, the big celebration. This is my sister, Rosa, and my mamma, and over here . . ." She pulled Nell from table to table and introduced her to what seemed like dozens of relatives. Aunts, uncles, cousins. At least three babies.

The smell of garlic and heavenly spices made Nell swoon. She couldn't wait for Angelo to serve the dinner. It started with a blessing in native Italian by the eldest relative that some of the children called *Nonno,* followed with pumpkin-filled tortellini floating in a savory broth. Rosa whispered, "Eel broth. In *Italia,* we feasted on eel and lamb, but we no have so much chances here in America. Angelo, though, he makes the best roasted chicken and potatoes to ever cross your tongue, and his roasted veal . . ." Her eyes rolled up as she inhaled and waved her hand in front of her face.

Nell practically devoured the food, so different from their British feasts of roasted goose with bland, congealed sauces. Angelo's food, with its rich spices, practically danced on her tongue. She ate until she thought she would burst amid boisterous laughter and spontaneous stories from the old country.

Rosa pushed away her plate. "We have to save room for panettone and *pandoro.*" Sweet breads, she explained, but they were rich and heavenly, the panettone filled with raisins and candied citrus peels, the *pandoro* a tall star-shaped cake dusted with powdered sugar. Nell indulged in both.

As the food and dishes were cleared, Nell noticed a table set with linen, china, and dishes of food. When she asked Felice if she was expecting more guests, Felice nodded. "We leave a place for the Madonna and Christ child. We would be so blessed if they came to taste the gift from Angelo's kitchen. If we don't leave the table set, it would bring dishonor on our family to forget the reason we have to celebrate this most wonderful occasion, no?"

The afternoon was spent with more chatter, the children shooed outdoors to play in the street. Not a single girl or woman in the crowd would be what Nell would call a potential customer with their plain cotton or wool dresses, heavy stockings, and shoes that had seen better days. Each one, though, wore a jeweled brooch or rhinestone necklace, some bit of sparkle, to dress up her attire. The day with the Salvatores entwined Nell's heart—a day to tuck in her memory. It wasn't home with Mama and the family, but it wasn't bad.

"*Buon Natale.* Merry Christmas!" Felice said as she kissed both of Nell's cheeks again as she was leaving. "And the hat, I will save it for my Ricky's wedding."

Nell laughed and told her she should wear it and not save it. As Nell climbed the stairs, she thought of leaving out a plate with a piece of Quentin's toffee in case the Madonna and Christ child should make a visit.

A note from Jeanette was propped against the electric toaster.

Going upstate for a few days. Mother thinks it will help Father's disposition. I called Greta and asked her to tag along. Be home Friday.

Jeanette

PS: Your mother called. I told her where you were and to try again later.

Five minutes later, the phone rang.

"Mama, I'm so glad you called."

"Nell? Are you all right?"

Nell assured her she was, that she'd had a lovely day with the Salvatores. "How was your Christmas?"

Her mother was full of tales about the snow that had fallen and the tree they'd chopped at Uncle Eli's horse farm. They had tied it to the top of Granville's roadster to take home to Louisville.

Mama said, "Iris has had the loveliest parties. A young man from Lexington has shown her an unearthly amount of attention. It wouldn't surprise me a whit if he proposes before her season is over. I'm so sorry you'll miss her grand ball day after tomorrow. She was counting on you being there."

"I know, Mama. But it's been frightfully busy here. Have her write and tell me all about it. What about Mittie? Has she b-behaved?"

Her mother's tinkling laugh sparked across the miles. "Oh, you know Mittie. Always the life of the party. So much like her mama that it's frightening."

"Aunt Sarah?"

"Oh, the stories I could tell. It's been a lovely Christmas. The only thing missing was you."

"I know, Mama. I missed you, too. Next year. I promise."

Nell put on the kettle, and when her tea was made, she changed into her nightie and wooly socks and propped herself up with pillows in the bed. She had a stack of magazines to look through. Now that delivering the hats for the wedding party was all that was left to do, it was time to be thinking about spring designs.

She tossed aside a couple she had already read and picked up the next one on the pile. *Couture Design.* She thumbed through it, making mental notes until she came to a section in the middle. Her breath caught—a write-up of the runway show with Soren with photographs. She flipped the page and saw all of the ensembles they'd done. She couldn't stop looking at them. Her designs. And Soren's. In a magazine. Captions *and* a rave review.

Some of the freshest creations from New York this fall.
Soren Michaels is a designer extraordinaire.
Millinery from Oscar Fields the perfect added touch.

She read each word, savoring them all. It was only a few paragraphs, but the reviewer was lavish with praise. A quote nestled on the last of the four-page spread said, "Oscar Fields has outdone himself by hiring Nell Marchwold, a hatmaker of British ancestry. She's a bright star on the fashion horizon."

Her name was mentioned. *Her name.* Mr. Fields said he would make her a star. She wasn't there yet, but after she'd read the pages a dozen times, it began to sink in. *Time will tell.* As she drifted off, she smiled. It was her boss's favorite motto.

CHAPTER 14

Mr. Fields made no mention of the magazine nor did Soren call. Perhaps it wasn't as spectacular to them as it was to her. And it was old news as she'd bought the magazine when she was looking for ideas for her client's wedding. She was bursting to show Calvin, but something held her back. He would start in on the Nellie March line again, and even though her heart ached for that, the nod needed to come from Mr. Fields.

Still, Calvin picked up on her merry mood. "You're quite the sparkler nowadays. Don't tell me Mr. Fields gave you a big bonus."

"Nothing like that. The wedding party hats have been delivered, and I'm just more relaxed."

"I was hoping it was because you were going to ask me out for New Year's Eve."

She gave him a quirky, fake smile. "Don't you just wish?"

"So do you or do you not have plans for New Year's Eve?"

"Maybe. I told Jeanette that if I survive this week, I might do something with her. Greta's going to a party with Spike and some of their acting chums, so she won't be coming. Jeanette would like it if you went with us, I'm sure."

"A double date then?"

She punched him on the arm and said she had an appointment with the Benchley girls.

"Maybe you could see if one of *them* is interested in a sharp, good-looking, but lonely guy from the other side of the East River."

"Come along and ask them yourself."

"They'd just think I was a kibbitz. Moving in on your territory."

She shook her head and left Mr. Lonely Heart doodling at his desk.

When she entered the consulting salon, she was surprised to find Mr. Fields with Mavis Benchley, the girls nowhere in sight. Mr. Fields pulled Nell into his grasp and presented her like he was showing off a trophy. "Here's our girl."

Mrs. Benchley gave her a hug. "Oscar's been telling me how happy the bride and her mother were with the hats you did."

"They did turn out well, but it's kind of him to say so. Are Daphne and Claudia here? I thought the appointment was for them."

"Oscar sent them to the fabric room to pick out colors. We're in a bit of a pickle. Daphne's been invited to a masquerade party at the Hornbilts' mansion. She's going as an exotic belly dancer—gracious, I don't know how the girl comes up with her ideas—but never mind about that. She needs a headdress of some sort."

"Certainly, I can do that. And Claudia, will she need something, too?"

"Just Daphne this time. Claudia will have to settle for going to the club with her father and me."

Mr. Fields nodded. "Excellent, my dears. I'm leaving you in Nell's capable hands." He kissed Mrs. Benchley lightly on the cheek.

When he'd gone, Mrs. Benchley shook her head. "Such a sweet man. And a tragedy that he's never remarried."

"Did you know Anna, his first wife?"

"Not personally. From what I gather, she was beautiful and talented, but timid as a church mouse. He would be quite a catch for some lucky woman."

Nell shuddered to herself. Today he'd been charming. Maybe he'd turned over a new leaf. There was always hope, but then his best behavior always surfaced when Mrs. Benchley was around. Jeanette's story about the way Mr. Fields treated Anna was evidently not widely known. Or it could be that Jeanette had it wrong. She was known to exaggerate.

They found the girls giggling, Daphne before a mirror swiveling her hips. She was a natural, and within the hour, they'd chosen a filmy peach fabric that would fall from a jewel-encrusted headpiece.

Daphne said, "I'll need it by Friday. Can you do it?"

"Most certainly." It would be simple after the relentless pace of the last few weeks.

As they were leaving, Mrs. Benchley whispered to Nell, "Looks like you're getting along grand at the speech clinic."

"Dr. Underwood's been very patient with me. And helpful. Thank you for the recommendation." She *was* doing well. Only a mishap here and there.

"Anytime, my dear."

Nell rested against the counter when they left. Who was she kidding? Her stammer had improved, but she'd pushed the last session with him out of her mind because of the unsettled feeling it induced. The thought of going back in January stirred up a new swarm of doubts.

Jeanette squealed when Nell told her she'd invited Calvin to go with them on New Year's Eve. "You're a doll! But, oh my goodness, I wasn't thinking. Are you and Calvin...I mean, you're not an item again, are you? I don't want to be a fifth wheel, you know."

Nell put her hands on her hips. "We were *never* an item. He's a friend, that's all. In fact, I'm hoping the two of you hit it off. Shall I tell Calvin to meet us at Lily's Place like before?" She blew on her tea, then took a sip.

Jeanette winced. "No, there's this new place—the Emerald Jungle."

Nell sputtered. "Emerald Jungle? Really?"

"You've heard of it?"

"Well, no, but it sounds…different…daring. Where is it?"

Jeanette scratched the back of her head and twisted one side of her mouth. "Harlem. And before you say anything, it's not dangerous. Greta and Spike went right before Christmas and said it was the absolute berries. Jazz music and dance contests. There will even be prizes for the New Year's Eve bash."

"Guess it's a good thing I invited Calvin then. You're going to need a dance partner." *And bodyguard.* Nell shuddered and finished her tea and asked if Jeanette's dad enjoyed the trip to the country.

"He did. We all did. At least he's breathing better and promised to take it easy on smoking. Thanks for asking."

Perhaps Jeanette needed to dance to escape reality.

On New Year's Eve, Calvin called for them in a taxicab rather than meeting at the dance club. As the cabbie honked and weaved through midtown and beyond the lights of Broadway, the air pulsed with expectation. Flashing lights in yellow and green splayed across the front of the Emerald Jungle when the car pulled to the curb and the driver opened the door for them. Ahead of them, a couple emerged from a swanky car, the woman wearing a long mink coat, the man in a tuxedo. Nell was glad she'd worn her buttercup dress and new coat.

Large windows flanked the double doors, people shifting like shadows behind them. Once they'd purchased their club cards, they entered the main room through a velvet curtain tied back with a serpentine cord. Music and smoke filled every corner, giving a blue haze like looking through filmy georgette. Once Nell's eyes adjusted to the light, she was surprised at how large it was. A room full of smartly dressed patrons from young people like themselves to paunchy men with bald heads and matronly women waving cigarette holders, their laughter tinkling like brass chimes.

Long tables with linen cloths were set out in rows on either side, leaving the middle for chorus girls dressed in glittery outfits and ostrich plume headdresses. They were in the midst of a routine when a waiter showed Nell, Jeanette, and Calvin to places and gave them a slim cardboard menu with a dozen hearty appetizer choices and drinks. They ordered sandwiches and colas, then leaned back to watch the performers. The air buzzed with frivolity as the dancers high kicked in their finale.

A pock-faced man with hooded brows sat next to Nell, his suit jacket taut across his back. He leaned over and said, "Ain't nothing like some good old jungle music to get your feet a tapping." He winked and said he had a little refreshment if she was looking to have some fun. He leaned back and puffed on a cigar the size of an overgrown carrot.

"Thanks. We just came for the music. And the dancing."

"That'll be coming up soon, I reckon. You save a dance for me, ya hear?" He sounded oddly out of place. Not a New Yorker. One thing she knew. She wasn't dancing with a stranger, even though she had to admit, it was hard not to feel the beat of the music.

Jeanette had no such reservations, and when the dancing started, she went with the first guy who asked her to fox-trot. Calvin whispered to Nell, "You want to give it a whirl?"

Nell realized she hadn't thought through the evening very well. She thought Calvin and Jeanette would just gravitate to one another, and she could sit demurely at the side and watch while she enjoyed the music.

Calvin's eyebrows were raised, waiting for her answer. It was only a dance, not a marriage proposal. She put her clammy hand in his and let him lead her to the dance floor. Calvin was easy on his feet, his embrace sure as he guided her through the motions, but Nell's joints were rusted hinges, stiff and out of practice. By the third song, the rhythm felt more natural, the steps easier. She'd never be nimble-jointed and footloose like Jeanette, but the tension fell from her shoulders, a sense of glee bubbling inside.

The bandleader announced a short break, and as they headed to the table, Nell was glad to see the waiter had delivered their order. The cola fizzed as it wet Nell's parched throat.

The stranger from earlier gave her a nudge. "You cut a pretty fine rug." He put a hand on his stomach and belched, the fumes of alcohol and cigar smoke making her eyes burn. "And you promised, sweetheart, you'd save a dance for me." He wiggled his eyebrows and reached for his glass.

Nell plowed into her sandwich and finished off her cola, turning toward Calvin so she wouldn't have to look at the stranger or smell his rancid breath. Calvin's hair shone like an iridescent raven, a trickle of sweat inching down his temple. Nell reached up with her napkin to blot it away.

Calvin talked around the food in his mouth. "So now you're my mother? You want to wipe the drip of mustard from my chin, too?"

"If you're messy, I just might have to."

Jeanette returned out of breath and grabbed her soda. "Is the food good? Did you hear? The dance contest starts at midnight, and I still don't have a partner. The last fruit I danced with mangled my toes."

Nell pointed to Calvin. "Here's your perfect match. You two have all the moves—I'll be the cheering section." Her stomach felt queasy, but she was still thirsty. The chorus girls pranced onto the staging area, dipping and twirling, waving exotic fans this time. Nell wished for a breeze to waft her way, her own head feeling like it was spinning. Instead of a breeze, though, it felt as if the air grew thicker. Smoke filled. Cloying at her throat.

She asked Calvin if he'd signal the waiter to bring her another cola as the dancers were making their final bows. The crowd clapped and cheered, then jostled past, elbowing one another to get to the dance floor. The waves in Nell's stomach now swam in her head. She was certain she couldn't dance if her life depended on it.

Jeanette was on her feet, and Calvin gave a desperate look toward Nell. "Are you sure you don't mind if I dance with Jeanette?"

Nell shooed them away and drained the last of her cola, which left a bitter aftertaste on her tongue. The waiter arrived with another cola and she wished she'd asked for ginger water.

The foul-breathed stranger draped his arm around her. "Looks like the little lady has a taste for giggle water. Can I freshen your drink?" He held up a flask.

She reached for her glass to put her hand across the top, but misjudged the distance and knocked it over, the cola spreading into a murky stain on the linen cloth. Realization dawned like a punch in the gut. She shot a glance at the disgusting man, shrinking from his grasp. A piece of lettuce was lodged between his two front teeth, his smile as green as her stomach.

She bolted from the table. The nerve of him to lace her drink with bathtub gin or whatever his particular preference of bootleg liquor was called. She needed air, but the front door seemed furlongs away, and the man might follow her. She yanked the arm of a cigarette girl in a skimpy costume and asked for directions to the ladies' room, then made a beeline for it.

Inside, the smell of urine and vomit assaulted her, the lavatory stained brown and no towels to wash her hands even if she'd dare to touch the faucet. Apparently the amenities out front didn't extend to the bathroom facilities. She stood in the middle of the floor and wrapped her arms around herself, tears hot behind her eyelids, her head stormy like her stomach. She swallowed to keep from heaving, then jumped. A noise, like a gunshot, shook the building. Plaster rained down on her. Screams followed, the cacophony of the orchestra screeching at first, then silent. Shouts echoed beyond the walls of her confinement. What on earth was happening?

She debated whether to stay where she was with the door bolted or venture out. What if Jeanette had been shot? Or Calvin? What if a gunman decided to fire more shots and she walked into a barrage of bullets?

"Fire! Fire!" Shouts and more screams.

She would burn to death if she stayed in the bathroom, so she unbolted the door and peeked into the hall. The burly stranger from her table was shouting orders to secure the holes. Whatever did that mean?

She flattened herself against the wall, hoping he wouldn't see her, but he turned suddenly and met her gaze. His eyes narrowed as he grabbed her arm. He hissed in her ear, "You! You didn't see or hear anything. No one messes with Louie and lives to tell about it." He gave her arm a wrench as he shoved her toward the dance hall.

A momentary thought flashed through Nell's head, but before she could place what it was exactly, pandemonium had broken out, an acrid smell of smoke hovering in the air. People slapped at smoldering linen cloths. Others were trying to get out the front door. Someone shouted for an ambulance. On the dance floor several bodies lay on broken glass, others bending over them. Nell feared they were dead.

"Police! Everyone stay calm. Please remove yourselves from the premises in an orderly manner." The officers had pistols drawn, waving nightsticks to direct traffic.

Nell cried in earnest now, the acrid stench searing her throat as she scanned the crowd for Jeanette and Calvin. A policeman nudged her with his nightstick and told her to keep a move on. He looked as if he would strike her if she didn't do as he said. As she followed the others through the front door, she looked back over her shoulder for some sign of her friends. It was impossible to see anything through the haze.

The night cold bit her lungs when she got outside, her arms at once freezing. Her coat, the one Mr. Fields had given her with the fox collar, was inside, no doubt ruined. Cars gunned their motors trying to get away; sirens wailed as two ambulances and a fire truck pulled up. Not a single taxicab was in sight.

"Hey, Nell! Over here!"

She rushed in the direction of Calvin's voice, still not seeing him, but he was at her side at once, pulling her briefly into his arms. "Jeanette's hurt. I've got her over here, but she's bleeding, and I'm afraid her ankle is broken. She needs an ambulance."

Nell dropped to her knees. Jeanette's hair was tangled, her face streaked with blood. She cried and clutched her leg. Nell cradled Jeanette in her arms and rocked her as they waited for help to come.

CHAPTER 15

The newspapers called it a "pineapple"—a bomb thrown through the front glass of the Emerald Jungle. Two people were in critical condition, dozens injured, including Jeanette who had to be stitched up at the hospital. Mrs. North, Jeanette's mother, had come when Nell called her to take care of Jeanette. According to the article, no arrests were made, and the people interviewed surmised that it was a war between mob bosses, that perhaps the Emerald Jungle, which had been open a mere two months, infringed on a rival's territory. No illegal liquor or contraband was found, and the identity of the owner hadn't been ascertained. When questioned, the spokesman for the jazz orchestra gave the name of the person who'd hired him. It proved to be a fabricated name.

On New Year's Day, Nell and Calvin went to see Jeanette at her mother's house, glad her ankle was only sprained and not broken and that her other wounds would heal quickly. Afterward they stopped at a coffee shop and read the newspaper account again.

"We'll be f-fired. I know it. It's what we d-deserve. Once Mr. Fields reads Jeanette's name in the paper, he'll figure out we were there."

Calvin ordered black coffee for himself, hot tea for Nell.

Nell corrected him. "C-coffee for me, too." When Calvin gave her a curious look, she explained, "My head feels like it's splitting in half."

"You have a hangover. Maybe we could see if they could bring a raw egg and some Worcestershire, a little ketchup, and I could whip you up a remedy. It'll be my mitzvah."

Nell shuddered. "Disgusting. Drinking a mitzvah sounds as nasty as whatever that horrid man put in my cola."

Calvin chuckled. "Ah, my *shayna maidel*, my pretty girl. A mitzvah is a good deed. I should pay penance for not paying attention to the louse who was chatting you up."

A wavy feeling rippled through her, sending an involuntary shudder. "He was pro-provoking, but there was something else, too." She told him about seeing the stranger in the hall and his shouts to shut the hole. "What do you think it could mean?"

"I've heard that the shrewd people who set up the speakeasies have trapdoors and such to stow illegal liquor. The police were too busy with New Year's Eve muggings to do a thorough check of the premises. My guess is that once the police left, the crooks snuck back in and cleared the joint out."

"Should I go to the police and give a description?" The thought of doing so sent cascading ripples down her spine. *No one messes with Louie and lives.*

"You'd have to give your name. Place of employment. Fields will find out for sure if you do that. No use getting the salon involved." He shrugged. "Tomorrow it'll be old news. And I'm sure the weasel has gone underground or fled the city by now."

"But what if it's the right thing to do? What about the moral obligation?"

"You'd be wise to let it be."

Nell drank the hot coffee before her. It was as bitter as the tainted drink Louie had given her. Without the fizz. *Let it be.* Calvin's way of handling matters. She couldn't even bring herself to admit to Calvin the man's name was Louie. And now that time had passed, she wasn't certain herself. The same fleeting memory from her encounter with Louie zipped through her head. When she tried to catch it, bring it to life, it was gone.

She went home alone, Calvin saying he wanted to check on Jeanette again. Something about the stranger's eyes and his manner was familiar. Not that she'd met him before, but more that he reminded her of someone. She just didn't know who. Uncertainty over what to do stayed with her as she rode the motor bus, but it was the fear coiled in her belly that told her to remain silent.

Nell and Calvin were summoned to Mr. Fields's office first thing when they returned to work after the holiday. Mr. Fields paced behind his mahogany desk, his face brooding, his nostrils flared. He picked up the newspaper with the article about the Emerald Jungle. Nell's heart was in her throat waiting for Mr. Fields to lash out at her and Calvin. They deserved it.

Instead, in a cool, steady voice, their boss said, "Do you two know anything about this?" He stabbed at the headline.

Calvin nodded. "A bit. I escorted Nell and Jeanette there."

Mr. Fields snorted. "I expected as much when I saw my niece's name as one of the injured." He glared at Nell. "You. This is how you repay me for the kindness I extended in bringing you to New York?" His eyes seared into hers. "You realize you've risked your own reputation by going to such a place, and by doing so, it's a direct reflection on me, on Oscar Fields Millinery."

He leaned across the desk and jabbed a finger into Calvin's chest. "I expected better of you, not carousing in some juice joint."

Calvin didn't flinch. "I understand your position, sir. Nell and I have nothing but regrets for having chosen the wrong place to celebrate the New Year."

"Yes, sir. What we did is r-r-regrettable. I have no d-defense for my actions."

"No defense? Jeanette's name is on the front page. The. Front. Page. A few questions by some nosy investigator could link the two of you and your relationship to this firm. A whisper here and there, and clients will start going somewhere else. It takes years to build a reputable business, and a single incident like this could destroy it instantly. It's not a pretty reflection on the two of you at this point in your careers."

He drew a deep breath, a hard edge to his jaw as his eyes rested on Nell. "You are aware that the show with Michaels set me back so that I'm not even sure we'll turn a profit this year? No, I don't suppose you are, having nothing in your head but fluff and not one ounce of common sense."

Nell's mouth was clogged with words she wanted to say, an apology for their poor judgment, a plea…but nothing would come from the honeycomb of her throat.

"Go on, both of you. I need to think this through."

"If it's of any w-worth, I truly am s-s-sorry."

Mr. Fields pointed to the door.

As they scuttled from their places, Mr. Fields said, "I meant to ask, how's Jeanette?" There was an odd catch in his throat, but his face remained stony as they told him Jeanette was home and would be fine when her ankle healed.

❧

The following day, Mrs. Benchley and her daughters paid a visit to the salon. Nell was still on edge from the New Year's incident when she greeted them.

"How was your costume party, Daphne?"

"Splendiferous! And I have invitations to four more balls in the next month."

"Oh, that's lovely."

Mrs. Benchley added that as soon as they got in touch with Soren, they'd like to have Nell work with him on matching head-pieces for Daphne's new gowns.

"Mavis, lovely to see you." Mr. Fields swept across the showroom lobby. "I was hoping you'd drop by soon. Has Nell seen to getting you some refreshments?" He oozed charm and manners, as if their conversation the day before had never happened.

"Nothing for us today, Oscar. We're on a bit of a tight schedule."

Several of Nell's hats that she'd designed before Christmas had gone through production and were shown on a tiered display. Nell's breath caught. She'd not seen them and they'd turned out lovely.

Claudia gasped. "Oh, Mother, I simply have to have this one." She picked up a lemon-colored cloche with hyacinth bugle beads in a fleur-de-lis pattern.

Nell laughed. "I might have had you in mind when I was design-ing that one."

When she tried it on, her brown eyes shone, eliciting a "Stun-ning, my pet" remark from Mr. Fields.

The girls ended up choosing two each, and Mrs. Benchley took one of the floppy-brimmed hats with a cluster of antique roses, declaring it would be perfect for her mah-jongg afternoons.

As the shopgirl wrote up the ticket, Mrs. Benchley pulled Nell and Mr. Fields aside. "I'm sure you've seen the news."

"What news, Mavis?" Her boss's manner was guarded.

Nell's palms went clammy. There was no way Mrs. Benchley could have connected her to the Emerald Jungle incident. *Was there?*

Mrs. Benchley pulled a magazine from her handbag, instant relief making Nell's underarms damp. *Couture Design.* "Oscar, my dearest, you scoundrel. This. This!" She flipped to the coverage of the show.

Mr. Fields stroked his mustache. "Oh, that. Yes, I saw it last month. Soren sent me a copy. I'm surprised he didn't send one to you."

"You're not getting the significance. This is the British edition. One of my friends went to London for the holidays and brought it back." She nudged Mr. Fields. "All the people in London are over the moon about Nell's hats. I think you've made a grave mistake in not going ahead with the Nellie March label. There's a mention somewhere that Nell hails from England's own shores. My friend says everyone wants to know how to get her hats. I'm surprised you haven't been getting calls."

Mr. Fields shrugged. "Can't say as I have."

Mrs. Benchley gushed, "Think of the international exposure. Looks like an opportunity to me." She folded the magazine and returned it to her purse, then wrote out her check and told the girls to hurry up, they were late.

When they'd gone, Nell said, "It was a nice f-feature, wasn't it?"

"Splendid, but surely you've better things to do than stand around hoping I'll take Mavis's advice and buy into that Nellie March nonsense." He spun on his heels and left.

Yes, she did have plenty to do. But it didn't keep Nell from dreaming.

CHAPTER 16

The second week of January turned bitter cold and drizzly. Jeanette had returned to the flat, and Greta was all in a dither about an audition for a vaudeville traveling troupe. She and Spike had put together a parody of Cleopatra and Mark Antony, and their funny antics cheered Jeanette up. In her spare time, Nell transposed notes from her beginnings as a junior apprentice into her new journal. She illustrated each concept with a line drawing and dubbed the project, *The Millinery Guide for Beginners*. She'd forgotten how much she didn't know when she came to New York and how far she'd come. She could always try and publish the handbook should Mr. Fields find her no longer suitable for his salon.

Her appointments with Dr. Underwood were canceled when he was called away on a family matter, and when she finally did see him later in the month, he commented on her increase in stuttering and asked if she had any insights on what might have caused a setback.

Nell shifted her position, then gazed at the doctor. His shirt was bright purple accented with a lime-green bow tie. How she'd missed it was a mystery, but of course, she'd been avoiding looking at him for fear he could see her shame, the actions of New Year's Eve ever looming in her mind.

She took a deep breath and told him about the Emerald Jungle.

"Sometimes we all need an evening out. There's nothing wrong with celebrating the New Year. Tell me more about why this bothers you."

"I should have r-refused to go to the d-dance club and suggested a m-moving p-picture or s-something else. I was uncomfortable with where we were, and then there was the b-bomb."

Dr. Underwood gave a tiny intake of breath. "That dance club? I remember reading about it in the newspaper."

"See? I was s-stupid for going there."

He held up a hand, palm out, to stop her. "First of all, I don't allow my clients to call themselves negative names. Let me ask you, would you have thought the same if there hadn't been a bomb?"

"Maybe not to the s-same d-degree, but there's m-more."

She had already decided she would tell Dr. Underwood about Louie, so she unknotted her fists, recounted his too-friendly remarks, lacing her drink, and then seeing him later in the hall. "He grabbed my arm and told me I'd b-better not tell anyone I'd seen him."

"So you had the misfortune of being in the wrong place, of seeing or hearing something you shouldn't have?"

"I didn't actually see or hear anything except his saying *shut the hole*, which I didn't understand then and still don't. But it felt f-familiar, like it had happened before."

"But the man was a stranger to you?"

She nodded. "He r-reminded me of s-someone." An ache throbbed behind her eyes. "I just…don't…know…wh-who."

Dr. Underwood tented his fingers and went into his world behind closed eyes. Nell tried to imagine that there was a blackboard in his mind where answers appeared. But when he opened his eyes, he didn't have an answer, but a question.

"Tell me, what is the emotion you're feeling right now?"

She had a kettle full. Regret. Shame. Insecurity. Frustration. Fear. She sifted them through her mind and whispered, "I'm afraid."

"I can hear it in your voice and see the tremble in your fingers. I'd like for you to close your eyes."

Panic filled her chest. She shook her head.

"It's all right. There's nothing here to be afraid of."

She chewed her lip. Shut her eyes, then opened them again quickly.

Dr. Underwood gave her a reassuring nod. "Don't fret. Fear can only hurt you if you let it. Does this Louie know your name or where you live?"

"Of course not. I didn't tell him anything."

"Then the fear isn't coming from him, but another source. Forcing it will not likely benefit you, so let's stop for today. The good news is that this event may have sparked the deep-rooted cause of your stammering. I want to deal with that the next time you come. I'll have you draw again. In the meantime, I want you to practice your breathing and visualizing words before you speak them." He closed her folder and bade her good day.

⚭

Like her thoughts, the trolley was crowded on the way home. She was glad she'd told Dr. Underwood about Louie, but the netting of apprehension clung to her. It wasn't as simple as just letting go of the fear, although she whispered a prayer asking for the courage to do so.

As she stepped from the trolley, a car honked and whizzed past. Her heart pounded. She hadn't even seen it. She waited for a break in the flow of traffic and made a dash between two cars and looked over her shoulder, half expecting to see someone behind her. When her feet hit the sidewalk, she stumbled, her legs watery. A stocky man in a business suit grabbed her arm before she tumbled to the ground, his grip firm on her forearm. Wrenching almost.

When she thanked him, he tipped his hat and strode away. She rubbed her arm where his touch had been, tears smarting her eyes. The urge to run rose in her chest, but the smell of apple turnovers from a cart vendor sent her reeling. Her head felt as if it were spinning, her heart thundering hooves. She shuffled to the nearest building and leaned against its harsh bricks until she could collect herself. Instead, she felt swept into another time, another place, another man's steel grip on her arm.

It was autumn. The smell of apples crisp in the air. Leaves clumped in piles against the cellar door and along the rock wall of the rose garden. Mama had shooed her out the door so she could finish the birthday luncheon.

A breeze picked up the leaves and swirled them as Prunella crouched behind a tree, her knees skinned from a fall on the rocks in the rose garden. She was trying not to cry, trying not to notice when her grandfather stomped past and grabbed Gramma Jo by the arm, hissed something at her.

Her grandmother lifted her chin, walked over to the cellar, and lifted the heavy door. "If you want another jug, get it yourself. Drink yourself into a stupor and see who gives a tick."

He charged at her grandmother. Burly but not tall. Whiskers on his face that burned Prunella's cheek when he'd given her a kiss. He raised his hand and smacked across Gramma Jo's face. He growled in a low voice, but Gramma Jo crossed her arms and shook her head. He raised his arm again, but she shielded herself and lowered her chin. That's when he pushed her into the blackness of the cellar.

Prunella cried out, then tried to suck the sound back in, shrinking into herself, hoping to become invisible. She didn't dare breathe. But then, reaching around the tree trunk, a beefy hand grabbed her wrist. Face close to hers, he said, "You didn't see anything, you hear me? You breathe a word, and I'll do more than bloody hurt you." He looked toward the cellar, a sneer on his lips. He shoved her away, then heavy boots stomped to the tool shed and slipped inside. Mama came from the house and said she heard a scream. Grandfather stepped from the shed and said he heard it, too. Mama glanced at the cellar. "What's that doing open?"

Prunella's grandfather shrugged. "No bollicking idea."

"I'm looking for Prunella. Have you seen her?"

"Not this morning. I've had m'self a bugger of a time working on them carriage wheels."

Mama peered into the black hole of the cellar. "Prunella? You down there? Come out now if you are. There's slimy, crawly things down there."

Prunella peeked around the tree to tell her mother she wasn't in the cellar, but her grandfather's squinted eyes sent her cowering back before she could utter a word.

A biting, cold gust of wind swept down the New York street, stinging Nell's bare hands and face. But the chill weather wasn't the cause of the guttural sound that rose up in her chest, her tongue thick.

A woman touched Nell on the arm. "Are you all right, miss? You look like you've seen a ghost."

"I'm f-fine, I think. Just need a bite to eat." Despite the cold, perspiration dampened her brow, the memory like a knife twisting her insides.

Grandfather killed Gramma Jo. Nell was there and saw it. She'd never spoken of it. Ever. Because until that moment, she had no memory of it.

She pulled her coat tight and turned in the direction of her flat. It explained the silence that descended on the room whenever Greystone Hall or the subject of her maternal grandparents arose. There must have been suspicions, and it probably explained why Nell and her mother never returned to Greystone. No one thought to question Nell, and if they had, she would have remained mum from fear she would be the next one shoved down the cellar steps.

By the time the red-and-green awning of Sal's came into view, Nell was convinced that somehow the buried memory was the root of her stammering.

Dr. Underwood confirmed Nell's suspicions when she called and made an emergency appointment with him the following morning.

His words were kind, soft as he told her he was sorry. "Sometimes a new trauma can trigger old wounds. I suspect that's what happened. And it could very well be the cause of your stammering. Perhaps time will bear that out."

Nell had hoped he would tell her she was cured, but instead he cautioned her about deeply ingrained speech patterns that could still surface, especially in intimidating or stressful situations. And it was disturbing that such a horrid secret had followed her grandfather to the grave, not that she felt sorry for him, but that Gramma Jo had been victim to such outrage. She longed to talk to her mother about it, but it seemed cruel to bring it up over the telephone.

Calvin was bent over his worktable when Nell arrived at the studio. She was an hour late but felt the time with Dr. Underwood was necessary. She looked over his shoulder and saw that he was working on a fedora.

He looked up at her. "What do you think of this for summer? Perhaps in willow banded with a narrow suede strip?"

"Very nice. Hard to believe it's time to get the spring line ready. I'm weary of cloches and itching to do some ladies' boaters—I think they're going to be the r-rage this season."

"You may be right." He went back to drawing, the only sounds those of the radiator clacking when it came on, the gentle hiss as it cycled off.

Just as Nell nestled in at her own desk to work, Harjo looked in and told Nell that Mr. Fields wanted to see her in the conference room next to the executive office upstairs. He held the door and waited for her. As she left, Nell looked over her shoulder at Calvin who mouthed, "Good luck."

A wave of apprehension sloshed in her stomach as Harjo waved her into the conference room, then went into his office. Hazel and Marcella from assembly jerked their heads up when Nell entered.

Hazel said, "You got any idea what this is about? I was telling Marcella that if we get the can, I'm marching straight over to Murdoch's and putting in my application."

Nell shook her head. "Mr. Pritchard didn't say." There was no sense in speculating as they would find out soon enough. It must not be about the New Year's Eve incident or Calvin would have been invited, and of course, Hazel and Marcella hadn't been anywhere near the Emerald Jungle.

Marcella, a petite woman with lavender eyes and salt-and-pepper hair, nodded to Hazel. "I've heard Mr. Murdoch treats his workers better anyhow. And they get an hour for lunch instead of thirty minutes. And production bonuses. We get squat."

Both women had worked tirelessly for the Soren Michaels show and neither made snide remarks like Steiger. And they both had families who depended on them. Nell prayed they weren't losing their jobs.

Just then Mr. Fields entered with Harjo Pritchard and a smartly dressed woman carrying a valise.

Mr. Fields stood at the head of the table and greeted them. "I'm sure you're curious about the nature of this meeting. Certain factors have made it necessary to remain quiet until all the pieces of the puzzle were in place." He stroked his mustache and smiled.

"It appears that Oscar Fields Millinery has been offered a unique opportunity. As you all know, Nell Marchwold, our junior apprentice, has been in the news of late."

Nell felt every eye in the room fall on her. She had no earthly idea where this was going. The base of her spine buzzed with a strange mix of anticipation and fear. She chewed on her lower lip, waiting for Oscar to continue.

"The opportunity of which I speak is one that happens rarely." He picked up a copy of *Couture Design*. "Last fall, I felt the urge to push Nell into an arena of greater responsibility and encouraged her to work with a couture designer here. The coverage has been quite spectacular, and now my salon"—he made a sweeping motion with his free hand—"*our* salon has been invited by one of the finest ladies' societies in London to set up a temporary shop in London. If they're pleased with our work, we have the chance to design their millinery for the upcoming wedding of Prince Albert, Duke of York, to Lady Elizabeth Bowes-Lyon."

Nell's head was spinning. *London? A royal wedding?* She took rapid, shallow breaths, her eyes wide, afraid that if she blinked she would wake up from this dream. Oscar was going on about the management of the New York store in his absence and hiring new designers to replace those who had left. But Nell barely listened.

London.

Her grandmother.

Home.

She was getting ahead of herself. But in the next breath, Mr. Fields confirmed that those gathered would be part of the entourage that would travel to London, meet with the ladies, and if things went well, remain there until after the wedding on April 26. They would depart from New York Harbor in three weeks.

Nell was sure that if she breathed, she would discover it was all a cruel joke. When Mr. Fields introduced Molly LaGrange, the woman with the valise, as the agent who would oversee their travel plans and secure accommodations for them in London, it slowly began to soak in.

Nell was going to London. To design hats. Maybe see Quentin. And she dared even hope to make a trip to Gloucestershire to see her grandmother.

Her heart overflowed.

London

1923

CHAPTER 17

Nell slipped a sapphire silk evening frock over her head and clipped on matching earrings that cascaded from her lobes, each dazzling with a dozen tiny stones. It was her third time to change that day, as it had been each day of the voyage. A simple day dress for breakfast, a stroll around the ship's deck, and then time in her first-class cabin to work on sketches. And her speech exercises. Either a silk or georgette gown with gloves for tea and a social time before dusk. Formal wear for dinner in the first-class dining room each evening. And with each change of costume, she wondered how long before the bubble would burst and she would wake up above Sal's Diner realizing it had all been a dream.

There had been endless forms to sign and plans to coordinate with Miss LaGrange before they left. Nell had been in charge of the supply list to pack from their own inventory, items that were more practical to take along rather than order in London. It was disappointing that Marcella and Hazel had been given second-class accommodations, but Mr. Fields had explained it wasn't a pleasure cruise for them, but a time to work and be ahead of schedule before their arrival. Each afternoon Nell delivered new sketches for them to work on. Their eyes twinkled, both of them quite content with sharing a room and the opportunity for their first trip anywhere beyond the boroughs where they'd grown up.

The first evening aboard ship, Mr. Fields asked that she call him Oscar. "People expect that of colleagues, and it will put them more at ease in our company. In cultivating connections, you just don't know which of the esteemed people we'll be dining with might require our services."

Oscar it was. Although training her brain to think of him as such caused a throbbing behind her eyes. It felt peculiar somehow, and she chided herself for being suspicious of his motivations.

Nell left a few wisps to curl about her face—the softer look Oscar thought suited her now shoulder-length hair—then put on the simple headpiece with delicate feathers in the same sapphire as the rest of her ensemble.

If her wardrobe had been her wedding trousseau, it couldn't have been more elegant. She prayed no one saw beneath the lovely clothes to the trembling inside. Excitement and opportunity, yes. But more than that, the possibility of failure. Was she ready to step back on the shores of her beloved England and present herself as a designer? This time she had to do more than smile and make small talk. She had to prove herself if she would ever be Nellie March.

Oscar waited in the small reception area at the end of the hallway leading from her cabin, erect and smiling in a tuxedo and top hat. Tonight he carried a cane, she supposed so he would appear more dapper for the banker and his wife who would share their table at dinner.

He pecked her on the cheek and offered his arm. "Stunning, my dear. That color brings out the fire in your eyes."

"Grandmama always said blue was my best color."

"She was right."

When cocktails were offered before dining, Nell asked for ginger water, her taste for alcohol forever ruined from her New Year's Eve experience. Oscar ordered a gin and tonic and oysters on the half shell for their appetizer.

After feasting on boiled turbot with shrimp sauce and quarters of lamb with mint sauce, Nell was certain she couldn't manage another morsel and that she would be letting out the seams in her dresses if she kept eating such rich food. But when the tray with desserts was passed, she couldn't resist the Albert cake, a confection of delicate pastry with almond and raspberry filling. It reminded her of the Bakewell pudding that was Grandmama's favorite.

Mr. Fields nudged her. "Mr. Fitzsimmons is waiting for your answer, my dear."

Nell shook the fog of memories from her head. "I'm s-sorry. I was enjoying the Albert cake so much I didn't hear the question." She swallowed hard. In truth, she hadn't heard a single bit of the conversation.

"Your family, they hail from England?"

"Yes, sir. The Cotswolds…in Gloucestershire."

"The country then? What trade were they in? Farmers? Dairymen? The potteries?"

"Not a trade, although we did have a flock of sheep and horses for the fox hunts. My grandfather ran the Marchwold estate when he was alive."

"Landed gentry then. Quite the mess with gentry now. I'm going to England to see about buying some properties let go to the dogs. Quite an upheaval since the war. I don't suppose your estate's still in the family."

It wasn't a question. But it *was* still in the family. Just not her branch. She explained that her uncle now ran the estate and that she was looking forward to visiting Marchwold Manor while she was in England.

She swallowed and looked at Oscar who encircled her shoulders with his arm. He nodded at Mr. Fitzsimmons. "If we get time, she means. We're going to have our hands full in London with the royal wedding first."

"So Miss Marchwold here got you an in with the royal family?"

Heat crawled up Nell's neck. "We weren't acquainted. What he m-means is that we're meeting with a ladies' s-society to see if they like our work. It will be grand, of course, if they commission us for their hats for the wedding. It's quite exciting, getting to be in London in the springtime and be part of such a g-grand event."

Mr. Fitzsimmons snorted. "If you like the soot and the fog, I guess it's a good time."

It was a relief when Mrs. Fitzsimmons said she had a headache and excused herself. Her husband followed, and Oscar suggested they take a walk on the promenade deck. Stars twinkled like diamonds on a velvet sky, the air crisp. At the end of the promenade, Oscar leaned on the rail and spoke into the night. "I didn't appreciate your correcting me in front of Fitzsimmons. Let him think what he will about whom we'll be making hats for. Your explanation added nothing to the conversation." His voice was even, as if he'd made a comment about the constellations overhead.

"I'm s-sorry. I only thought—"

"You leave the thinking to me. And don't get any ideas in your head about skipping all over the country visiting long-lost aunts and uncles and playmates from days gone by." His tone was as cold as the night air.

What you have to say is important. Dr. Underwood's kind wisdom came back to her.

She drew a deep breath that burned her lungs. "I had hoped to c-connect with a childhood friend who's now a banker in London. And it would be a shame to come so far and not at least visit my grandmother. A few days at most. I'm sure we can work that in."

"Surely your grandmother could travel to London."

"I'm afraid not. When I wired that we were coming, Jane—that's

her lady's maid—reported back that my grandmother's quite frail."
Nell had to see her. Even if it meant getting on the wrong side of
Oscar. She never dreamed he would refuse her request.

"Perhaps after the wedding. Time will tell. We may be needed
back home."

"After the wedding then. I can accept that." It was a small consolation, but she was certain if things went well, he would come
around.

Shouts rang out when land was sighted. It was only Ireland, where
they would stop first, but after Ireland...home.

A few hours later, Nell stood on deck and inhaled. She was certain she got a whiff of lavender and woodsmoke and grassy meadows, but as the dock at Southampton came into view, the smell
turned to coal oil and fish odors.

Still, Nell was overjoyed when she set foot on British soil, a joy
that nestled against her ribs as a hired motor car took them from
Southampton to the city that awaited them.

Home. Only it wasn't. It was London, a live, throbbing melting
pot of wealth and poverty, cobblestone and opulence, shadowed al-
leys and merry laughter, the clashing of Dickens and high society.

Their hostess, Lady Abigail Haversham, represented the finer circles, the ones Oscar crowed about, and she was lovely. Robust yet
refined. The founder of the London Noble Women's Society.

"You're finding your accommodations satisfactory?" Lady Haversham lifted her glass of sherry, having dispensed with introductions
and settled at a table in the Royale Hotel dining room on the day
after their arrival.

Oscar returned her toast. "Splendid. We're most grateful for your
hospitality."

Nell agreed. Her cozy one-room flat had a hot plate in one corner with a narrow bed and chest that occupied most of the room. A door that she thought was a closet revealed a private toilet and wash basin. A chintz-covered chair in a tiny alcove overlooked Hyde Park, and if she craned her neck, she could see Kensington Palace. Hazel and Marcella shared a similar arrangement across the hall with Oscar and Harjo having flats on the floor above.

But it wasn't the room or the view that made Nell's pulse race; it was snatches of conversation, a bit of Cockney from the driver of their car, the refined formality of the doorman of their building, the soft lilt in the voice of Lady Haversham. Nell didn't realize how starved she was for the voices of her countrymen.

Twenty minutes into the lunch, another dawning came. She hadn't stammered a single time.

Lady Haversham dotted her napkin to her mouth. "Nell, we weren't exactly sure what type of studio you would need, but I think you'll be pleased. We'll go there straight away after we've had dessert." She signaled the waiter for a menu, and when they'd made their selections, she said, "To be quite frank, you're our secret weapon, so I hope I don't frighten you by saying that we have great expectations. The other women and I feel it's our responsibility to set the standard for excellence for those who've become, shall we say, a trifle set in their ways in regard to fashion. When I read about you in *Couture Design*, I told my husband, Bannister, that even if it took a motion on the floor of Parliament, we were getting you here, royal wedding or not."

Her laugh was breathy, her chatter tinkling. A women who was self-assured and reminded Nell of the women who used to come for tea or dinners at Marchwold Manor. A touch of merriment as they'd gossiped about fashion and scandalous happenings they'd read in the *Tatler*.

Nell laughed along with her. "I think you'll be pleased. And such an historic occasion."

"There's nothing like a royal wedding to bring out the claws of even the finest bred women. And their husband's checkbooks, of course."

The shop in Mayfair was in a plum location in the heart of a posh shopping district. It was a small shop, two rooms on the ground floor, but another large space upstairs for the workroom, an office for Oscar with a marble fireplace and Queen Anne desk. A smaller room—a cubbyhole, really—would be for Harjo. Two local women had been hired to handle reception, retail sales, and to be Nell's personal assistants.

An array of hats from the New York inventory was already on display in the window and scattered throughout the salon. As Lady Haversham showed them around, Nell noticed two women peering through the front glass and trying the doorknob.

"May I?" She posed the question to Lady Haversham, but Oscar nodded to go ahead. By teatime, Nell had made three sales and two appointments for later in the week. Before leaving, Lady Haversham handed her the list of consultations she'd already acquired.

"It's a trial period, you understand, but if what I've seen thus far is any indication, I believe my instincts were correct."

When Oscar took her to dinner at the hotel near their flat, he complimented Nell on her remarkable day. "Maybe all we had to do was get you on familiar turf to bring out the best in you."

"I've always given my best, but thank you for bringing me to London. For everything." She lifted her water glass. "To much success."

CHAPTER 18

Oscar stopped at her desk at the back of the consulting room as Nell organized the orders for the day. "A good day, I see. Mind if I have a look?"

She handed him the stack of work orders and receipts. Two of Lady Haversham's friends had each ordered hats for two upcoming galas the Noble Women's Society was hosting the week prior to the wedding. A garden tea for the eight bridesmaids of the wedding couple and their circle of friends. A dancing ball for the members of Parliament. Nell's heart fluttered with the enormity of it. And all in just two weeks.

Oscar handed them back. "I'd like to see your sketches in the morning. This could be quite a turn of events."

"It's Friday. I was hoping perhaps I might call Quentin, the friend I mentioned who lives in London. I can work on the sketches tomorrow evening and Sunday when we're closed."

"I'm sure I don't need to remind you that time is of the essence. You have to stay ahead of schedule to allow for those who procrastinate. We can only compete with the established businesses in London if we offer services above and beyond what they do. I'll meet you for breakfast at seven sharp to see what you've done." He started toward the door to leave, then turned around. "I almost forgot, we have tickets to a show tomorrow night. I'd like you to wear the sapphire-blue gown you wore on the ship. You never know when a reporter or one of our new clients will see us." He popped his fedora on his head and sailed out the door.

Oscar had a point, and she did adore meeting with clients, listening to their chatter, the way they turned phrases and called her *love*. But an evening or two on her own didn't seem a lot to ask.

The Gaiety Theatre on the Strand was magnificent with its gilded dome ceiling and curtained balconies, as was the musical revue on stage with talented singers and beautiful costumes. What Nell enjoyed most, though, was noting what the theater patrons wore. To Oscar, the evening was about being seen, but for her it was taking in ideas that she could incorporate into her designs.

As Oscar's hand guided her deftly toward the exit, a voice rose above the crowd. "Well, if it's not Prunella Marchwold."

Nell would know that voice anywhere. Simone Honeycutt from Heathdown. The girl who'd taunted her in confirmation class. The girl who tried to lure Quentin away from her when they planned a picnic or walk on the village square. The last girl in England Nell wanted to see.

Simone elbowed well-dressed theatergoers like a trout swimming upstream until they were face-to-face.

Nell inhaled silently, a small tick in her jaw. "Hello, Simone. You're looking well." At least that was the truth. Simone's hair was no longer in ringlets but pulled into an upsweep, a headband with iridescent peacock feathers adorning her forehead at the hairline. But her smile was the same, red lips tilted at the corners in a permanent smile. Angelic almost.

"What a shock to see you. Last I heard, you had moved to New York to be a salesclerk so you could send money home to your family. How's your mother?"

"She's fine. Not starving."

Simone's gaze traveled from Nell's head to her feet, then a raised eyebrow as she looked at Oscar. She leaned in close to Nell's face. "You always did go for older men, didn't you?"

"My apologies. Oscar, this is Simone Honeycutt from my village in Heathdown. Simone, Oscar Fields, my c-colleague."

Oscar nodded. "Always my delight to meet one of Nell's friends."

"Likewise. Prunella's been one of my dearest chums since we were wee ones. So, tell me, Mr. Oscar Fields, how did a shopgirl rate a trip to London?"

Nell didn't answer. She couldn't. As Simone was talking, Quentin Bledsoe walked up.

His russet mop of hair had grown a shade darker, his face fuller than when he was a teen. But the smile was the same, and the glint in his eyes remained.

"Here you are, Simone. I lost you in the crowd." When his eyes met Nell's, his face faded to the color of paste. "Nell…Nell…You're here. In London."

An awkward moment passed, a flapping of butterflies in Nell's stomach at the sight of Quentin and Simone together. She nodded. "We've been here a couple of weeks. You l-look well. How are you?"

Mr. Fields cleared his throat, his grip on her elbow firm.

She apologized and made the introductions again. Simone crossed her arms, a pouty look that Nell remembered all too well.

Quentin ignored Simone and opened his arms. "How about a hug for your old friend?" He took her in his arms briefly, but it was long enough to catch a whiff of his cologne. Woodsy. Warm.

They were blocking the flow of people exiting the theater, so Oscar suggested they move along, and Quentin fell in stride beside Nell. "I can't believe you've been here two weeks and not called me."

"I did plan to. We've been very busy getting organized. And we've had quite the rush of clients already. I would like to see you, though…and Simone, too, if we can find a time."

"You have a shop here?"

"Yes. Oscar Fields Millinery of London. On Clifford."

"It's providential seeing you here," he said. Simone tugged him toward an exit door. As people streamed between them, he looked over his shoulder. "You look smashing. Give me a call. You have my number."

When Nell and Oscar made it outside, Nell looked up and down the sidewalk, hoping to catch up so they might talk further with Quentin. She hadn't expected her fondness for him to surge through her like it did. And she certainly hadn't expected to see him with Simone. The two of them, though, had disappeared into the damp night air.

As the cab pulled away from the curb, Oscar said, "Was that the boyfriend you were telling me about?"

"I…I don't re-re-recall saying he was m-my b-boyfriend."

"Good thing for both of us that he won't be a distraction from your work. Although I do question his taste in women. Did you notice your friend's ensemble? Simone, wasn't it? Cheaply made. From one of the street fairs, I would imagine. Tell me, did you enjoy the theater?"

Nell ignored the question and watched the fog gathering in the trees of Hyde Park.

Gloomy, wet days followed, and instead of walking to the shop in Mayfair with Hazel and Marcella, Nell took the bus with them. Her assistants joked and pointed out sights along the way. The horses on their morning exercises in Hyde Park. The street markets. Bobbies with their rounded hats and whistles. Hazel giggled and asked if they remembered to bring a *jumper* and a *brolly*. A sweater and an umbrella.

Riding the bus, Nell scanned the streets for an incidental sighting of Quentin. She debated whether she should call him. He'd said she should, but perhaps he was merely being polite. He hadn't contacted her. The thing that galled was that he'd chosen Simone. Or perhaps it was just a friendly relationship. Nell wanted to know more, but then again, she didn't. And she knew that's why she wouldn't call him. He knew where she was. She would wait.

She did, however, enjoy talking to her grandmother on the telephone every Sunday afternoon. Nell smiled when she remembered the first telephone being installed at Marchwold Manor and her grandmother's amazement at the "newfangled" invention. Her grandmother still hadn't gotten over shouting into the mouthpiece.

"You don't have to shout, Grandmama. I'm not on the other side of the Atlantic, you know."

"I know you're not, dear. But you're not here, either. Why don't you put that dear man you work for on the line so I can have a word."

"His room is on another floor. And besides, we're building our client base, hoping to get some commissions for those who've been invited to the royal wedding. A lovely woman was just in the shop yesterday who I think is close to engaging us for her royal wedding hat. It's quite exciting, isn't it?"

"Such a to-do. Your aunt Vivian's got herself worked into a right lather about it. Fretting she and Preston wouldn't be invited, and now stewing like a pot of prunes that her gowns won't arrive from London in time to get alterations done if they're needed."

"If she comes to London, be sure and give her my number. Maybe I could make a hat for her." She knew that would never happen. Aunt Vivian, a London socialite before marrying her uncle Preston, had always treated Nell like she was an orphan someone left on the doorstep.

"And one for Josephine. She looks lovely in a hat. Something in blue to match her eyes."

Josephine? Gramma Jo had been dead since Nell was four years old. Just the mention of her name brought a sour taste in her mouth. Had Grandmama gone daft? Jane had mentioned frail, not that her mental faculties were failing, too. And Nell desperately hoped Grandmama would be able to verify if what Nell remembered—or thought she remembered—held any truth.

"Grandmama, don't worry. It will be perfect, I promise. I have to run now. I love you."

"I'll see you next week then." *Click.*

No, not next week. The wedding wasn't for another month, and there was still work to be done.

❧

Quentin finally did call to invite Nell to dinner. She arranged to meet him at a tiny restaurant across from the Marble Arch she'd seen from the bus, in easy walking distance from her flat. She arrived at eight thirty, half an hour past when she told him she would be there, but a flurry of customers and a surprise visit from Lady Haversham had kept her late. When Oscar popped his head in to say he would be joining the Havershams for dinner, it was an unexpected stroke of good fortune. Nell had fretted all day about what to say should Oscar invite her to eat with him. She'd decided she would tell him the truth—she was dining with an old friend.

A friend. Her emotions were a knot, and now her calves ached from walking too fast. Quentin might have even given up. She ducked into the doorway under the awning, the smell of the wood fire overtaking her. Candles flickered on heavy oak tables, an aproned hostess greeting her. She explained that she was to meet someone, but she was late. Her words caught on her tongue, her stammering so frightful it was any wonder she was understood at all.

"Ah, yes, the gentleman over here. He's just having a pint while he's waiting."

Quentin rose to meet her and held the chair for her to sit next to him rather than across. Their knees bumped as they settled into their chairs and the hostess said, "The cook is featuring prawns and scallops in lemon sauce and shepherd's pie. Or if you fancy, our regular plate with bangers and mash."

Nell and Quentin asked for the seafood dish at the same time. A pot of tea for Nell. Another pint for Quentin.

"Quaint little place. Don't know as I've ever seen it." Quentin adjusted the tie at his throat.

"I hope it wasn't in-in-inconvenient." She took a deep breath. What was wrong with her? She never stammered around Quentin.

"Too far, you mean?"

"Well, it is late, and you have to work tomorrow."

"I work late most evenings, so this isn't unusual, if that's what you're asking." His voice was deeper than she remembered, the tone that of his father in the pulpit.

"I suppose. So you like your job? Tell me about it."

"Let's see. I'm an overseer for a few accounts but am acquiring more each week. The atmosphere is lively with the economy soaring like the wind one month, crashing against the rocks the next, but as long as people have money or can borrow it, I have a job. And yours?"

The waitress brought the tea and the ale with a cheery "'Ere you go, loves."

She shrugged. "A lot like yours, actually. Busy. And I'm working very hard to build my reputation, and as you say, it can have its ups and downs."

"So busy you didn't even have time to call your oldest friend?"

Ouch. It was the sort of thing he might have teased her with when they were younger, but even though he had the old, good-natured grin on his face, the words had a bite to them.

"I should have called, and I even told Oscar—Mr. Fields—that I wanted to spend time with you. The truth is, this is a very important assignment. It could mean international exposure for the salon as well as a boost to my career."

"Do you fancy coming back to England then?"

"I'm not sure. Mama's in Kentucky, so it would be hard to leave the States. With me in New York, we can visit a couple times a year. If an opportunity came along, I don't know. I would have to weigh the options."

He studied her, his gaze the one she remembered. Thoughtful. Caring. Her insides tumbled. She was blathering on, not giving him a chance to tell her about Simone. Or perhaps he was encouraging her so he didn't have to deliver bad news.

The taste of copper lolled on her tongue from biting her lower lip. "Sorry, I carry on so. I haven't even let you get a word in. How's Simone? She looks well. Bright and quite lovely."

"Same old Simone. She talked me into going with her to the theater."

"So, you're not…umm…I thought p-perhaps…"

"Perhaps what? That I'd finally given in to her wiles after all these years? She's swell, don't get me wrong, but…no. There's nothing going on with Simone and me except in her head."

Nell laughed, her shoulders relaxing. "That's a relief. You had me worried. You deserve someone much nicer."

Their food arrived, the seafood swimming in a rich, creamy sauce, the smell of citrus enticing. Quentin gave her hand a squeeze and bowed his head, asking a simple blessing for the food and for God to find their hearts worthy.

Nell whispered, "Amen," more in gratitude about Simone than the blessing of the food.

"How about you? Any beaus in New York?"

"I'm afraid not, much to Mama and Aunt Sarah's chagrin. It's not that they don't applaud my career as long as it doesn't interfere with finding the right husband."

Quentin spooned in a mouthful of the seafood concoction. "Oscar seems like a decent chap, watching out for your best interest. Taking you to the Gaiety for a show."

"He thinks it's important to circulate in the right crowd."

"And you? Do you enjoy that?"

"Occasionally. It gives me inspiration to see the current fashions and hairstyles, what elements might work in a hat."

"You're happy then designing for a nice salon and getting your name in magazines?"

"How did you know about the magazine?"

"My mother sent it to me. Said everyone in Heathdown was crowing about it."

She gave him a playful touch on the forearm. "I'm not happy just because of the magazines, although that's nice. It's a combination of things. Not all women have perfect features, but they all have an inner beauty, and it's pure bliss to see the transformation when someone with, say, plain features gets a glimpse in the mirror in one of my hats and feels beautiful. For some, I suspect it may be the first time. It's not about my happiness, but other women discovering their own beauty and carrying themselves with poise."

"You've always been passionate about hats. Remember the time you drew the Easter lambs and put a bonnet on every one of them?"

"Whatever made you think of that?"

"I saw the drawing when I went to see your grandmother. It's in a gilded frame hanging above her writing desk."

"I can't believe she kept that. Oscar has promised me a couple of days after the wedding to visit her. I just hope we have enough business to keep us afloat here and stay that long."

"You'll be fine." He leaned close and kissed her on the cheek.

"Aren't you two the little lovebirds?" The waitress clucked her tongue. "I wish I could get my Johnny to look at me that way instead of that wretched bottle he's in love with. What'll it be? A nice tart for dessert? Some port for the gentleman?"

Quentin said, "Both sound divine, but we'd better be going."

The night was damp but warm as they strolled on the walk and then crossed to the Marble Arch. As late as it was, people still ambled about, most of them with beagles and greyhounds and wiry-haired terriers on leads. Lovers holding hands. Frolicking newsboys still hawking the evening paper. Stooped men with canes and businessmen cutting across the park, going home to wives and children. Nell and Quentin.

Quentin talked about his family in Heathdown and King's College in Cambridge where he had taken his accounting degree. She talked about her roommates, that she thought Calvin might be sweet on Jeanette and that she'd had a postcard from Greta, who'd finally landed a role with the vaudeville troupe and was playing Philadelphia.

"You'd like Greta, Quentin. She's energetic and determined to make it as an actress."

"Sounds a lot like someone else I know."

"Do you think I'm daft for wanting to make women beautiful?"

He sidestepped something on the walk. "Not at all. Without dreams and passions, mankind would wither into nothingness."

Somewhere in the distance, a clock chimed twelve times, and Quentin asked if he would see her again.

Nell hesitated. "Not for a while. We've only a few weeks to make an impression and worlds of hats to make. New customers every day. I'll call if I find a time that I'm free, when Oscar doesn't have something arranged."

"You do sound happy."

"It's what I've always wanted."

As his warm hands surrounded her and his lips brushed her cheek, a figure turned up the walk to their building. *Harjo.*

He eyed them, then strode up the steps without a word.

CHAPTER 19

"This isn't the hat I chartered you to make." Lady Blythe-Perkins drew her lips tight, hands on her hips. "I'll be ridiculed for wearing something so hideous. The style and that bilious chartreuse would make the king himself weep."

Nell stood by, waiting for the willowy woman to finish. And to give herself time to think. She remembered the session distinctly. The woman had come on a hectic day demanding to be worked in. She'd brought neither fabric swatches nor her dress design, but said she'd send them by courier later. And she'd not so casually mentioned that her husband was an influential member of the House of Lords.

Now, as the irate woman stood before her, Nell said, "I'm ce-certain this is your order...but I w-will...check it against the o-o-others." The all too familiar failure of her tongue to deliver the words brought a scathing look from her client.

"If I'd known I was dealing with a moron, I wouldn't have bothered. *Highly recommended. She's one of us,* Lady Haversham said. Just because some distant relative of yours was an earl doesn't make you capable."

Nell looked up to see Oscar standing in the arch between the two rooms of the salon. "A little problem?" He swept in and lifted Lady Blythe-Perkins's hand to his lips. "I'm Oscar Fields, owner of this salon. How may I be of assistance?"

"By sorting out this mess, for starters." She repeated what Nell had already heard.

"Yes, m'lady. The satisfaction of a beautiful woman like yourself, one of your stature, means the world to me. As I know it does to Nell. Whatever we can do to make amends—"

"You can start by finding the hat I ordered."

Nell stepped forward. "If you have a m-moment, I'll fetch the original receipt."

"I don't have all day."

"Yes, ma'am."

Nell retrieved the purchase order file from her desk. She thumbed through the orders, the attached sketches and fabrics, and pulled out the one for Lady Blythe-Perkins.

Odd. The description on the order sheet didn't match the hat made for Lady Blythe-Perkins. The next form had the details for a Mrs. Fortner, but again it didn't match the hat Hazel had made. Nell's palms grew damp. She must have transposed them on the workroom sheets when she'd attached the swatches. Mrs. Fortner's hat would be all wrong as well.

Nell swallowed hard and braced herself to face Lady Blythe-Perkins.

"Again, my apologies. This is indeed not the hat you ordered. We still have the swatches in the workroom and will remake your hat. Would tomorrow be c-convenient?"

"I'll be back at nine in the morning."

Oscar offered his hand. "And rest assured, you won't be charged a farthing for your inconvenience."

"I should pray not. And I'm certain Lady Haversham will be most interested in what I have to tell her. There's no telling how many other orders you've gotten wrong, and my friends have been too kind to bring it to your attention. We will all think twice before securing your services in the future. Shoddy, that's what it is."

When she flounced out the door, Oscar asked to have a word with Nell in his office upstairs.

After Nell explained what happened, Oscar said, "You do understand the gravity of your error?"

"Of course. But she was rather beastly if you ask me." *Tattling to Lady Haversham indeed.*

"A rudimentary principle I taught you from the moment I took you on—the customer is always right."

Nell nodded, her face still hot. "And you know I work hard to make sure every hat is up to your finest ex-ex-expec—"

"Expectations? Is that word you're looking for? Perhaps you are a simpleton and crumble under the slightest pressure."

"We've been overrun with new orders."

"Which is always a good thing. When did Lady Blythe-Perkins come in?"

"Last week. On Wednesday."

"The day after you were out three-quarters of the night with your childhood sweetheart."

"Not three-quarters. And his name is Quentin." His name was sweet on her tongue, and although she hadn't stayed out late as Oscar implied, she'd lain awake long into the night thinking of Quentin, recalling his touch, his eyes, the catch in his voice when he chuckled. She smiled and lifted her chin.

Oscar flicked a piece of lint from his sleeve. "I know I don't need to remind you the work here comes first."

Nell fanned through the order forms still clutched in her fingers. "I know you're right. It was entirely my error. I'll work all night if I have to remaking the hat. And the one for Mrs. Fortner."

Oscar's eyebrows shot up. "So there are other mistakes as well?"

"Only the two. And contrary to what you say, it wasn't my evening with Quentin that caused the error. Lady Blythe-Perkins came in while I was helping Mrs. Fortner and demanded to be seen. She had no p-patience for measurements and said she was late for a meeting at the palace."

"Buckingham?"

"She didn't say."

"This is precisely why you should have exercised more caution. This is the clientele we need to cultivate."

Grovel for, he meant. Nell nodded, knowing in her gut he had a point. "I'll present Lady Blythe-Perkins with a bouquet of flowers when she comes in the morning for her hat. From my pocketbook."

"We only have two weeks left. From now on, I expect you to be available day and night." He picked up the telephone and made a shooing motion with his hand.

❧

Lady Blythe-Perkins arrived half an hour late, but Nell quietly withdrew from the customer at the consulting table and greeted her warmly. When Nell opened the hatbox, Lady Blythe-Perkins sniffed.

"At least you got the colors right. May I try it on?"

"Please do."

The hat truly was spectacular. Just the right mix of sophistication and flair with the brim tacked up on one side and secured with a cluster of ruby bugle beads and sparkling crystals, an embellishment that had taken Nell three hours to create. Lady Blythe-Perkins smiled at her reflection, then removed the hat and handed it to Nell to box up. She tucked the bouquet Nell had given her under one arm, grabbed the thin cord of the hatbox, and left without a thank-you.

Nell stood in the shadow beside the window and watched her

step into the backseat of her driver's car. At the intersection, the rear window was cracked open and the flowers tossed onto the street below.

By the time Mrs. Fortner arrived that afternoon, Nell had decided there would always be people who were impossible to please. Thankfully, there were also those like Mrs. Fortner.

"Marvelous, my dear. Not everyone likes chartreuse, you know, but I've always felt it had a warm earthiness about it. And the poppies are lovely."

Nell was glad she'd stayed up until four in the morning and redone the hat. The wide brim was the perfect balance for Mrs. Fortner's heavier build. They chatted about the wedding and Mrs. Fortner's interest in growing herbs and her work with an orphanage.

"Suitable and worthy pursuits for a matron. My mother is smiling from her window in heaven, I'm sure. But my real passion was to be a cook, a chef in one of those charming sidewalk cafés in Paris."

"What kept you from it?"

"Marriage. Children. My own reluctance to assert myself. Running a home has given me ample practice to experiment with cuisine and such, but nothing I could fall back on should I find myself alone and my dear husband's fortunes fallen by the wayside."

"You sound like my mother. Only it did happen to her."

"Oh, gracious. What did she do?"

"Sailed to America and found another husband."

As Nell boxed up her hat, Mrs. Fortner asked, "Would you and your colleague Mr. Fields be available on Saturday before the wedding? I'm having a small party and would be delighted if you could come."

"How k-kind of you. I'll have to check our diaries. Any particular occasion?"

"It's for my longtime friend Cecilia, who you may know as Countess of Strathmore and Kinghorne."

"Elizabeth's mother? The one who's marrying the Duke of York?"

"The same. Just the dearest of people. I'm doing a soiree for her and a few friends. Fifty or so. If you can work it in."

Nell's fingers trembled as she tied the ribbon of the hatbox. "I'm honored. I'm sure we'll be delighted to attend." She handed over the box.

Mrs. Fortner gave her a card in return. "My number."

"Thank you."

When she left, Nell wobbled to the nearest chair and sat down. Lady Blythe-Perkins and all her airs had caused Nell to lose a night's sleep while it was Mrs. Fortner she should have been concerned about. But Mrs. Fortner, bless her, would have never made such a stink.

Connections, Oscar always said. Nell huffed out a breath. What did he know?

❧

Nell was putting the finishing touches on a new window display when Lady Haversham dropped by the Mayfair salon.

After exchanging pleasantries, Nell said, "Oscar's out on an errand, but I know he's been anxious to see you. Would you care to wait?"

"Actually, it's you I came to see. Could we have a word?"

Instantly the image of Lady Blythe-Perkins came to Nell's mind. "I hope all is well, that your friends have found the hats to their liking."

"Most assuredly." She sat in the chair Nell indicated. "All except one. I think you know who I mean."

"I hoped we'd resolved her dissatisfaction."

"It would take more than you and all the king's men to bring an ounce of satisfaction to the dreadful woman of whom we speak."

Nell's jaw started to drop, but she caught herself and chewed her bottom lip instead. "As Mr. Fields says, the customer is always right."

"Not in this case, but that's not the purpose of my visit. I came to tell you that, on behalf of the London Noble Women's Society, we'd like to commission you to make our hats for the wedding. About two dozen or so if you can work us in."

Nell's heart soared. And Lady Haversham had come to her and not Oscar, but she knew he would be thrilled. "Absolutely. Since we've already done designs for a few of the women for other occasions, we have measurements on file so the consults will go much quicker."

Lady Haversham nodded, smiling, and in that moment, Nell realized how much she reminded her of Mrs. Benchley. Gracious. A leader of her social set. *And* encouraging to Nell as a woman in business.

Lady Haversham said she was on her way to tell the society the good news.

"It's good news for us as well. I'm most grateful. You've been a pleasure to work with from the moment of our arrival. I think I can speak for Mr. Fields, too, when I say how much we a-a-appreciate you."

"You're very kind as I suspected you'd be, well-bred and from a noble family."

When Mrs. Haversham left, Nell spun around the room. She couldn't wait to tell Oscar that all of their hard work had finally paid off.

CHAPTER 20

Oscar stormed through the showroom and straight to Nell's desk. "Is everything all right? I just saw Lady Haversham's driver pulling from the curb as I was returning from the tailor. Was something amiss? Another mix-up on an order?"

"Calm down, Oscar, or you're going to give yourself an attack of some kind. It's not going to do any of us any good if you work yourself into a lather." Inside, Nell trembled. She'd never talked to Oscar in such a flippant way, but Lady Haversham's news had buoyed her spirit.

Oscar stiffened, his thin lips clamped into a straight line. "I'm not working myself into a lather. I merely asked you a question for which I'm waiting to hear your answer. What did the dear woman want?"

Nell couldn't help herself. Her face broke into a wide grin. "We—Oscar Fields Millinery of London—have just been commissioned to do the hats for the London Noble Women's Society for the royal wedding." She put her hand on her hip in what she knew was a cocky pose and enjoyed watching Oscar's eyes widen and his mouth fall open.

Nell continued, "Two dozen or so hats for the cream of London society. Hats that will grace the halls of Westminster in two weeks."

She'd never seen Oscar speechless, nor the particular shade of beet red that his face had become. He gaped, fish mouthed, gathering his thoughts, it seemed.

He lifted his chin. "And what terms, exactly, did you agree to?"

"Terms?"

"Payment. Materials. Appointments. Details, Miss Marchwold. It's quite one thing to receive the news, but another entirely to negotiate the terms. If we have to special order materials and pay a premium for a courier to deliver them, it will affect our net profits."

"Of course. I'm familiar with our regular suppliers and what they carry. And I'm certain that none of the women will flinch at the cost."

"We have to be competitive, but we don't want to offer our services for an amount that will make us look inferior. Like I said, details. You should have insisted that Lady Haversham speak directly to me."

"I told her you were out, but she seemed quite satisfied with speaking to me. I gave her your regards and told her you would be appreciative of the commission. You are, aren't you?"

"But of course. And let's hope that your giddiness doesn't elicit errors like it did with Lady Blythe-Perkins. We can't afford another unhappy customer."

"Yes, sir. I'll be most c-careful and commune more closely with Hazel and Marcella."

"See that you do." He brushed past her on his way to the door that led to the stairwell.

"W-wait. I didn't tell you the other exciting thing that happened."

"What? You wait until I've stepped out, and then you garner one piece of good news after another. What, pray tell, could be more exciting than getting what we came to London for in the first place?"

She handed him Mrs. Fortner's card. "We've been invited to a party."

"When do you think you'll have time for a party with the new orders?"

"This is one I think we'll want to make time for." She gave him the details and said Mrs. Fortner requested a reply. "I can call her with our acceptance if you wish."

"Absolutely not. I will handle it." And this time when he started out the door, she didn't call him back.

The next day, Oscar had an array of dresses delivered from a couture shop around the corner. "I want you to look your loveliest for the royal family."

"It's not the royal family. Only the friends of the bride's mother."

"There's always the chance the betrothed will make an appearance. It would be the cherry on the top of our time in London to be treated to such a surprise."

"Lady Elizabeth wasn't mentioned, and Prince Albert would have no reason to come without Elizabeth. But thank you for sending the dresses. They're lovely."

Nell chose a chiffon gown in a melon color that went with a pair of emerald earrings she already had. It was neither too provocative nor too severe, one she hoped would give the impression that she was stylish and approachable. Then she met with the first of the women's society friends to begin their designs for the wedding.

By the night of the party, she was weary with exhaustion from the long hours of consulting, then working alongside Hazel and Marcella to give the right flair to each hat. Nell's assistants, who'd become her friends during their time in London, offered to help her get ready.

As Hazel did the buttons up the back of Nell's dress, she said, "It's too bad you're not stepping out with a beau tonight. You ask me, your beauty is wasted on the likes of Mr. Fields."

Nell told her it was a thrill no matter who her escort was, but the truth was, Quentin had been on her mind all day. Every day, in fact. Not that he would care for such pomp and circumstance, but she did wish she had more time to spend with him. And at night, he filled her dreams, not as a childhood friend, but as someone she wanted to spend time with and let the matters of the heart take their course.

Oscar was resplendent in his tuxedo when they met in the foyer of their building. Handsome enough to turn the heads of any unattached woman. He still fussed at her over each detail of the hats and grumbled about the cost of the French ribbon and special flowers she ordered for some of them. Listening to him was a small price to pay for the experience and respect she was gaining as a designer.

In the cab, she took in the lights of London until the driver pulled onto a street lined with carriages and automobiles, chauffeurs assisting well-dressed passengers from their conveyances. The walks on both sides of the street teemed with onlookers.

The cabbie thumbed toward the crowd. "Royalty gawkers. Snip in the paper this morning about all the hobnobbing spots. Got me and the missus a spot picked out to watch the fanfare come wedding day. She wouldn't miss it for naught." He pulled up beside a Rolls-Royce, then came and opened the door for them.

While Oscar settled the fare, Nell looked at the long row of soot-stained brick homes, each one distinguished by a stoop with tall, heavy doors and gaslights on either side. Modest, but with a special elegance like Mrs. Fortner herself. Oscar put his arm around her shoulders and leaned in close. "It's not the dress I would have chosen, but your perfume is quite alluring."

Nell turned her head toward him, their faces close. Someone stepped from the shadows and held up a black box, a blinding flash lighting the night air. Nell stumbled, her shoe catching on the hem of her dress, but the photographer reached out and caught her by the arm.

"Sorry, miss. Didn't mean to make you take a tumble. If I could just have your name, please, for the caption in the paper."

Oscar answered for her. "This is Nell Marchwold and I'm Oscar Fields. My assistant and I are guests of Mrs. Fortner."

With the camera slung over his back, the man—a reporter, Nell now realized—wrote it all down and said, "Got it. Name sounds familiar. You're not British, are you?"

"American, but my lovely Nell is a born and bred Englishwoman."

Someone shouted that the Duchess of Sibley had arrived. The reporter tipped his hat and dashed up the walk. Nell smiled to herself. Oscar was always trying to get his name in the paper for publicity. Nell was quite content to remain in the shadows.

Mrs. Fortner greeted them and invited them to make themselves at home. Nell had never been keen on circulating in a roomful of strangers, but she encouraged Oscar to go and visit with some of the men clustered around an elegant buffet. Nell skirted the room and sat on a brocade settee next to a woman with chestnuts for knuckles and loose skin under her chin that swayed like a velvet drape as she sipped her champagne.

"Tell me again, love, how you're related to our Prince Albert."

"I'm not related. I'm a hatmaker, a milliner."

"So you're German then. I didn't know Cecilia knew any Millers." A maid with a tray in her hand walked past, and the elderly woman signaled for a fresh champagne.

Poor dear. Her memory and hearing were both gone, but not her taste for champagne. All attempts at engaging in conversation were met with the same misunderstanding, and for once Nell was glad when Oscar rescued her.

With his arm around her waist, he led her to a group of women gathered near the ornate fireplace. "Here you are, ladies. Miss Marchwold, my apprentice whom I was telling you about." To Nell, he said, "We were discussing the bride's gown, and I knew you'd want to hear all about it."

While Nell had been keeping the tipsy octogenarian company, Oscar had no doubt been working the room. She turned her attention to the ladies who gave an animated description of the simple gown made of a deep ivory chiffon moiré embroidered with pearls and silver thread.

One said, "Madame Seymour created it and has even sewn in a strip of Brussels lace that's been in the family for generations."

A sprightly woman with dark hair interrupted. "I've heard it's from the gown of one of Lady Elizabeth's ancestors who wore it to the grand ball of Bonnie Prince Charlie. Isn't that the loveliest thing?"

"Are you certain about that? I don't believe I recall hearing that."

"Yes, Cecilia told me herself. Of course, Lady Elizabeth doesn't want to make a grand showing, sweet like she is and not taken to all the fuss." The woman turned to Nell. "Are you married? Or promised to some bright young man?"

"M-married? No...I have..."

Oscar clutched her hand and drew it up. "What Nell means to say is she's dedicated to her career. At least for now. Isn't that true, dear?"

One of the women clucked her tongue. "I don't understand the ways of today. Women and their careers. Who will run our homes if the women are all in offices and wearing business suits every day?"

"The same ones who always have. Our housekeepers and governesses."

Nell said, "Until misfortune strikes. Sometimes women are forced to work. Having a skill to rely on can come in handy."

"You speak from experience?"

She nodded. "When my father was killed in the war, my mother was displaced from the position she would have had as the next Countess of Marchwold. Lucky for us, her sister invited us to move to America to be near them." *Lucky for us.* An icy finger ran down Nell's spine. She'd never considered her mother's choice good fortune. Only one that had taken Nell from all that she loved. She willed herself to look at the dark-haired woman who'd posed the question.

"Marchwold? You must be related to Vivian Marchwold then."

"She's married to my uncle."

"The daughter of Constance and Oxley Wentworth?"

Nell nodded, the conversation taking a turn that made her neck itch. Vivian and her mother, Constance Wentworth, had a lot in common with Lady Blythe-Perkins, not the least of which was putting Nell in her place. Both Vivian and her mother treated Lady Mira like she was an object that stood in the way of Vivian's rightful place. What future would Nell have had in such a house? Had her mother, in fact, done the noble thing, the one that required strength, by moving an ocean away?

Choice words about Vivian lolled on her tongue, but she wouldn't speak ill of her. Her grandmother's voice whispered softly in Nell's head. *We all have a bit of good and evil in us. Let your words and your deeds show the world what dwells in your heart.*

As Nell tried to think of something nice to say about her aunt Vivian, the woman leaned in and whispered, "No wonder you moved to America." She turned her attention to Mr. Fields. "How about you, Mr. Fields? Is there a Mrs. Fields?"

"There was. She was a victim of the Spanish flu in nineteen."

"Then you're surely in need of another wife."

Relieved to have the spotlight off her, Nell said, "If you know of any prospects, I'm certain Mr. Fields would be delighted to have an introduction."

The woman with dark hair said, "You don't have eyes on him yourself?"

Nell chuckled. "Oh no, ma'am. Like he said, my career is my priority for the moment."

One of the women who'd been silent throughout the conversation said, "I just might know of someone. Perhaps I could give you her number."

Oscar's Adams apple bobbed up and down. "I certainly didn't expect to happen upon a group of matchmakers. I do appreciate the kind offer, but I'll only be in London a few more weeks; then it's back to New York and the old grind of running a salon." He pulled Nell into the crook of his arm. "With Nell, of course." He graciously extricated them from the clutch of women and asked Nell if she'd care for a glass of champagne.

"No, but a drink of water would be nice."

Mrs. Fortner intercepted them as they made their way across the drawing room. "Oh, good, here you are. Cecilia would like to meet you before she leaves. She's making it an early night so she can save her strength for the big day."

They spoke briefly to Cecelia, who was both charming and gracious and said she was happy to make their acquaintance. When Cecilia had gone, others began to leave as well. Oscar said he'd changed his mind about the champagne, and together they thanked Mrs. Fortner for the invitation and stepped out into the cool, clear night. Oscar offered his arm and suggested they walk for a bit.

Nell kept her arm tucked into the crook of Oscar's arm, the warmth through his jacket welcome. After a time, he asked if she was chilled, and when she admitted she was, he removed his coat and draped it around her shoulders.

After another block of walking, he said, "You certainly made it clear to that bag of old gossips that you've high aspirations."

"If you mean becoming a designer, yes. You've been more than gracious in taking me in, keeping me on even when I've made terrible mistakes, and teaching me about the business. Perhaps I've not shown my appreciation, but I'm sincere when I say that it means a lot."

"And what other aspirations do you have?"

In the dark, it was difficult to tell what he was implying. Did he think she was going to beg to get the Nellie March label? Perhaps he thought she had aspirations toward him. That she wanted to be the next Mrs. Fields.

The traffic was heavier now as they came upon a section of nightclubs and eateries. A gas lantern above the sign of a small establishment caught Nell's eye. Plutino's Ristorante. In smaller letters beneath the name, it read: *Ravioli* and *Manicotti*. The place Quentin said was just around the corner from his flat. Her knees went weak, and Oscar took her faltering for being too tired to go any farther and offered to buy her a warm drink or a bite to eat.

"I'm all right. Perhaps we can find a t-taxicab now."

Oscar stepped from the curb, hand raised, and yelled, "Taxi!" and when they'd settled into the seat, he turned to her. "You didn't answer my question."

"About my aspirations?" Then it hit her. Did he think she was using him to advance her career and then leave Oscar Fields Millinery?

She placed a hand on his arm. "The only thing I've ever wanted was to make fancy hats. And that's still what I aspire to. But since you asked, I'll tell you. I want my designs to stand for something— to bring out a woman's best features and give her confidence."

"That's a rather lofty way of saying you want your own label."

"A label could accomplish that. With the Oscar Fields insignia behind it, of course. Perhaps refine what I'm already doing into a distinctive style, one with a certain artistic flair so that it would be recognized as a hat that makes its owner feel beautiful inside and out."

"It's obvious that all the attention of late has gone straight to your head. While you've turned into a decent designer, I'm not interested in specializing. There's no money in it, and I have to think about keeping the business afloat." He huffed. "You might want to ask Nora Remming what happens when you get fanciful ideas."

Her face flamed as if he'd slapped her. The next time he asked, she would keep her aspirations to herself.

CHAPTER 21

Nell rose early on Sunday morning and made a pot of tea using the hot plate. While the leaves were steeping, she picked up the telephone and gave the operator Quentin's number, trying to remember what it was like to sit beside him in church. If he was agreeable to joining her for the service, then perhaps they could take a walk or picnic in Hyde Park afterward. Depending on the weather, they might even venture to Westminster and stroll through the cloister gardens.

"There's no answer for the number you requested. Have a lovely day."

Nell dropped the receiver onto the hook and drank her tea. Well, then.

She walked to St. Mary Abbots on Kensington High Street alone, the familiarity of the service a balm for her weariness, but also a reminder of Quentin and the faith they shared. Nell joined in singing "A Mighty Fortress Is Our God," her throat thick with emotion and memories of sabbaths in their tiny church in Heathdown. Only a few more days until the wedding…and then a visit with Grandmama. And now she knew, time also with Quentin and whatever possibilities God had for them. Whether she would leave Oscar and stay in London to be near Quentin or not, she didn't know. A part of her thought she might, but jumping ahead of herself was futile.

She took her Sunday stroll on her own, and as she crossed the intersection before her block, a young boy handed her a bright yellow tulip from the bucket he carried on his arm.

She reached for her handbag to give him a tuppence, but he shook his head. "Naught for me, miss. You look like you could use some cheering up. It's me good deed for the day."

She touched his weathered cheek, rosy from the cool morning, and thanked him. As she walked away with her nose to the tulip, for some reason she thought of Calvin. Jeanette had written that they'd seen each other a few times. Nell had been right. Something wonderful was blossoming for them. And Jeanette had scrawled across the bottom that Greta and Spike were still traveling with the vaudeville act.

The warm thoughts vanished the moment she arrived back at her flat and found a note on her door.

NM, Needed at once at the shop. OF

Her first thought was that the note was another ploy to play with her emotions and test her loyalty, and if it hadn't been four days before the wedding, she would have ignored it and spent the afternoon on a park bench writing letters. But the day had grown cloudy, moisture teasing the air, so she changed from her Sunday dress into a simple drop waist and low-heeled shoes, then grabbed her brolly and raincoat and walked to the bus stop.

She let herself in the Mayfair shop with her key and went to her desk to stow her things. Her feet were leaden as she climbed the stairs to Mr. Fields's office.

Harjo Pritchard growled a "Took your sweet time getting here" as she swept past.

Mr. Fields and Lady Haversham sat relaxed with cups of tea, and Mr. Fields had a smug look about him. Lady Haversham patted the seat of the chair next to her for Nell. "I was just telling Oscar that Mrs. Fortner called with the most marvelous suggestion. As you know, I'm having the bridesmaids' luncheon on Tuesday, and she thought—and I concur—that the young women would enjoy having a souvenir hat to remember this momentous occasion. I know it would be quite impossible to make eight new hats from scratch, but perhaps some from your stock downstairs. And it would be lovely if you could add a rose-and-silver thistle like that featured in Lady Elizabeth's gown."

Nell swallowed. Eight hats before Tuesday? It would be murder getting them done. Then again, it would confirm what she told Oscar. All she wanted to do was make hats. And these would be spectacular!

"What a splendid idea. I'll call for Hazel and Marcella to come and see what we can do."

Mr. Fields gave her a wary look. "I've explained that it might be quite pressing on your time."

"Oh, I think it will be quite manageable and such a pleasure." Nell turned to Lady Haversham. "Do you have a photograph or facsimile of some sort for the thistle? I like to be authentic whenever possible. And I believe the wedding gown has Brussels lace. Perhaps we could add a bit of that for an extra touch." She rose and offered her arm. "Let's go down to the salon and see what we have."

"I've not had this much fun since my dear Bannister took me to India and I rode an elephant."

As they left, Nell turned and gave Oscar a tiny wave, touched her fingers to her lips, and blew a kiss in his direction.

By first light, throngs of people streamed along the streets of London, elbowing and jockeying for the best positions along the routes that would take the Duke of York from Buckingham Palace to Westminster. Lady Elizabeth Bowes-Lyon would be whisked with equal fanfare from her home on Bruton Street.

Mr. Fields wanted everyone in the salon together and chose Buckingham Palace as their viewing post. Bright banners were festooned from one light pole to the next, the smell of cherry blossoms and fried fish from vendors wafting in the air. Cheers went up when the palace gates opened and a charge of royal horsemen preceded the royal coach.

The duke waved to onlookers who fanned handkerchiefs in return and shouted blessings. In moments, all that was seen was the back of the two rearguard horses. The crowd shifted and moved into an ever-changing sea of faces, dressed in their finest as if they had front-row seats. Nell scanned the crowd hoping to catch of glimpse of Quentin, knowing the improbability.

Oscar whispered, "Why so melancholy?"

"Just thinking of the hats we made for this day. It's gratifying to know we had a small part."

"Of greater importance is knowing the lovely women wearing them have ringside seats inside the abbey. The *right* kind of people, my sweet."

"It would be fun to see at least one of them so I could keep it as a memory of this day."

"You weren't being melancholy then, but sentimental." He kissed her lightly on the cheek. "That's what I want you to remember from this day. Our time together."

She forced a smile. It was hard not to question his motives. She'd hoped that his seeing her joy in making the hats for the bridesmaids would send the message that she was adaptable and in love with her work. Becoming an "item" with Mr. Fields, as Jeanette might say, made her groan.

"They're coming! They're coming!" Shouts echoed through the crowd like water rushing through a canyon, the rumble of wheels on stone streets faint, but unmistakable as people called out to their beloved Duke of York and his bride. The horsemen, a dozen or more, sat erect on the beasts, their spears pointing to the heavens. Onlookers threw rose petals and kisses as the coach carrying the bride and groom and Lady Elizabeth's bridesmaids passed. When the last of the processional clip-clopped inside the palace grounds, the gates were closed, but the cheers continued. Rumors that the royal couple would appear on the palace balcony crackled like electricity down a wire.

When the couple emerged a short time later, a roar went up. Nell watched in rapt attention as Lady Elizabeth, now HRH the Duchess of York, stepped to the rail, the flutter of her veil behind her. Smiling, almost shy, her groom joined her, resplendent in his RAF dress uniform with gold braids across the right side of his chest, medals pinned to the other. He tenderly helped the duchess with her veil, the look of adoration apparent even from a distance.

A hush fell across the expanse as the couple thanked everyone for their loyal support and their gracious wishes. The veil fluttered again, this time caught by Queen Mary. But Nell doubted that Elizabeth noticed. She had eyes only for her husband. And for an instant, Nell imagined the unspoken love in that gaze was between her and Quentin.

Nell brushed away a tear, feeling the fool since she'd promised herself she wouldn't cry. Mr. Fields encircled her in his arms and said, "It's quite contagious, isn't it?"

She shot him a puzzled look.

"Love. The thrill of romance." Whatever longing had been in her heart fled. Oscar was flirting with her or he had his own longings.

"A thrill, yes. My grandmother would have loved seeing this. I can scarcely wait to tell her."

A young lad walked past, calling out, "Pasties for sale! Only a shilling. Get your beef 'n' onion pasties while they're hot!" He reached into the covered tin box hung around his neck and fished out two newspaper-wrapped pasties for a customer.

Hazel pulled on Harjo's arm. "Buy us gals some lunch, okay?" She looked back at Nell. "You two hungry?"

Mr. Fields gave the go-ahead to Harjo who handed the lad a handful of coins and asked for five pasties. They cupped the newspaper under their chins to catch the crumbs while pigeons pranced at their feet snatching every morsel that fell.

They then turned in the direction of Hyde Park where fruit wagons and trolley carts with bottles of ale were scattered. Each had a long queue of ladies in fine hats, ruffians with holes in their pant knees, gentlemen with babies on their shoulders, young and old, rich and poor, waiting to spend a few pence on their wedding dinners. Farther down, a confectionary cart bore a sign that said, "Wedding Cake: Congratulations to Bertie and Lady Elizabeth." Nell craned her neck but couldn't see the end of the queue.

Hazel said, "I still wish we'd gone to where they're showing the real cake. Ten foot tall, that's what I heard."

Marcella said, "You'd stand in line all night to see a lousy cake? You ask me, you've seen one, you've seen 'em all."

"Well, I've never seen the cake of a duke before. Who knows? He just might be the King of England someday."

"And I'm going to be the Queen of the Bronx." She laughed and kept walking.

"Hats for sale! First-rate! Finest in London!" A toothless woman with rheumy eyes walked beside a cart as a baggy-trousered man gripped the handlebars and pushed it. Ladies' hats hung from brass poles at the corners with men's hats lining shelves along the side. A mangy yellow dog sprawled on a ledge across the front.

Nell stepped from the group. "Do you have anything for children?"

"For little birdies or lads, m'lady?"

"My younger sister. She's five."

Already the man had lifted the lid from a wooden compartment and was pulling out hats. He lined up four along his arm like it was a display rack. "Ten bob apiece, m'lady. Ye won't get naught better in all of London town."

Nell surveyed them and told the man she'd take the blue one—a slouched cloche the color of the sky with a daisy on the side.

"And fer yourself, m'lady? Special today. Two fer fifteen bob. Gotta feed my mongrel, ye know."

She shook her head and counted out ten shillings, then dropped it in his grimy palm. "And here's a little something for your dog." She added another ten pence.

"Thank ye, m'lady. Pleasant day."

The woman was already down the street shouting, "Hats for sale!"

Oscar indicated they should turn into the park. After a few paces, he said, "Hope your little sister doesn't get head lice from that."

"I'm not worried. Grandmama bought me one at the rose fair when I was about Caroline's age. I wore it every day until my grandfather's dog chewed a hole in it. It's one of my favorite memories."

Oscar made a grunting sound and kept walking. Marcella tapped him on the shoulder. "I don't mean to be impertinent, but we've done what we came for. Have you booked our passage back to New York?"

"A perfectly reasonable question." He paused, the five of them mingling in a circle. "We sail three weeks from tomorrow. It will give us time to finish any orders that weren't for the wedding and"—he winked at Hazel and Marcella—"give you girls time to take in a few sights if you've half a mind to do so."

Hazel sighed. "I was hoping to be home by the middle of May for my Bennie's birthday."

"Buy him a souvenir instead. Only I wouldn't recommend a fleabag hat from a street trolley." He cleared his throat. "Harjo and I have a few last-minute obligations, which we'll take care of as soon as Nell and I return from the country. She's desperate to see her grandmother in Gloucestershire, and I'm anxious to meet her family as well...as you might imagine."

Nell's knees felt like they'd been hit from behind with a hammer.

CHAPTER 22

Nell reminded herself that there were worse things than having Oscar accompany her to Heathdown. He could have refused to give her the time off—after all, he was paying all of her expenses while she was in London. Or he could have long ago fired her over the incident with Percy. Or the New Year's Eve disaster. He had the authority to run his salon anyway he chose. And she could choose to stay or go. She knew in the depths of her heart, though, that it was because of Oscar and a divine plan that she had been given the chance to become a milliner.

The news from New York was that her spring line was selling so well that the assembly workers had been put on overtime to keep up with the demand. In her gut, Nell knew Oscar's motive in going to Heathdown with her was to keep an eye on her every move and keep her at Oscar Fields Millinery. She just didn't relish the intrusion on her time with Grandmama, and deeper still, her need to find out if Gramma Jo's death had occurred as Nell's new memory revealed.

As the train sped through the countryside, she yawned and told Oscar she wanted to rest. She turned facing the window and watched the landscape fly by. The church spires of distant villages and rolling green hills pierced her heart. Willow trees made winding paths along the rivers, which nourished them, and as they neared Heathdown, they came upon a series of hills forested with beech trees, ancient oaks, and sweet chestnuts. Nell was surprised she still knew them all, but how could she not after all the time she'd spent on the project her governess had given her? She even remembered the title she'd given the assignment. *Home in the Cotswolds.*

The porter stood at the front of the railcar and announced, "Heathdown next stop."

Nell's skin tingled. *Home.*

She gave a wan smile to Oscar. At least he wouldn't be staying under the same roof since her grandmother's house in the village was modest in comparison to the manor and had only one guest room. When Nell had called to say they were coming, she asked Jane Alistair, the lady's maid, to reserve a room at the White Hart on the village square for Oscar.

The first person Nell saw when she stepped onto the platform was Davenport, the old butler from Marchwold Manor. His hair was whiter around the temples, his jowls a little fuller, but his eyes lit up as he walked along the rail, then swooped her up in arms that were still strong.

"My sweet Prunella." He set her down and held her at arm's length. "Your grandmother says I'm not to call you that anymore, that now you are Nell." His sinewy hand rested on her cheek. "But you'll always be sweet Prunella to me."

"And you'll always be the best friend a scamp like me ever wanted."

"Aye, we'll not have any of your tricks with bringing dogs with muddy feet and newborn lambs in the house, will we?"

"You never know."

Mr. Fields cleared his throat. Nell jumped, then apologized for her thoughtlessness and made the introductions.

She said, "We'll drop Mr. Fields at the White Hart so he can settle in. I'd like to see Grandmama by myself for a while."

Oscar said it would give him a chance to stretch his legs while he explored the town. Davenport put their luggage in the trunk of the Rolls and took Oscar's out again when they arrived at the White Hart. Oscar said he could manage from there.

Davenport said, "I'll be by to fetch you at seven. Lady Mira likes to retire early, so dinner will be at half past. It will only be the three of you this evening, so nothing formal is required. Unless, of course, that is your custom."

"I'll be waiting." His tone was terse, an odd look on his face. Nell smiled inwardly. Oscar wasn't used to their country life. Or maybe he thought they were going to be inseparable the entire time.

Jane Alistair met them at the door, her eyes fresh with tears as she held Nell by the shoulders, then gave her a long hug. "You've grown into a beautiful young woman with a mature elegance about you."

"I think your eyesight is failing. But thank you. Where's Grandmama?"

"Resting in the conservatory. Davenport fixed her a wee nook with a cot so she doesn't have to climb the stairs when she's weary. And she can keep a watch on the birds building their nests in the arbor. Do you want me to wake her?"

"No, let's get my things to my room and you can tell me all the news."

When Nell peeked into the conservatory half an hour later, her grandmother was stirring. Nell swept across the floor and knelt beside the cot. She stroked the blue lines on the back of her grandmother's hand, then leaned over to kiss the deep lines of her cheek. A lump grew in her throat, her eyes misting. With her handkerchief she blotted the tears.

"You're here." Thin lips, parched with age, tilted into a smile.

Her grandmother rolled to her side and swung her legs over the side of the cot to sit up.

Nell helped Lady Mira into her damask slippers. "You want to sit by the window?" She held her arm for her grandmother, but Lady Mira pushed it away.

"I may be old, but I'm still plenty capable of walking without help."

"I didn't say you were old."

"But it crossed your mind, I'm sure." They sat near the window in matching chairs with a cheery cabbage rose pattern and a view of the garden outside.

"You have a nice view here. You've always liked watching the birds."

Lady Mira waved away the comment. "Davenport said a young man was coming with you."

"Not a young man. My boss, Mr. Fields."

"I once knew a Fields or maybe it was Fielding. Lecherous old toot, he was." Her gaze clouded and shifted from Nell to the garden. "A pair of nightingales are nesting in the yews." She pointed a bony finger to the place she meant. "I hear them singing and caught sight of one yesterday."

"Would you like to go into the garden? Perhaps we'll see your nightingales."

Lady Mira shook her head. "Jane fusses at me when I want to go out. Says it's too cool. Or too damp. Or too close to dinner. I say it's too much trouble for her to bundle me up."

"There *is* a little nip in the air, and I'm sure Jane just doesn't want you to take a head cold."

"So she says." Her voice was sharp, and it was unlike her to speak ill of Jane who'd been in Grandmama's service since before Nell was born.

The soft shuffle of footsteps came from the hall. Zilla Hatch entered with a tray set for tea and placed it on the table between Nell and Lady Mira.

Nell jumped up and held out her arms for Zilla. "Oh my. You've not changed a whit." It was only a small lie. The former cook from Marchwold Manor had grown plumper, her formerly streaked honey-and-gray hair now without a trace of color. But she wore the same ruffled cap and smelled of cinnamon and bacon and something sweet. Oranges perhaps.

"Don't you just go on, Miss Prunella? Jane told me what a vision you were, and she was right. I'm looking forward to meeting that young man of yours."

"As I've already explained to Grandmama, he's my boss, nothing more. And he'll be here for dinner."

"Aye. Davenport told me. I made your favorite."

"Don't tell me, let me guess. Lamb stew?"

Zilla's chuckle came from deep in her belly. "I never could fool you for an instant. Go on now and have your tea." She bent to make eye contact with Lady Mira. "Don't forget your kidney pill, m'lady."

Lady Mira shooed her away, then pulled a fine silver chain that hung from her neck and withdrew a pill from the tiny silver case attached to the chain. She took it with a swallow of water and said, "For my digestion, but I can't tell it's made a mustard seed of difference."

Nell poured the tea, her mouth watering as she eyed the china plate piled with scones. She knew they'd be warm from the oven. She put one on a saucer for her grandmother and another for herself. "Quentin Bledsoe wrote that he'd been to see you."

"Not recently."

"No, a while back."

"It was nice of him to come, brought a sweet young girl with him. Colleen, I think. Or Corrine. We had tea in the garden."

Nell choked on her tea. Quentin was seeing someone? The

thought had occurred to her, of course, but he hadn't mentioned it when she saw him. An ache came in her chest.

She bit back the urge to cry and said, "He's quite fond of you."

"And I of him. When the miss went in to the powder room, I told Quentin to tread carefully in matters of the heart. Whether he paid attention or not is anyone's guess."

Nell had no answer. She did know that in his letter, he'd omitted any reference to bringing a friend with him when he visited Grandmama.

Her grandmother's shoulders sagged as if the effort of taking tea had been too much for her. Then, just as quickly, Lady Mira straightened. "Like you. If you'd listened to me, you wouldn't be in the scrape you're in, Josie."

Josie? Gramma Jo. Grandmama's childhood friend, and the one from whom Nell, Aunt Sarah, and Iris had gotten their fine bones and flaxen hair. The one Nell hoped to learn more about. Would Grandmama even remember? Now wasn't the time.

Nell patted her grandmother's hand. "I'm Nell, remember?"

"I know that. What do you think, I'm an imbecile and have to be reminded who you are?" Her eyes flashed, but in the next instant, her brows puckered and she gazed toward the garden where the afternoon shadows had lengthened. "He's no good for you, you know."

Was she talking about Oscar? Quentin? Or had her thoughts traveled far beyond the tiny flagstone garden to a place and time from long ago?

❧

Nell's grandmother changed into a gown of polished silk with a high neck and lace at the cuffs. She was still the picture of elegance, her silver hair framing her face. Nell, too, had changed from her traveling clothes into a navy frock with a sheer scarf, one end thrown over the shoulder.

Oscar greeted Nell with a kiss on the cheek and one on the back of Lady Mira's hand when Nell introduced them. They lingered in the parlor until Davenport came in and bowed, announcing dinner.

Nell's pulse throbbed in her neck at the sight of her grandmother's china, the crystal candlesticks that had graced every formal dinner at Marchwold, a bit surprised that Aunt Vivian had let the china go. Even the flowers reminded her of days gone by, the vast urns that graced the rambling halls and great dining room of Marchwold.

After Davenport served the first course of leek soup, Oscar commented about his walk about the town. "I noticed you only had a mercantile for clothing. And no millinery shops."

Lady Mira said, "It's not our custom. Those who like fine dresses—*couture*, you would say—take the train to London and frequent the shops there."

"That must be difficult for you."

"It would be tiresome, I'm sure. But a local dressmaker knows what I like and does quite elegant work. Jane, of course, still makes my hats."

"Jane?"

"My lady's maid—the one who saw Nell's talent when she was a wee girl and taught her all that she knows."

"Ah, yes. Nell told me about her. Of course, I'd like to take an ounce of credit for helping refine Nell's skills and blending in my firm's model for success." He cleared his throat. "I would even imagine that you might be interested in investing in Nell's continued success at Oscar Fields."

"In what capacity would that be?"

"A shareholder, perhaps. A capital investment, so to speak. We're privately held and give dividends to our investors."

"And how many *investors* are we talking about?"

"Myself, of course, as the majority owner. Business owners and a few of my trusted staff hold shares as well. I would be happy to discuss it with your business manager. It would be a nice token for Nell's future, which is quite promising, I assure you."

Lady Mira scoffed. "Indeed. Perhaps you'd like me to sign over Nell's inheritance to you as well."

Oscar laughed softly. "You make it sound as if I'm ruthless. It wasn't that at all. It was only for her sake I even mentioned it."

The leek soup, so delicious moments ago, now churned in Nell's stomach, giving her the urge to heave. Oscar's motives crystallized in that moment. He'd kept Nell on even though she made grave errors because she was from a noble family, one of means whose coffers he might tap. All he had to do was cultivate the right relationships. His recipe for success.

Lady Mira stirred the lamb stew that Davenport served and said, "I've no idea if you're ruthless or not, but I can clearly tell you're cheeky. My sincere hope is you treat my granddaughter well. With her skills, she would be in high demand, I would imagine."

Nell's throat constricted. An argument wouldn't do her grandmother's liver or stomach or whatever it was she took the pills for any good. Oscar, though, seemed nonplussed.

"I feel confident Nell is quite content where she is." He wiggled his brows again. "Aren't you, darling?"

"For now, yes. And I'm shocked—dumbfounded, really—that you would even suggest such a thing to Grandmama." Nell knew she shouldn't have said it, but she wasn't a piece of property to be argued over. Let him simmer in his own juices for a while.

The lamb stew was everything Nell remembered, but the mood had been shattered and a pall hung in the air. When Davenport brought in the roast beef and Yorkshire pudding with its golden puffed crust, Mr. Fields said, "This certainly is a feast. I didn't expect to be treated in such a grand manner."

Davenport nodded. "Thank you, sir. I'll convey your appreciation to Mrs. Hatch. Nothing is too grand for our Prunella."

"I couldn't have said it better myself." He lifted his wineglass. "To Nell. And I'm sure that a meal at Marchwold Hall couldn't hold a candle to the one we've just eaten."

Lady Mira said, "Manor. It's Marchwold Manor. You can make your own comparison after our luncheon there tomorrow. Their new cook is some wonder chef from Paris who makes dishes that are impossible to pronounce. I just hope he doesn't serve that wretched eel again." She folded her napkin and asked Davenport to ring for Jane. "I'll leave you young people to have dessert on your own."

Nell rose and gave her a grandmother a kiss. "We won't be long. I'd like to read for you when you're all tucked in."

Oscar ate his lemon custard in silence, and when they'd finished, Nell asked if he was ready for Davenport to drive him back to the White Hart.

"It's only a few blocks. Or I could wait in the parlor until you're finished tucking your grandmother in. We need to discuss our plans for the upcoming week. I rang Harjo to see if anything was new, and we've had several inquiries at the shop. I think it best that we take the afternoon train tomorrow and get back."

"Tomorrow? You're joking. Not that I would keep you from something important, but I'm going to stay a few more days. Maybe even a week if you're going to be busy."

"I hope you haven't forgotten that it's on my account you're here at all."

"No, you don't let me f-forget that. And I am g-g-gr—"

"Grateful. Yes, well, if you are, then I expect you to be packed and ready to go when we finish this luncheon tomorrow. Perhaps you can have your servant pick us up from there." He folded his napkin and set it on the table, then rose.

Nell put her palms on the table, her heart in her throat. "And if I'm not ready?" She met his gaze.

His eyes widened as the familiar clench came in his jaw. It felt like hours ticked by, but presently, he smiled and said, "You'll be ready. If not, then your friends Hazel and Marcella will be looking for new employment the moment we dock in New York Harbor."

"You w-w-wouldn't. Not after their years of service to you. Good assembly workers are hard to find."

"No one is irreplaceable. It would be prudent of you to remember that. We'll discuss our new business on the train."

His shoes clicked on the polished oak of the dining room as he strode out the door.

Nell clenched her own jaw, her heart turned to stone. She wouldn't cry. Nor would she let Oscar know that she, too, might be looking for another position. She shoved hard against the table and climbed the stairs to her grandmother's chamber.

CHAPTER 23

Outside her grandmother's room, Nell gathered her wits and smoothed her dress, but she knew she couldn't keep her fury from her grandmother. She turned the knob to the bedchamber and found Lady Mira already dressed for the night, sitting against the headboard as if in anticipation of Nell's visit.

Her grandmother patted the bed next to her. "How was your dessert?"

Nell bit her lip, her insides still trembling. "It was lovely, as always. I'm afraid I have terrible news, though."

"Oh, gracious, what is it, dear?"

"Mr. Fields just informed me that we have to return to London tomorrow."

"Whatever for? You just got here."

"A new business opportunity. When I told him I wasn't going…" She pursed her lips, still angry about the hold Oscar kept on her life.

"I pray that ruffian hasn't hurt you."

"Not in a physical sense, no. He's quick to point out my faults, in particular my stammering, but he's given me a chance to succeed and brought me to England, which he reminded me of when I told him I wanted to remain here a few days."

"It would do my heart good to have you."

"I know. Mine, too."

"What would happen if you didn't go?"

"He says he'll fire Hazel and Marcella, my assistants both here in London and back in New York. They're both lovely and have families who depend on their income. I can't do that to them."

"No, of course not. You don't suppose he thought you might decide to stay in Heathdown, start a little business of your own here?"

"Right now, there's nothing I'd love more—"

"Pffft. I wouldn't allow it." She lifted Nell's chin with her finger. "You've a splendid career ahead of you. There will always be people who want to dictate your life, but you must learn to stand your ground. You're a very capable young woman. Clever and beautiful."

"You're my grandmother, so you're entitled to be biased, but I'm afraid I do let him get to me. I've come so far with my skills and techniques, and I can't deny that without Mr. Fields I wouldn't be half the designer I am."

"It's all you've ever talked about, so I know you've weighed the cost of accomplishment. Anything worth pursuing involves sacrifice. You're learning that firsthand, it seems. The Lord won't abandon you if you abide in him."

"I do cling to that, and I've never questioned that my desire to create comes from God. But you're right, it's not easy. What I regret is that Mr. Fields's announcement has overshadowed something else I wanted to talk to you about."

"What is it, love?"

"One of my clients last fall commented on my stammering and gave me the number of a clinic." Nell told about Dr. Underwood's unconventional methods and trying to link it to some trauma from her past. "Over the past few months, my speech has improved, and even more so since I remembered an incident that happened long ago. On my fourth birthday, to be exact."

Her grandmother cocked her head, her eyes drifting like they'd gone to a faraway place. A twinge of guilt knotted Nell's insides. It had been a long day for both of them, but she should have been more considerate of her grandmother's fragile state.

But then Lady Mira shook her head. "You haven't always stammered. And I've always thought that Josie's death might have played some role. What did you remember?"

Nell told her about hiding behind the tree at Greystone Hall and witnessing the exchange between her grandparents and the fatal shove given to Gramma Jo. "When Grandfather wrenched my arm and told me he would do more than hurt me, I was afraid to tell anyone. So much so that I apparently blocked it from my memory."

Grandmama held a frail hand over her mouth and closed her eyes. When her eyes opened, they glistened with tears. "We all knew he'd done it. You've no idea what my poor Josie endured at the hands of that despicable man. And your mother and Sarah and Spencer as well, though not to the same degree. There was no proof that it was anything but an accident, so what you remembered is most likely accurate. Have you talked to your mother?"

"Not yet. It seems a ticklish subject for the telephone, but I do want to tell her the next time I'm in Kentucky. I hope it's not too painful for her."

"The truth has cleansing power. She'll be glad you talked to her."

"I am sorry I didn't tell someone." Nell shuddered. "But he was so vile…so frightening."

"That he was, and he would've called you a liar, of course. The trauma for you might have been worse. What I do know is that for several months after that, you didn't speak at all. Gradually, with your mum and dad's coaxing, you began to speak, but you stammered."

"I didn't talk at all?"

"Not a whit. We were so thrilled that you'd regained your speech that we were quick to overlook the stammer." She tilted her head, that ethereal smile gracing her lips once again. "When you were a wee sprite, you knew every Mother Goose rhyme backward and forward. Once you even stood up in front of the congregation and recited, *Christmas is coming, the geese are getting fat.*"

Nell laughed and finished the saying. She did remember the rhyme, but not the incident her grandmother spoke of. A deep sense of longing settled in Nell's bones. Being here with Grand-mama had filled an empty spot in her heart.

Lady Mira dabbed her eyes with the corner of the sheet and looked at Nell. "We had some grand times, didn't we?"

"We did."

"The fox hunts. The house parties." Her eyes gleamed, but Nell knew that something had shifted, that the grand times of which her grandmother spoke were those of long ago.

Nell picked up her grandmother's Bible, its pages yellowed, the cover creviced and worn. "Shall we read now, Grandmama?"

The early morning fog lost its battle with the sun, leaving a glimmer on the yews in the garden. Zilla brought a fresh pot of tea, and Jane hastened with a downy lap cover for Lady Mira. Nell and her grandmother laughed and talked until the teapot was dry. Then they strolled along the path, peeking into the branches where the nightingales were nesting, but the songbirds had been clever and hidden their nest well.

"And you, darling Nell? What will you do now?"

"See what Mr. Fields has for me in London and explore several new ideas. I can hardly wait to sketch a nightingale for a beaded hat I want to call Lady Mira's Songbird."

"At least I was good for some drop of inspiration."

"You've been good for more than that. Much more."

Jane stepped out from the conservatory and said it was nearly time to go to Marchwold Manor for lunch. A quiver rippled through Nell's stomach, but she didn't know whether it was from excitement at being in her childhood home or the dread of leaving.

Davenport took her bags to the car and settled them in the back of the Rolls, then drove to the town square to White Hart. While they waited for Davenport to collect Oscar, Nell drank in every detail—Heathdown's cobblestone streets, the lampposts with their gas lanterns, the rose garden at the center of town where two old men sat on a bench throwing crumbs to the pigeons, the corner tobacconist where her grandfather sometimes took her to pick up his favorite cherry-laced pipe tobacco. She wondered if the stooped man behind the counter still had the macaw that called her *pretty girl*.

The hair on Nell's neck prickled when Oscar slid onto the leather seat beside her, a hint of whiskey on his breath. She still seethed over his threat to fire Hazel and Marcella, but making a scene would accomplish nothing. Determined to remain aloof, Nell remarked on points of interest as Davenport drove through the village.

"The church where I was confirmed. Quentin Bledsoe's father has been the vicar as long as I can r-remember."

"Your friend from London with the striking girlfriend?"

"That's the one. And straight ahead is the entrance to the estate." The iron gates stood open, the rolling green of the grounds unfurling like an emerald sea, the rooftops of the barns in the distance. The oak-lined road curved until it crested the hill and the walls of Marchwold came into view, stately and solid. An unfamiliar footman opened the door and ushered them into the drawing room. Nell blinked, the familiarity of it gone, replaced with furniture and wallpaper and draperies of modern design. Stark and geometric, the warmth no longer there. The great fireplace, at least, bore some resemblance to the one she remembered, orange flames flickering in the firebox beneath the carved stone of the mantel. The painting above, though, was a massive framed artwork of misshaped animals and people in colors that hurt her eyes.

"I see you're admiring our latest acquisition."

Nell turned. "Hello, Uncle Preston. Thank you for having us. And yes, I was observing your painting. An original?"

"A piece of rubbish, that's what." Her grandmother removed her gloves and asked where Vivian was.

"She'll be down shortly." Preston extended his hand to Oscar. "Allow me to introduce myself. I'm Lord Preston Marchwold, and apparently my mother and I have different tastes in art."

"Oscar Fields. And as they say, beauty is in the eye of the beholder. My lovely Nell has told me much about your fine home."

"Nell? Oh, you mean my niece, Prunella. She's blossomed from the frightfully awkward child I remember. No doubt you're responsible, my good man."

"I would like to claim the credit, but—"

Vivian swept in and made a beeline for Nell. "Oh, you darling girl. I'm so glad it worked out that Preston and I were here for your visit. We just returned from the royal wedding yesterday. I would have never guessed that's what would bring you back to England."

Nell nodded toward her boss. "It was all Mr. Fields's doing. Come, let me introduce you."

After the introduction, Vivian rested her hand on Oscar's sleeve. "We'll have to compare notes about the wedding. I hope you got a good view of the ceremony. What section were you in?"

He cleared his throat. "We preferred to observe the return of the bride and groom to the palace. Not so stuffy, and it gave my staff an opportunity for a holiday." He took a champagne flute from the footman's tray. "To the royal couple."

Vivian returned his toast. "Indeed. Duchess Elizabeth is quite charming. I met her at the bridesmaids' luncheon a few days before the ceremony."

"You weren't a bridesmaid yourself, were you?"

"Aren't you charming? My mother's in London and was most fortunate to secure us an invitation. A delightful time, and it seems Prunella might've had a wee part."

Nell nodded. "The bridesmaids' hats? I hope the girls liked them."

"They adored them. I'm almost tempted to have you make something for me, but I couldn't dare hurt anyone's feelings at Malone's Salon. Their designers are from Paris...and you know what superior materials the French use."

A bubble under Nell's ribs that started as irritation now boiled. Aunt Vivian might have changed Marchwold Manor into a place Nell no longer recognized, but she hadn't changed herself a bit.

Nell swallowed, gathering words in her head, but they tumbled out of her mouth unchecked. "Whatever makes you think our hats are inferior? Mr. Fields has always insisted on only the most superb quality, not just in his m-materials, but also in his d-designs."

Vivian batted her eyelashes. "Gracious, you're just as prickly as you were when you were a child. I'd hope that a few years might have transformed you into a swan. Preston, would you ring the footman and see if lunch is ready?"

"Yes, dear." And as Nell passed him with her grandmother on her arm, Preston said, "You'll have to pardon Vivian. She's under a great deal of strain managing the staff and planning the summer season of guests right on the heels of the royal wedding."

Lady Mira gave him a steely look. "I can only imagine."

At lunch, Preston engaged Oscar in conversation about business, and Nell held her breath, hoping her boss didn't hit him up for an investment on Nell's behalf. Her uncle would laugh them right out of the manor. The conversation, though, veered toward real estate prices and the fluctuating economy. When the footman brought dessert, Nell declined and said she'd like to amble about the garden.

Vivian said, "If you would wait a few minutes, we could all enjoy our coffee in the garden together."

"No thanks, I'd like to be alone, if you don't m-mind."

"Well, of course, we mind, but I suppose you'll do whatever you want the same as always. Would you like for me to ring the footman to escort you?"

"I remember the way."

Nell stepped into the glow of the afternoon and across the flagstone to the rose garden that had been her mother's favorite place. Melancholy stirred in her chest as she wove her way among the paths, the fragrance intoxicating. A cloud drifted across the sun disorienting her for a moment. The beds were laid out around the fountain with water bubbling through a cherub's fingers as it always had. Memories flooded her thoughts. Mama's endless work tending the roses. It must've been her refuge, too, the place she grieved her own mother's death and her abhorrent childhood.

Nell knew now that she'd somehow woven the two gardens together in her drawing for Dr. Underwood. They both bore sorrow, the rose petal drops of blood that appeared when Nell had let her fingers draw what her mind commanded. *Nothing comes without sacrifice.* Grandmama's words whispered to her spirit. Gramma Jo's life was cut short, but she gained eternity where pain and sorrow were no more. Mama's sorrow was transformed into a new life in America, choosing to take her daughters into an unknown future.

For Nell, heeding the demands of an impossibly difficult man ensured the jobs of two dear friends. Tears beckoned and she offered no resistance. Nell lowered herself to a nearby bench and wept, letting the tears wash away her own deep sorrow.

"Are you all right? You look wretched." Mr. Fields hovered over her.

"I'm fine. Just reliving a few memories of this place." She sniffed, then slid her handkerchief from her pocket and blotted away the drip on her nose.

"We don't have time for you to go on a crying jag if we're going to catch that train."

"Yes…yes. No, w-wait. I have to do something first."

"We don't have long."

"It'll only take a minute." She dashed across the grass to the potter's shed behind a line of yews, grabbed a pair of shears, then returned to the roses. She snipped a dozen or more blooms. The thorns bit into her flesh, but she gripped the stems anyway, took the shears back, and told Oscar she was ready. Pressed between layers of parchment, the roses would be a gift to her mother.

The good-bye to her grandmother lingered with hugs, hearts torn, tears. And more tears. When Oscar coughed to signal his impatience, Nell's grandmother whispered, "Guard your heart, my dear. Remember, strength and honor." Ah, the passage from Proverbs she'd read to her grandmother the night before. *Yes. Strength. And honor.*

Davenport said he would come back and retrieve her grandmother once the train had come, so Nell thanked Preston and Vivian for the lunch, and on legs as heavy as lead, she walked to the waiting car.

The train was just pulling into the station when they arrived. Davenport and Oscar took the luggage to the platform, and after a quick good-bye to Davenport, Nell entered the passenger car, taking the first seat she found by the window. Davenport remained on the landing, speaking to a couple who'd just arrived. The man turned, a lock of reddish-brown hair falling across his forehead as he lifted his gaze to Nell's compartment.

Quentin. A young woman stood beside him. Shapely. Brunette. And beautiful.

Quentin's arm rose in a wave as the train pulled away from the station. The chug of the engine and the blast of the horn filled Nell's ears, the clacking on the track going faster and faster.

CHAPTER 24

Ten minutes out of the train station, Oscar pulled out a sheaf of papers to discuss business. Nell balked, her stomach a cauldron of the emotions from the last two days. Self-pity didn't suit her, but neither did she feel like talking to Oscar.

He plunged in anyway. "Leo informs me our final tally in London is on the mark, and with several new requests, we're moving toward a successful run."

It sounded like something they'd say on Broadway, and for a moment, Nell wished she was back in New York, catching up with Jeanette or watching Greta doing her act. She pulled out her diary and scribbled down the appointments as Oscar rattled them off. A concert at Royal Albert Hall. A dinner with the London Noble Women's Society on Saturday.

Quentin. She thought she would be seeing him, but the unexpected sight of him with the girl at the station gave her pause. Perhaps the comely brunette was, like Simone, a friend. Or perhaps they'd only met up on the train. Nell penciled his name in the margin of her diary. She knew his phone number by heart.

She snapped the appointment book shut. "I'm curious about the books. Mind if I see the numbers?" It wasn't the first time she'd thought of it, and since her hats were a principal source of their income, it was only prudent for her to be informed. She'd simply never asked before.

Oscar quirked one brow. "The figures are not something I would expect you to grasp."

"You might be surprised." She didn't expect Oscar to show her the accounting books, but to imply that she couldn't understand them miffed her. "I've handled the ordering for the suppliers, so I'm aware of some of the costs and what we charge our clients. I think I could be an asset to you if I had a better understanding of both the debits and assets."

"Is this another of your fanciful ideas? Your job is to make hats. For Oscar Fields Millinery. It's quite simple, really." He signaled for the porter and asked for a Scotch on the rocks. End of conversation.

In spare moments each day and every evening, Nell rang Quentin's number without reaching him. When there was still no answer by Friday, she called his bank and was told employees weren't allowed personal calls.

"Can you give him a message then? Tell him Nell Marchwold called and would like to speak to him."

"Is it a matter of urgency?"

"You might say so, yes." They sailed in ten days. Ten days to settle the matter of her heart. Not a moment went by that Quentin didn't appear in her thoughts and send a flutter to her chest.

She thanked the bank receptionist and waited.

And waited. She ate an apple at her desk for fear he would call during lunch and she would miss his call.

At a quarter of five, the shop clerk peeked around the screen that separated the showroom from Nell's office space. "Pardon, Miss

Marchwold?" She extended an envelope with Cablegram stamped across the front. "This just came for you."

"Thank you." Nell's stomach pinched, followed by a sigh of relief when she saw it was from New York. It wasn't news of her grandmother or a message from Kentucky. She slit it open and read words just as disturbing.

```
Mr. North passed in hospital STOP service Monday
STOP Jeanette wanted you informed STOP worried
about her
Calvin
```

A lump the size of Manhattan filled Nell's throat, her eyes hot with tears. Poor Jeanette. Guilt crept over her. She'd only written two brief letters and hadn't even asked about Jeanette's father.

Her heart was still heavy when she and Oscar went to the promenade concert at Royal Albert Hall. On the way there, she delivered the news of Mr. North's death to Oscar. His lips tightened, and when he said, "That's a shame," his tone was shallow. In the next breath, he reminded her of the meeting the next day, the preliminary sketches for a new client, and the women's society dinner later in the evening.

A few moments before the concert began, the scent of Quentin's cologne wafted by. Nell froze, afraid of an encore from the night of the Gaiety Theatre and seeing Quentin with Simone. Only this time the vision Nell had was of the girl at the train station. She held her breath, afraid to look around, but when the scent grew stronger, she slowly pivoted her head. The woodsy smell was that of the man next to her. Bald and rotund.

She scarcely heard the music nor Oscar's bantering during the dinner that followed.

"Tomorrow should be a lively evening with the Havershams and the ladies' society. And of course you and Hazel and Marcella will be needed in the workroom early in the morning. It's vital we end this trip on a positive note."

Nell's shoulders sagged, but she forced a positive tone in her voice. "It will all be done. You know I'm always p-prepared."

"And for which I pay you a pretty penny." He rattled off a few other last-minute engagements that Harjo had put on the calendar. Time was running out to see Quentin, but as long as they were in London, she wouldn't keep from trying to contact him no matter how much Oscar grumbled.

Oscar called for the check. "You're not ill, are you?"

"Just tired."

When the cab delivered them to their Hyde Park address, Nell forced herself to walk the few steps to the entrance. Oscar stopped suddenly and drew her arm tightly into the crook of his. Nell snapped to attention and saw a figure in the shadows step from the recessed entry. She knew before he spoke that it was Quentin.

"Nell, I'd almost given up." His voice was strained. He took a tentative step toward her, but stopped when Mr. Fields held up his free hand, the other still clamped tight around her.

"What do you mean, lurking about? And what do you want with Nell?"

"It's Quentin Bledsoe, sir. I was hoping to speak with her."

"She's not feeling well."

Nell tried to shake off Oscar's hold on her to no avail. "I'd like to talk to Quentin for a few minutes."

"Nell, it's late, and we have an early day tomorrow." To Quentin, he said, "I don't take kindly to this sort of intrusion. And certainly not at this hour."

"My apologies. I've been here most of the evening." To Nell, he said, "I received your message, but too late, I'm afraid. The shop was already closed. The bank receptionist said it was urgent."

"Not urgent. I just dearly hoped to see you before we sailed."

Oscar said, "Perhaps you should call at a decent hour."

He ignored Oscar, and in the dimness of the gaslight, Nell couldn't read Quentin's expression, but her heart soared at the nearness of him. She only hoped he could read in her eagerness how truly glad she was to see him.

"Yes, Nell, I'd love to see you. Are you free for lunch tomorrow?"

"I have appointments beginning at one, but I could meet you at the Plum Tree Restaurant across from the shop. Noon?"

"I'll be there."

Nell's stomach was a swarm of butterflies all morning, but Oscar hadn't hovered like she expected him to, nor had he mentioned her lunch with Quentin. She kept an eye on the clock, groaning as the minutes crawled by. Finally, at half past eleven, she collected her bag and told the clerk she'd be back after lunch.

Quentin was waiting when she arrived and stood to welcome her with a handshake and a quick peck on the cheek. She had to remind herself to breathe. "You're early."

"Anxious, I suppose."

"Me, too. I thought the c-clock had s-stopped." *Calm. Let the words come naturally.*

"It's been a while."

"I saw you getting off the train in Heathdown. Family visit?"

He shrugged. "Of sorts. Just overnight."

She waited, her eyes riveted on Quentin's face, his strong jaw and wide mouth. His freckles had dimmed with age, but his boyish charm was more endearing than ever.

"We're here now." He cleared his throat and sipped his water.

"I'm sorry if this seems awkward. We've always had an easy way between us, and I know things have changed."

"We both grew up."

"I'm not here to make things difficult for you...and your boss. I guess that's the proper term."

She nodded.

"Like you said, we grew up. While I nursed the hope that things might remain as they did when we were younger, I do understand that things don't always happen the way we imagine they will. Sometimes God leads us in a direction we didn't expect."

"What are you saying?"

A pained look settled in his eyes. "Nell, I'm glad you called. I've wanted to call you, but quite frankly, I've not known how to tell you my news." He took a deep breath and rubbed the back of his neck. "The truth is I'm engaged to be married."

The air in the restaurant grew thin, the space between them a chasm.

"Oh." Her voice was a squeak, all the conversations she'd imagined now thick on her tongue, unspoken.

"It wasn't an easy decision, but one fate seems to have thrown in my path. I've prayed earnestly for God's answer, and he's been faithful. When I saw how you've bloomed and the joy on your face in doing what you love, it was confirmation. I'd been seeing Colleen a while before I got the telegram that you were coming to London. She was ready to advance our relationship, but I was hesitant. I've always had a soft spot for you, and I wanted to make sure I wasn't making a mistake. There was just something in your voice and the glow on your face that told me you'd found your calling. And it wasn't me."

Nell gripped the edge of the table. "Oh. Oh." She bit her lip to keep from crying.

Quentin was getting married. But not to her. Her love for him had rekindled or perhaps it had been there all the time, but now it was too late.

She gathered every bit of courage she could find and smiled. "Colleen is a very lucky girl, I hope she knows that. Congratulations, Quentin." His name on her tongue was like honey, and she wanted to reach across and kiss him on his lips that were full and always so inviting. And it grieved her that she would never have that chance.

Quentin leaned back, relaxed now that he'd broken the news. "So tell me, have you had a successful trip?"

"Beyond our wildest expectations."

"I always knew you were something special."

Nell was unaware of how she made it back to the salon, but she did remember Harjo opening the door for her and asking if she'd had a nice lunch. He could have been sitting at the next table and she wouldn't have noticed. The afternoon was a blur, the chatter of the client and her sister who she'd brought along for company nerve-racking. Oscar stood silently in the background, his manner approving, but his presence like a needle under her fingernail.

That evening, Sir Haversham asked for champagne, and when the waiter popped the cork, Nell jumped like she'd been shot.

Lady Haversham said, "You're a bit skittish tonight. Has dear Oscar been working you too hard?"

Nell forced a laugh and denied it, then steeled herself to have a good time. After all, Quentin and Colleen were probably sipping their own champagne at that very moment.

Glass raised, Lady Haversham proposed a toast. "To goodwill between our countries and the success of the royal wedding."

Nell let the bubbles fizz on her tongue, the bite welcome, as their hostess continued, "We can only hope there'll be another such occasion in the near future for which you'll always have an open invitation."

Mr. Fields said, "Hear, hear. To the London Noble Women's Society. To good business and much, much more."

Nell hoisted her glass. "To good business." She let her narrowed eyes rest squarely on his gaze without flinching. "Wherever it may take us."

His face looked frozen in a smile. He drained the glass and held it out for the waiter to refill.

Along with the women, Nell laughed at the men's jokes and made glowing comments about the food. They dined on escargot, asparagus soup, fillet of sole, and gâteau cake with brandied fruit. It was rich and opulent, each course accompanied by the appropriate wine. Nell took a sip of one, willing it to settle her stomach and her nerves. It did neither. Nor did it ease the sadness that skirted the fringes of her heart.

As they stepped from the restaurant into a drizzly night air, Sir Haversham approached Oscar. "Glad to have you here, chap. My wife has spoken highly of you." He cleared his throat. "I don't mean to burden you, but there is a small matter of compensation."

When Oscar gave a small jerking motion with his head to Nell, she slipped away a few steps, but not so far that she couldn't hear the low tones of the conversation.

Oscar said, "I thought we were flush."

"Up to a point, yes. Real estate's taking a thrashing right now. Leasing rates increasing, and we did set you up in a higher price bracket in Mayfair at your request." Sir Haversham handed Oscar an envelope. "I've estimated the expenses until your sailing date. Some of the figures ran a little steeper than projected, but with your good return, I'm sure it won't be a problem."

Nell rubbed her arms to chase away the chill, but it wasn't from the night air.

The last few days were spent packing the workroom, putting supplies in trunks, and seeing a couple of late, straggling customers who had to choose from the stock inventory. Mr. Fields came in as they closed the lid on another trunk, and Nell told him she had an errand to run and would be back by five o'clock when they closed the door for the final time.

"I'd be happy to accompany you, stretch my legs a bit."

"It won't be n-necessary."

"Not going to say good-bye to your friend? What was his name?"

She shook her head and said nothing, then left before Oscar could make any objections. Without any concrete plans, she clipped along the street in Mayfair, turning corners when the mood struck. She drank in the sights, memorizing the sounds of people's voices and breathing her last of London. After a while, she slowed her pace and took notice of the shops. A bookstore with a yellow tabby curled in the window. And in the reflection of the glass, she saw Harjo across the street milling about.

A slow burn started under her ribs. Oscar didn't trust her to even take a simple walk around town. An image flashed in her head of Harjo holding the door for her after her lunch with Quentin. A coincidence? She didn't think so. What was Mr. Fields afraid of? That she would decide to stay in London? Or maybe it was just a sick thrill for him. Well, she could play games, too.

The door chimed when Nell went in, a musty smell assaulting her. A young man with jug ears sticking out from a driving hat asked if he could help her.

"Do you have any Agatha Christie novels?" A mystery to read on the ocean liner might take her mind off Quentin. She glanced over her shoulder and made out a wavy image of Harjo still standing across the street.

"Dead cert. Brand-new Hercule Poirot novel just came in."

She took it and while the shopkeeper rang it up, she checked on the whereabouts of Harjo. He hadn't moved. Nor had the cat in the window when she went out and reversed directions, going back the way she'd come. She passed a shoe shop and an apothecary with window advertisements for tonics and medicines to cure all ails. If there was one to cure a broken heart, she would buy enough to drown in.

She picked up her pace. If Harjo was following her, he would have to hurry. She crossed to Harjo's side of the street and clipped along for a block, then made a quick decision to turn a corner and flattened herself in the recess of the door to a tobacconist. The scent reminded her of her grandfather. She kept her eye on the intersection, and when Harjo careened around the building, she turned facing him.

He pulled up short, his eyes darting from side to side. "Nell. What a surprise."

"Isn't it?"

"Ah, here it is, the place I was looking for." Harjo nodded toward the tobacco shop.

"I didn't know you s-smoked."

"There's a lot you don't know, Miss Marchwold." He tipped his hat. "Out for a little shopping?"

"That and a few other things." She ambled down the block knowing he'd probably only wait a few minutes before following her again. At least he knew she was on to him.

Around another corner, she discovered a row of couture shops. Malone's Salon. She stopped and peered at its oval awning, the elegant gold lettering on the door. This was where her aunt Vivian bought her hats—the ones made by French designers. A bell dinged when she entered. A salesclerk with a tiny black mustache and feet that pointed inward reminded her of Charlie Chaplin from the silent screen.

"How may I assist Madame today?"

"Just seeing what's new for summer."

"Ah, this way then." He pointed out the section. She noted the styles and colors, tried on one or two, moving from section to section.

"Is there a particular style or color you're looking for, Madame?"

She shook her head. What she was searching for wouldn't be found in a millinery shop, but she decided on two headpieces for Jeanette and Greta and a jaunty cloche for herself. The total was enough to make her head spin. Two weeks' wages. Oscar would be livid to see her with a hatbox with Malone's insignia, but it gave her another idea.

On the way back, she popped into three other millinery salons. She had no doubt Harjo would report back that Nell was looking for another place of employment.

New York City

1923

CHAPTER 25

Nell stood on deck until the last glimmers of land faded, the ache even deeper than the first time she'd left her homeland. Each billow carried them farther out to sea, farther from Quentin, and she knew the next time she saw her grandmother's sweet face, it would be on the heavenly shores, not in Heathdown.

Her fingers grew numb from gripping the rail. The wind whipped her hair into a frenzy, but still she stood. An hour. Maybe two. A deck captain touched her forearm and asked if she was all right, but she didn't answer. There were no words.

Then Oscar was there, loosening her fingers, coaxing her along to her quarters, and asking a female attendant to assist her. When the woman left, Nell retrieved a dressing robe from her trunk and changed, then curled into a ball under her covers. Her teeth chattered, and a groan came from her gut. Cutting. Sorrowful. She fought the urge to cry until she thought her chest would explode and then let out the first sob. Tears for Quentin. Tears for her grandmother. And hot, angry tears that sprang from the depths of her soul. When exhaustion overtook her, she drifted in and out of sleep, jerked awake by dreams each time she relaxed. Hours passed, but she couldn't bring herself to rise from the haven of her bunk.

Eventually a knock sounded at the door, but she groped for the spare pillow and covered her head.

A voice shouted. "Nell. Wake up."

Nell pulled the pillow tighter over her head, but strong hands removed it. Through squinted eyes, she made out Hazel's form.

"Can you hear me?" Hazel's face was inches away from hers.

"I can hear you and smell the onions on your breath."

"Mr. Fields sent me to check on you. Says he hasn't seen you since we passed Ireland."

"What time is it?"

"You should be asking what day it is. Two days since we set sail. Do you have a fever?"

"I don't think so. I think I just needed the sleep." She yawned and stretched her arms over her head. "What day did you say it was?"

"Saturday. Do you need help getting dressed?"

"No, I can manage. I must smell like a sailor. I'll get washed up and be out soon." Her bones ached, but she felt a surge of energy pulse in her veins, and her stomach rumbled.

"What do you want me to tell Mr. Fields?"

"Tell him I'll meet him in the dining room in an hour. I'm starved half to death."

Hazel gave a throaty laugh and said, "Aye, aye."

"Thank you for coming to check on me."

⚜

Oscar and Harjo rose to meet her when she went into the dining room. Rich smells wafted from the plates of other diners making her even more hungry.

Harjo closed the ledger before him and dropped it into his valise. "Good afternoon. You had us worried. A touch of the sea in your stomach, huh?"

"Something like that." He could think whatever he wanted. She wouldn't be discussing her grief over Quentin with Harjo and Oscar. While she wolfed down the lobster bisque, she asked what she'd missed during her confinement.

"Harjo and I have been evaluating our finances and trying to decide where to go from here."

Harjo gave a sharp look to Oscar.

Nell eyed them each in turn, trying to gauge what passed between them. "London was productive, was it not?"

Oscar ignored her question and told Harjo he would meet him on the deck later. "Nell and I need to discuss the fall line." Harjo gulped the last of his whiskey and told Nell to enjoy the remainder of her lunch.

When he'd gone, Oscar leaned forward. "I hope your rest was restorative. You had me worried."

"I didn't realize how long I'd slept, but I'm feeling quite chipper now, and I have worlds of new ideas." Diving into work would keep her mind off Quentin and what might have been. She knew that, but the ache in her chest told her nothing would take away her thoughts of him.

"That's good to hear as I have some news I think you'll like."

Her antenna went up.

"We've had an inquiry from Soren Michaels. I must say it surprised me after the ordeal with Percy, but he's requested teaming up with us again for a late summer show."

"That is good news. Soren's a genius when it comes to fashion and business."

"A rising star on the fashion front, it would seem."

The words had a familiar ring—Oscar had uttered them enough times. Still, Nell was happy to hear that Soren was making a name for himself.

"There are a few clauses in his proposal we need to clarify before we move forward, but I've a good feeling about this. With the proper planning, we can make an even bigger impact this time." He took her hand, his touch as warm and soft as doeskin. "Your three-year anniversary with the salon is coming at the end of July, and I've decided to give you an early gift, an advance from apprentice to designer."

She blinked, not sure she'd heard right, but Oscar's raised brows and lips curved into a smile seemed authentic. "It's my turn to be surprised. I'm…uh…speechless. And grateful."

"I thought you'd be pleased. I've always had faith in you and believe this is only the beginning of what we can accomplish together."

"Thank you. You won't regret it, sir." A knot formed in her throat. All she'd worked for hadn't been for naught. Or perhaps her popping into the millinery shops in London with Harjo spying on her had indeed prompted Oscar into action.

❧

The ship's hairdresser lifted the tresses from Nell's neck and ran his fingers through them. "Are you sure a bob is what you want?"

"Absolutely. Carefree and fashionable. Just like this." She pointed to the model in the magazine. She didn't add that she was also hoping it would make her look more professional. Someone to take seriously with her new position.

She closed her eyes when the first snip of the scissors cut off a sizable chunk. Another snip sent a flurry of doubt through her middle, but when the woman gave her a mirror to look at the results, she gasped. It was glorious! Sleek with just a fringe of bangs. She stared wide-eyed and tipped the hairdresser double the customary amount. She sailed out the door, a new energy in the swing of her hips.

Even Oscar commented that it gave her a more mature look when she showed him her newest designs. And as the shore of North America drew nearer, Nell's excitement mounted. She was ready for the new challenges ahead. When she stepped from the cab in her neighborhood, the smell of garlic and sausage and the sounds of Italian shouts and laughter and the rush of traffic assaulted her. Funny, but in its own way, it felt like home.

The flat was empty when she entered, but a vase of daisies sat on the tiny kitchen table, a note propped against it.

Welcome home! Can't wait to hear everything.
Dinner tonight at Sal's. Gotta run. Class.

Signed in Jeanette's unreadable signature.

Nell looked around, unsure what to do first. She put the kettle on, then went to change. A handful of letters were on the bedside table. She fanned through them, looking instinctively for a London postmark. Her heart sank. There would be no more letters from Quentin. But her mother and Aunt Sarah had written. The remaining mail was a reminder to make an appointment with Dr. Underwood along with two advertising flyers.

When she'd put on a comfortable skirt and low-heeled shoes, she took the letters to the kitchen and made her tea. Her mother wrote at length about the abundant flowering of all the spring trees and her new rose varieties. Nell smiled, remembering the pressed roses from Marchwold she still needed to put on parchment and tie with silk thread to make a keepsake for her mother. Caroline was thriving and taking swimming lessons, and Granville was busy with his summer teaching schedule. She closed by saying, "I trust your trip was lovely. We are anxious to hear about it. With love and prayers, Mother."

Nothing about looking forward to Nell's visit to Kentucky. Perhaps her mother had given up on the notion of Nell ever getting away from New York. Her family had their own bustling lives, and Nell would likely be an interruption anyway. Sadly, Nell also realized the likelihood of a visit was slim in the near future. Her talk with Mama and what happened at Greystone Hall would have to wait.

Aunt Sarah's letter was much the same. News of Iris and Mittie. The sad news that Iris had not received a proposal during her season in spite of many eligible candidates.

Now she's determined to go to Vanderbilt University and is trying to convince Mittie to join her. Whatever has gotten into you young girls is beyond me. Careers and being independent. The girls and I are planning a dash to New York in July to shop for their college wardrobes. And to hear of your trip, of course.

Love and kisses, Aunt Sarah

Nell placed a call to Dr. Underwood's office and had just hung up when Jeanette burst through the door and slammed her purse on the table. "You're home! And your hair. What have you done?"

They both talked at once, laughing and crying and hugging until Jeanette finally said, "Tell me everything. Did you have someone in London do your hair? Oh, I bet Oscar just had a basket of kittens. He's such a prude about change. So how was everything? Did you have fun?"

"Jeanette, give me a minute. Please, I just got here and there's so much to tell you. Where shall I start?"

Nell told about the shop in Mayfair, Mrs. Fortner's party, and the horrible Lady Blythe-Perkins. The excitement of being in London on the day of the royal wedding and her trip to see her grandmother. And at last, she told her about Quentin.

"Oh, you poor thing. So he wasn't just a friend like you said."

"He was a friend. And so much more. I just didn't realize it until..." She widened her eyes to stop the tears, but the mere mention of Quentin was akin to being ripped in half.

"I'm sure Oscar's keeping you occupied all the time didn't help. He thinks it's his mission in life to go around tripping people."

"Yes, I was busy with Oscar. And he was difficult. I can't help how he is, but on the ship home, he gave me quite a shock. I've gotten an advancement—from apprentice to designer."

"What? Get out."

"More responsibilities. A tiny hike in pay. It's progress, don't you agree?"

"Sure. Good old Oscar." Her voice wasn't convincing, and a silence fell between them. It took a while before Nell figured out what was different, and then it struck her. The Victrola wasn't playing. No music blaring and no Jeanette turning circles in the room. When Nell mentioned it, Jeanette shrugged.

"It's on the blink, and I don't have the money to get it fixed. Besides, I've been so busy I haven't had time."

"Busy with school?"

"Actually, no. I dropped out."

"But your note said you had to go to class."

"Well, sort of. I'm helping out at Miss Beverly's School of Dance and taking classical ballet and tap practically every evening. Dance class. Isn't that the niftiest?"

"But what about getting a diploma?"

"It's just not my cuppa tea, you know. I adore working with the kiddos. It's really what I've wanted to do my whole life—I was just afraid to go after it."

"You're joking?"

"No. While you and Greta were off having your own frolics, I was sorting out some stuff here. With my dad and all."

"I'm so sorry about him. What happened? I thought he was doing better after your holiday."

"Yeah, but then he got pneumonia and three days later he was gone. Just like that. Just like Aunt Anna when she got the Spanish flu. And now it's killing my mom." She took a deep breath and brushed away a tear. "Not literally, but she's worried about money and how she's going to make it."

"Did your dad leave anything?"

Jeanette shook her head. "A stack of doctor bills and a few stocks that Mother had to cash in to pay for the funeral. I'm not sure we would've made it without Calvin helping out."

"Calvin's helping your mom pay bills?"

"No, not giving her money, but moral support. When Calvin came over after my accident, both my parents sort of took to him, you know. Said he was just a decent chap and all."

"He is nice."

"Calvin sat up at night at the hospital with my dad so Mother and I could go home." Tears glistened in earnest in her dark eyes. "Before he died, Daddy motioned for me to come close, and in a raspy whisper told me that Calvin was a good man and that I should hang on to him. So I'm trying."

"And you're in love?"

"Ain't it the berries?" Jeanette's face broke out in a grin.

"I'm thrilled for you, and Calvin deserves someone really nice. Someone like you."

"But he wanted you first."

"Only because he didn't know you."

Jeanette puffed out her cheeks and let out a long, slow breath, obviously relieved to get it off her chest. "So, tell me about the wedding. Did you get a personal introduction to the king and queen?"

Nell laughed. "No, it wasn't like that at all..." Nell told about the wedding and the people she'd met, the horse guard with riders who carried spears, royal carriages, and the peddlers on the street. When she told it, it sounded like a fairy tale. But the only handsome prince was the one who got away.

CHAPTER 26

Nell tucked her handbag under her worktable in the studio on Monday morning and laid the gift-wrapped box with the necktie from Carnaby Street on Calvin's desk. She hoped he wouldn't think it a consolation gift since she'd been promoted, and in her heart, she knew he'd be happy for her. None of his usual clutter topped his work space so she wondered if he had moved to the workroom. She pulled the sketches she'd drawn on the ship from her attaché case and tacked a few of them on the corkboard. Excitement buzzed along her spine as she viewed them from different angles. Some of her best work yet.

She especially like the one with a mushroom brim and scribbled a note to check on braided trim, adding other supplies she would gather for the mock-ups. The metallic lace for the flapper cloche would have to be ordered, but it could be added later.

A quick glance at the clock told her Calvin was either late or had an early consulting appointment downstairs. Odd, though, that he didn't stick his head in and at least say hello. Or maybe he got confused on the day they were returning from London. The places where Nora and Percy had once worked showed signs of activity, no doubt that of the two new designers Oscar had hired on the eve of their departure for England. It looked as if they were settled in, and Nell was anxious to meet them. Where was everyone? She looked at the calendar and groaned. The first Monday in June. Their monthly staff meeting, and it wasn't Calvin who was late but her.

She pulled the sketches from the display, put them in a folder, and scuttled to the conference room upstairs.

"Oh, so you decide to grace us with your presence." Oscar stopped midpace at the end of the conference table and nailed her with a dark look.

"I apologize. I was here early, getting organized...waiting for Calvin." She scanned the faces of those gathered, expecting to see him. Leo, the firm's accountant, sat on one side next to Harjo and Steiger, and on the other side of the table, a man and woman she didn't know but assumed were the new designers. But no Calvin. "Where is he anyway?"

Oscar threw up his hands. "Gone. Doesn't work here any longer."

"What? Did you let him go?"

"No. He left on his own, but I was hoping you might shed some light on his leaving. You two are thicker than bees in a honeycomb, so I assumed you have information we don't."

"I haven't seen him...or talked to him. Did he give a reason?" *And why hadn't Jeanette mentioned this?*

"None. Turned in his notice and left. Steiger thinks he may have gone to Murdoch's." Oscar spat out *Murdoch's* like it was vile on his tongue. "Some thanks I get for taking the no-count on. Not a lick of talent, but he did keep the old bats happy and handled the men's line without too much supervision."

"Not to disagree, sir, but he presented you with several ideas you r-rejected."

"Children's stuff. Nothing that fits the clientele of our store. It wouldn't surprise me if he absconded with half of our designs."

"Calvin wouldn't do that."

"Time will tell. Murdoch's better not have a single hat in their showroom that's one of our exclusives or they'll be hauled into a court of law for industrial espionage. No one leaves Oscar Fields Millinery unless I boot them out myself."

Nell dropped her folder on the table and took a seat.

Oscar picked up apparently from where he left off when Nell entered. "That trip overseas has netted us a profit that would make my father cry in shame. Leo, do you have the report summary?"

Leo looked at the ledger before him. "In the final analysis, total sales exceeded our predictions by eighty percent. The expenditures, however, were double our projections once we'd issued checks to Sir Haversham's realty company, which, in my opinion, were inflated figures. I've settled the accounts with the couture houses and tailors, costs not in the original budget. We do have a net profit, albeit slight."

Nell suspected as much after overhearing Mr. Fields and Sir Haversham at the society dinner.

Leo continued, "Without the backing you originally predicted, I'm afraid it could take the rest of this fiscal year to be back where we were. If that."

Nell recoiled. Leo didn't have to be so subtle. Why not just say that Nell's noble heritage had proven a disappointment? She could have told them that her grandmother, while comfortable, needed to preserve what allowance she had to live graciously in her twilight years.

When the show with Soren was mentioned, Nell asked if it would be out of line to offer Hazel and Marcella a small pay raise. "They were valiant in London, and it would be a shame to lose them also to Murdoch's. We need their ex-ex—"

"Experience? Is that it? Or expertise?" Oscar took out a handkerchief and mopped the sweat from his forehead. Anytime there was talk of finances, Oscar stewed.

"Both. I trust them to do good work. They probably even deserve a bonus."

With lips stretched thin, Oscar said, "No bonus. But perhaps a small hourly increase if we get on board with Michaels, providing you guarantee they don't leave. If they do, your pay will be docked accordingly."

Nell agreed. Oscar knew she would vouch for them. She'd missed spending time with her grandmother because of his threat to fire them. They were worth fighting for. She showed him her preliminary sketches and promised to have samples done by the end of the week so production could begin. By lunchtime, four designs had been approved. She gathered the supplies and took them to the workroom to get started.

Hazel looked over her shoulder, then said in a low voice, "Is it true about Calvin leaving?"

"Looks like it."

"Lucky duck."

"I'm sure it was a personal choice, not because he was unhappy here."

"He'd be the only one."

"What would you say if I told you Mr. Fields is considering a pay increase for you?"

"It'd be a miracle, that's what."

"And Marcella, too. I'm counting on both of you to get our new fall line off the ground."

"It'd be nice to be appreciated. Too bad you're not running the salon—we'd be a sight better off."

"I'll take that as a compliment, but Mr. Fields is still in charge. Always will be."

Nell showed her the new designs, and from the way Hazel's eyes lit up, she knew she had her cooperation, at least for now.

Nell shut the door of her flat behind her and turned the key in the lock. The first thing she intended to do was put Jeanette through an interrogation of why she didn't tell her about Calvin leaving the salon.

The flat was empty, and as Nell put the kettle on, she remembered Jeanette was going to spend the evening with her mother when she finished at the dance studio. She'd spent the better part of the weekend there, too, saying her mother needed her. Or perhaps she was avoiding Nell because of Calvin. It wasn't like Jeanette to skirt around the truth. So be it—she would go to Sal's and have a bite to eat as soon as she'd changed. On her way out, she remembered the kettle and turned back as the phone rang.

"Hey, Nellie March. Guess you made it back." *Calvin.*

"You. You! I'm so mad at you I could spit. What do you mean by going to Murdoch's?"

"Well, I didn't expect I'd get hugs and smooches when you got back, but I was hoping at least for a pleasant hello."

"Sorry. You caught me off guard, but I want some answers."

"Maybe you were expecting a call from someone else? Oscar perchance?"

A snakelike shiver slithered up Nell's spine. "Why would he call me at home?"

"Rumor has it—"

"What rumor?"

"All those parties you went to across the pond. Steiger had a heyday talking about how he heard Oscar was wooing you, buttering you up to be his next wife."

"That's r-rubbish. What does Steiger know? Yes, we went a lot of places, but the only moves Oscar made were making sure all the right people saw us."

"You're right. Steiger probably invented it to stir up trouble."

"Guess you didn't have anything better to do than believe false rumors and look for a new job."

"Back up. Let's start this over. I called to talk to Jeanette."

Nell winced, a pinch in her gut. "Oh."

"You did know I've been seeing Jeanette?"

"She mentioned it. But she didn't tell me you were a traitor."

"Could we talk about something else?"

"Not until you tell me why you left."

"Hey, what happened to the timid Nellie March?"

"More than you'd like to know, and don't call me Nellie March." She stopped. Calvin was her friend. Jeanette's boyfriend. With effort, she softened her voice. "I am interested in what you have to say, unless you'd be breaking some confidentiality clause from Murdoch's."

"Not at all. How about I buy you lunch one day this week and talk about it? For old time's sake. Murdoch's is only a couple blocks from Oscar Fields."

They picked a time and place, and Calvin asked again to speak to Jeanette.

"She's not back from her mother's. And sorry to be so prickly. I'm truly glad you and Jeanette are seeing each other."

"She's a swell egg. Like you, *Nell*. You gonna tell me about your trip?"

"At lunch. If you're nice."

"Always."

He hung up. And of course, he was right. Calvin was nice. Always.

She dropped onto the settee, still feeling irritable. Calvin's remark about Steiger nagged at her, his prediction that she would be Oscar's next wife. Is that what the promotion was about or was it because she'd stuck it out and earned the position of designer? Steiger just liked to stir things up. No wonder it was so easy for Calvin to leave.

Instead of going to Sal's, Nell meandered through the neighborhood and stopped for a tortellini and cup of tea when her stomach started growling. The days were growing longer with the advent of summer. She found a bench at the edge of a green park and watched a gaggle of young boys kick a tired rubber ball in the street, their laughter and shouts a symphony.

A teenage couple strolled by, adoring eyes on each other, their fingers clasped. She and Quentin had been like those two once. Until they both grew up. When the familiar pangs of regret swallowed her, she rose and went back to the flat.

The least she could do was thank Quentin for his honesty and wish him happiness. Perhaps he was never hers to begin with. It was time to let go. But it felt as if she were severing a limb.

She spent the evening thumbing through a stack of fashion magazines, letting her imagination drift, but all the while she was drafting the words she wanted to say to Quentin. She went to her desk, her grandmother's sampler with the words *Strength and honor are her clothing* giving her courage. She whispered a quick prayer; assembled her stationery, pen, and ink; and wrote, "Dearest Quentin."

She scratched through "Dearest," then tore up the page and started over.

Dear Quentin,

    It was a pleasure to see you again in London. You're looking well, and I enjoyed reminiscing with you. We had an uneventful voyage back to the States, but already new plans for the work ahead are under way, and there's the possibility of doing another runway show with the couture designer Soren Michaels. I believe I've told you about him.

    I owe you an apology. In my state of surprise at your engagement, I failed to ask when the wedding would be. Will you marry in Heathdown or London?

Should you and Colleen get a chance for a trip to New York, I would consider it an honor to show you the sights. There are many I've not seen myself in this vast city, so it would be a pleasure to discover them with the two of you.

I'm expecting a visit from Aunt Sarah and the twins next month.

I'll always be grateful that I was able to return to England and especially to see dear Grandmama. If you go up to Heathdown, give her my love, won't you?

Although it may be unseemly to mention, you'll always have that special place in my heart as my first love.

With my kindest regards,
Nell

CHAPTER 27

Soren Michaels came in the next day with sketches and to discuss the preliminaries for the runway show he called *spectacular*. Whatever negotiations there were between Soren and Oscar had apparently been worked out, and Oscar was up to his usual criticism of the hemlines of Soren's designs.

"Nell and I value your opinion, Oscar, but no one is doing Edwardian anymore. This is the golden age of jazz, and if we aren't at the forefront, we'll be edged out."

"Tasteful evening wear will never go out of fashion. We witnessed that in England, didn't we, sweetheart? The Brits hold to their traditions, their conservatism."

Nell shuddered at the *sweetheart*, which she knew was for Soren's benefit. "Our clients were conservative, I agree, but the events they were attending were more formal, too. The couture shops leaned toward the shorter hemlines and less coverage on the top. I can see this one appealing to the free-spirited American image." She pointed to a frock with a black tulle skirt and a sheer top with pink beaded florets in a diamond pattern. The underbodice was a simple flesh-colored chemise, but the placement of the rosettes and the sparkle spoke of detail and elegance. A bit provocative, but brilliant, too.

Oscar scowled but held his tongue.

Soren said, "Girls today want something that can go from the opera to a speakeasy without a change of costume. Flirty skirts that swing. The boxy look that falls from the shoulders with unrestricted movement. I just spent a delightful evening at a new club in Harlem. Glitter and glamour are all the rage."

Oscar mulled it over and said, "As long as it brings in a steady flow of customers, I have no objections."

"To placate you, Oscar, I have several designs for the mature women in the crowd, like our mutual friend, Mavis Benchley. Jeanne Lanvin in Paris has done quite well with her line that's a bit longer with fuller skirts. I just don't want to veer too far from my trademark look. I know you understand the importance, Oscar, of having something that sets you apart from the other milliners here in town."

Nell wanted to kiss Soren, but Oscar only nodded and asked what date he had in mind to do the show.

"I have a couple of chaps who are trying to get inside information on when the other houses are having their runway shows so we can schedule accordingly—the first show of the season is the one people remember."

"Certainly. I'm sure Nell can be ready whenever you are."

As before, Soren told them he would have copies of his designs sent over for Nell to begin working on them. "I want to know this time I can trust you not to let them fall into the wrong hands. I still shudder when I think of those shabby imitations in Phillip Price's window. And the nerve of him to call it couture."

"Your sketches will be kept in my suite of offices. I'm sure Nell won't mind working next door to me on this project." Oscar's look dared her to disagree, but it was fine with her. It worked both ways. She could keep an eye on him, too.

"It was a business decision. Sort of a slap against the head when I had time to think it over. Plenty of time while you were gone, you know." Calvin took a bite of his corned beef on rye. They'd spent the first minutes of their lunch with Nell giving Calvin the tie from Carnaby Street and a few awkward starts, but both of them knew the real reason for their meeting.

"I thought you'd take advantage of our being in London to come up with something dazzling."

"I did." He winked. "Only it went in the portfolio I took to Murdoch's. Keen for me that they liked it."

"So this was your plan all along?" She stirred her minestrone, the barley bits popping to the surface.

"No, my plan was to become a premier designer, like you." He leaned in and took another bite. "Congratulations, by the way. Jeanette told me you got a promotion, that you're officially a designer now."

"Thanks. I feel bad that Oscar always overlooked your ideas."

"Don't be. That's the way it is in this biz. It's swell now that I'm working for someone who's not a schmuck."

"But Oscar owns all your designs. At least the ones you made for him."

Calvin shrugged. "Nothing done on Oscar's time went to Murdoch's, but I did have a few late nights at home putting a portfolio together. I never knew it could be such fun."

"I know you haven't been happy at Oscar Fields, but why now?"

"Something's bothered me for a long time. I always thought there was something fishy about how Mr. Fields took me on with barely a glance at my portfolio. I thought my degree in textiles was proof enough at the time. Then a month or so ago, Steiger cocked an eye at me and sneered, said my old man hadn't done me any favors getting me a job at the salon."

"Your dad got you the job?"

"Yeah, before I joined Fields, I was on the outs with my dad about my career choice. I told him if I couldn't get a design job in New York, I was going to Paris. My mother went on a crying jag about me leaving, so a few days later, my dad asked if I'd considered Oscar Fields Millinery. To make a long story short, I landed the job."

"How?"

"That's what I wondered at the time, but then I forgot about it. You came and everything was good at first, but Fields never gave me the time of day. After the remark in the workroom, I asked my dad. He and Fields went to the same club, and Oscar was on the verge of losing his membership for not keeping up his dues. My dad bailed him out and mentioned I was interested in millinery. *Voilà*. I got the job."

Nell laughed. "Oscar always says it's about connections and who you know."

"That's for sure. If I hadn't known you, I wouldn't have ended up with a swell girl like Jeanette. I was just too dense to see it at first."

"I'm glad you did."

"So tell me, anything new you're working on?"

"I can't tell you that. You're the competition."

He held up his hands. "Not trying to steal any secrets." He pushed away from the table. "Better get back or Murdoch will wonder where I am."

He gave her a brief hug and said, "Stay strong, Nell."

⚬⚬⚬

Jeanette jumped when Nell walked in. "Criminy, you scared me."

"Because I'm early?"

"No, I was going over the routine for the dance class in my head.

Miss Beverly says that picturing the moves and memorizing the positions and order of the steps will make it second nature."

"What? Are you going to be in a recital or something?"

"No, just leading the class for the first time while Miss Beverly observes. I can't remember being this nervous in my entire life."

"They're just schoolkids. They won't know if you have a misstep."

"No, but I will. The little girls are so energetic and enthusiastic, I just get tingles when I'm working with them. I sort of understand why you get excited about your hats sometimes."

"So you really love it?"

"Oh, you know it. And I've noticed a difference in Calvin, too, now that he's doing what he loves and doesn't have Oscar breathing down his neck. How was your lunch?"

"Strange."

"Really? I always thought you and Calvin got along."

"We did. I guess we still do, but...I don't know. It's not the same at the salon. No one to share a joke with or show my designs to..."

"You haven't even been working with Calvin for the past four months. Did he tell you his big news about the Paris designer?" The minute she said it, Jeanette clapped her hand over her mouth. "Never mind. What *did* you talk about?"

"What Paris designer?"

"I can't tell. Sorry, it just slipped out."

"Is Murdoch's working with someone from Paris?"

"You didn't hear it from me. Promise you won't say anything."

"I wouldn't dream of it, although I could get on Oscar's good side by slipping him the information."

"Please don't."

"You know I won't. Could I ask you something about Oscar, though?"

"Sure. What do you want to know?"

"I've noticed that he's always talking about money—if this show is profitable, if the fall season is successful. And when I've tried to ask him to see the books, he bristles. Says it's not my place. That, I do understand. I have no seniority, but while we were gone, I kept the supply room and did the ordering, so I wanted to know if what we took in on the hats balanced the expenses."

"You're losing me. What's the question?"

"Do you know if Oscar has financial problems? Or had them in the past?"

"I'm not sure. He's sort of slippery, you know. Acts like he's flush with dough sometimes, then tight as a drawstring on a coin purse the next. I told you he paid my rent for a while. Maybe a few months. Then he said he couldn't afford it. When Anna married him, they lived in a nice flat on the Upper West Side, but after she died, he moved back to his club."

"He doesn't have his own place?"

"I don't think so. Oh, get a load of this. Mother said he dropped by the other day to pay his condolences and gave her a hundred dollars. Like you, she was leery, but she took it. She said he even hung around and had coffee with her. Why the interest in Oscar all of a sudden?"

"I'm just trying to figure him out. He was slippery, like you said, in London. Buying me expensive clothes—by the way, you might want to check out my closet sometime—and then acting like he didn't have two farthings to rub together."

"You ask me, staying there is just going to bring you misery, promotion or not."

"The thing is, Oscar's been decent lately, and I have a steady string of clients. Mrs. Benchley's been a love, encouraging me. If I left, I would lose those contacts, the ones who are loyal to Oscar. They've become my friends as well."

"Unless it turns out that Oscar is really a snake and is just waiting to strike."

"You're too harsh, you know that. I'm just trying to see it from all sides."

"I wouldn't worry. You've got this show coming up with Soren. See what happens."

"Thanks. I feel better. It's nice to have someone to talk to."

"Did you mean it about the dresses?"

"Absolutely."

CHAPTER 28

Soren slung his briefcase on the conference room table and glared at Nell and Oscar. "Seven weeks! Those blasted Frenchmen don't know that in New York, we do the fall shows in August and the holiday shows in November. No one is in any humor to look at fur collars in July. Half of the patronage will still be in Martha's Vineyard or over in Jersey taking their summer vacations."

Oscar frowned. "What Frenchmen? I didn't know any of the Paris houses did New York shows."

Soren waved his fingers. "They do now. Murdoch's has teamed up with the House of Perrault the last Saturday in July."

Oscar turned to Nell. "Know anything about this?"

"Me? How would I know?" She wasn't sure whether it was worse to tell a lie or break a promise. She hoped this straddled the line.

"Your little tête-à-tête with our former employee comes to mind. I'm sure the two of you swapped a few trade secrets."

Nell drew back her shoulders. "T-trade secrets? Certainly not. Although it surprises me that you knew about my lunch with Calvin. Were you sp-spying on me?" *Calm. Breathe. Don't stammer.*

"I make it my business to know what's going on."

Before she could think of a retort, Soren said, "If their show is the end of July, we'll have to move ours up to the third weekend in July. Every hotel in town is booked so I've no idea where we'll have it." He pinned Nell with a look of desperation. "Or if we can even be ready by then."

"It won't be easy, but I think we can be ready. Hazel and Marcella have promised me their time as long as Oscar is willing to pay overtime."

Soren paced. "Which leaves us with finding a place."

Oscar stroked his mustache. "There's always the Stottlemeir Club. Unless you think it's bad luck. We can't afford another disaster."

"It's not my preference, but we may not have a choice. I'll get in touch with Mavis Benchley. Besides, it's less expensive than a hotel."

Oscar nodded and said, "Generous of you to consider the cost, and in light of the overtime and extra expense of rush orders on materials, it's imperative we cut corners somewhere."

The rest of the meeting went quickly with Nell getting Soren's approval on the two mock-ups she had done. She worked through lunch since it was Friday and her appointment day with Dr. Underwood, and by the time she locked Soren's designs in the cupboard of the conference room, she sighed. It had been a productive day, her newest designs both exciting and she hoped compelling. Six weeks. She didn't have time to worry about Oscar's financial woes or him spying on her.

❧

Nell resumed her visits with Dr. Underwood, who wore a poppy-colored shirt and a bowtie with zebra stripes for her first appointment. He listened intently as she confirmed that her memory did, in fact, happen. "Grandmama said it was always suspected but never proven that Grandfather pushed Gramma Jo to her death."

"Was she surprised by what you told her?"

"Maybe at first, but she always knew something didn't ring true about the accident. And for several months afterward I didn't speak at all, which concerned them. When I did start talking, I stammered, but they never questioned me about what happened that day."

"You seem to have lost the stammer now. Are there times when it recurs?"

"When I'm under stress and quite often when my boss frustrates me. Sometimes I think I need a psychotherapist to deal with that." Her attempt at humor brought a chuckle from the doctor.

"Sometimes we're all in need of that."

"I do wish I'd had the courage to tell what I saw that day."

"You were a frightened child. I'm sure no one holds you accountable for it. Your grandfather, he is deceased?"

"Yes. Drank himself to the grave, Mama said."

"It's normal your stammer surfaces now and again, along with residual fears. A trauma such as yours often follows victims into adulthood, but the effects are lessened because you're aware of what caused it. If you need me for anything, you can call." He looked at her folder. "Is there anything else that concerns you or that you want help with?"

"Not unless you can make hats."

"You got me there."

It was her last appointment, and as she boarded the trolley that afternoon, a warmth nestled in her breast. Stammering had tormented her most of her life, but it led to Lindy and Dr. Underwood. She would miss them.

Late Saturday afternoon, Nell called her mother in Louisville to tell her about the upcoming show with Soren, but her mother sounded rushed and said they were just leaving for a faculty dinner party.

"I have meant to call you, though. Jane Alistair wrote and said your grandmother's not doing well. A heart condition of some sort. You might write her a letter if you can spare a few minutes. It would cheer her up."

"I'll do that."

Nell changed clothes to go to Sal's Diner for a bite to eat, and before she left, she tucked the designs she was working on under the mattress. It wouldn't do to leave them out in the event Jeanette and Calvin happened to show up. It was overkill; Calvin wouldn't dream of stealing her designs.

Nell sat at the table in the corner where she could see everyone in the diner and those who passed by on the street.

Felice brought her a glass of water and winked. "Angelo's nephew from Philadelphia is visiting. You want I should call him up and have him come over to meet you?"

"Not tonight, but nice of you to think of it."

"A sweet *signorina* like you should be out dancing, doing a little smooching in the park with a *giovane*." She puckered her lips, which made Nell laugh. She promised Felice that maybe next time she'd take her up on her offer, but she knew she wouldn't. She wasn't ready to risk another broken heart.

That evening she wrote a letter to her grandmother, keeping the tone light so as not to aggravate the heart condition Jane had written about. She described some of the hats she was making, and under her signature, Nell drew a tiny nightingale.

Nightingale song wafted through her sleep that night as they darted in and out of the yews' soft fronds. The melody went off-key, the fluttering of bird wings a blur as they lit from branch to branch, then burrowed deeper into boughs of the shrubbery. In her dream,

Nell searched for the nest, but she only came up with emptiness and shadows.

Nell woke with an ache in her chest. The taste of garlic filled her mouth, now sour, and she thought of the richness of Angelo's cooking. The combination of the ravioli sauce, the session with Dr. Underwood, and news of Grandmama were undoubtedly to blame for the strange dream.

Still, dreams were a way of untangling the knots of the day's toil, her grandmother used to say. A wavy feeling came over her. The moon outside her window cast a thin shaft of yellow through the gap in her curtains, landing on the sampler above Nell's writing desk. She couldn't read the words in the dimness, but she knew them by heart.

Strength and honor are her clothing; and she shall rejoice in time to come.
In time to come.

The future seemed vague, hidden from her. She had the show with Soren to look forward to, but then what? Her stomach clenched.

Then what?

Tomorrow she would take a day off. Go to church, then take the ferry out to the Statue of Liberty to see the lady who heralded freedom...and the land of opportunity.

Maybe the wind that blew across the harbor would bring her the answer.

CHAPTER 29

On Monday morning, Nell felt a lightness in her step that had been missing for a long time. Her day of rest had been restorative. Invigorating. She arrived at the salon early, tucked her things in the conference room, then with new designs in hand went to the workroom where she took her place in the corner. She checked the head measurement on the block, then positioned the buckram on the block for the foundation of her newest idea. A basic cloche to which she would add a rolled brim and cover with scarlet velvet. She hummed as she pinned the buckram into place.

"Something's got you happy today." Hazel came in with Marcella and nodded as she leafed through her stack of orders for the day. "Can't say Mondays ever make me feel like humming."

"There's a lot to do, and the work goes faster when I hum."

Hazel waved one of the order sheets in the air. "Thirty more of the Summer Breeze numbers. The rate we're going through them, every girl of means in New York City will be wearing one of your straw cloches."

"That many? Another reason to hum a tune, I guess."

"That and being a bona fide designer now. High time, if you ask me. Sure gave old Steiger a jolt when I had the pleasure of breaking the news to him."

"I wasn't aware you were the one who told him, and why would Steiger care whether I'm an apprentice or a designer? The workroom routine doesn't change because of that."

"Maybe so, but the old goat darn near got the apoplexy when I told him that first day back. He hightailed it out of here like he had a train to catch."

"And here I thought it was Steiger who liked to stir up trouble, and I find out it's you. I hope you've smoothed things over. We can't afford for you to be fussing at Steiger and fall behind with the work right now."

"You sound like Mr. Fields. But don't you worry, the work will get done." Hazel squirmed into her smock and worked the buttons.

Nell shook her head. Hazel and Steiger had been at each other's throats for as long as Nell had been around. She doubted her reprimand would change that.

"Hazel, I know you and Steiger have been here the longest, but were you here when Oscar's dad was alive?"

"I most assuredly was."

"What was it like then?"

"Are you asking about the conditions or the old man?"

"Both, I suppose. Just curious."

"Old Mr. Fields was a hard man, expected miracles sometimes. No such thing as unions or overtime then. We worked long hours for a pittance, but the paychecks were regular unless the salon got in a financial pinch."

Nell nodded as Hazel continued. "Rumor was the old man got himself in a corner he couldn't get out of, and being assembly line, we weren't privy to the particulars, but the stress of it killed him. That's when our Oscar took over. Is that what you wanted to know?"

Nell nodded. "Was Oscar happy about taking over the business?"

"Poor man was still wet behind the ears, didn't know beans about business or designing hats." Her face scrunched in concentration. "I came to work every day expecting to find a Closed sign on the door. Around then Harjo came, and business picked up. He's pretty sharp, that Harjo, despite his barking. Surprised me no end that Mr. Fields got the salon back on track. I know I threaten to quit every other week, but I'm sticking around. Got my eye on Steiger's job when he retires. Though heaven knows when that will be."

The door opened and two workers drifted in, put on their smocks, and gathered their tools from the wall bins.

Nell didn't know much more about Oscar than she did before, but the part about Harjo piqued her interest. Was he just Oscar's secretary or did he have an influence?

Hazel and Marcella talked about their Independence Day plans, then asked Nell about the hats for the fall line.

"Lots of sparkle and some interesting lacy patterns." She finished pinning the buckram, then put the block on a shelf to dry.

Marcella put her hand on her hip and said, "Guess Hazel will be sticking me with the beadwork."

"You bet your bottom dollar, I will. All that close work strains my eyes."

Nell shook her head and told them she'd get the plans to them by Wednesday. She started for the notions room, but on a whim, she made a pass through the showroom to ask how sales were going and to check the display with her hats.

The doors had only been opened ten minutes, but already several customers were in the salon, and both salesgirls were busy, so Nell decided to check in another time. The front door jangled, and Nell looked back over her shoulder. Mavis Benchley. She hadn't seen her since their return, so she went to greet her.

"Don't you look smart?" Mavis stood back and surveyed Nell. "Oscar tells me you had a grand time over in England."

"Yes. Quite nice. And you're the one who deserves the credit. If not for you—"

"Pooh. A girl like you is like cream in a pitcher. Always rises to the top, you know. Like I tell my girls, you've got the rest of your life to be married. Make something of yourself today."

Nell blushed. "Is there something I can help you with?"

"No, I just came in for my weekly survey, to see if there was anything new." She glanced around. "And I wanted to go over the details of the upcoming show with Oscar. Is he here?"

"I'm not sure. Would you like me to take you up?"

"Heavens no. I know the way."

Nell went to the notions room and took inventory of what she needed, then spent the rest of the day finishing the scarlet cloche. The rosette made of filigreed braid was the perfect complement. She was nearly finished slip stitching it in place when Oscar came in and stood behind her, his hand resting lightly on her shoulder.

"Lovely. I could never quite master a fine slip stitch."

"It's easier with the silk thread and finding the right needle."

He bent over, his breath on her neck. "Having delicate fingers is an advantage, too."

"I'll be done in a tick. Was there something you wanted?"

"I thought if you'd like, we might take an early dinner. We've not officially celebrated your promotion, and I know a Greek place that does an early seating."

"I'm not dressed for dining out."

"You're always a vision, my dear. Just knock on my door when you're ready."

Candles flickered between them, their plates empty. Oscar lifted his water glass.

"To Nell. And to us."

She returned the toast with a click of her glass, uncertain what "to us" meant and chided herself for her suspicion. There was nothing untoward in Oscar's actions, but the toast seemed personal. Perhaps he was just lonely. They'd talked about the upcoming show with Soren, and Nell had asked how Mrs. Benchley was doing with the arrangements.

"She's most accommodating as always."

When they left, Oscar kept his hand at the small of her back and hailed a taxi for her.

"Thanks for the dinner."

"I'm glad you could join me. We should try this more often." He gave her a peck on the cheek and held the cab door for her. When she looked back, he gave a friendly wave, then turned and walked in the opposite direction. To his room at the club?

Emotion welled up in Nell's chest, an odd blend of apprehension and empathy.

With only three weeks until the show, Soren grew more nervous. He popped in every few days with suggestions, wringing his hands over getting everything done on time and endlessly querying her about keeping it all under wraps.

"Hazel and Marcella are reliable. And I've not breathed a word about what the dresses look like." She flashed him a smile. "You worry too much."

"Easy for you to say. You don't hold the reputation of your firm in your hands."

"But what I do reflects on Oscar, and I have a personal stake in this as well—my first show as a designer."

Soren paced the length of the conference table, his breaths audible. "I know that, and I've been thinking of something along those lines. What would you think if we were to share the spotlight as master of ceremonies. Two mics? One on each side of the stage. Having a knockout like you gracing the stage would have a certain appeal—"

"No! I could n-never...not the way I talk." Her insides twisted.

Soren snorted. "Give yourself some credit. You're not nearly as mumbledy-mouthed as you used to be. Going abroad has given you confidence."

"Oscar would never agree."

"I'll talk to him. Like you say, you have a personal stake in this as well. Even though it's Oscar's name on the label, people will see you on the stage and associate the hats with *you*, the designer."

Her hands went clammy and her throat dry just thinking of it. But he had a point. She *was* a designer and should act like one.

"I know you're right, that I need to shoulder the responsibility as a designer, but it still gives me the shakes. And I should be the one to approach Oscar. He'll probably still say no, but—"

"Attagirl!"

Nell was a mass of nerves when she knocked on Oscar's door the next day. She took a deep breath, trying to remember the speech she'd prepared.

"May I have a word, sir?"

"I hope you've not run into a snag with Michaels? Harjo just informed me how much this is costing us. A diamond cluster for one of the hats?"

"Yes, sir, one of the h-hats you approved." *Deep breath. Be confident.* "And to answer your question...no snags that I know of.

Things are going splendidly. I do realize the materials are expensive, but it's also an important show."

"I do agree on that. So what's on your mind?"

"Soren suggested that he and I share the duties of master of ceremonies. Two microphones on either side of the stage."

"You? He wants *you*?"

"Yes, sir. Since I've done the designs, it would naturally be my responsibility to present them. It would add a personal connection with the audience."

Oscar slammed his fist on the desk and glared at Nell. "Absolutely not. I'm still the owner of this salon, and I will never approve of a woman taking my place on the stage. If anyone is going to moderate the show with Michaels, it's me."

"I won't be taking your place. Only sharing my part of the burden for the success of the show. I really want to do this. For us."

"What do you mean for us? Did you think my taking you to dinner was some sort of romantic gesture? That I had other intentions?"

Nell felt as if she'd been punched. "N-no...I...of course n-not." She pressed her fingers to her lips. She *had* thought he might have those intentions even though the idea repulsed her.

"You would make a fool of yourself on that stage. Probably get tongue-tied and make me a laughingstock."

A coil of determination took hold. "There's always that possibility, but you'll never know unless you give me a chance. Women want to see other women making a positive impact. I'm certain this will be good for our image."

Oscar's gaze turned to stone. "Never has a designer asked such a thing. I may have promoted you, but in case you hadn't noticed, it's still my name gracing the front of this store. Designers come and go, but it's my name that people speak of when conversations drift to the topic of fine millinery."

"I understand that, and I'll abide by whatever you say. But I hope you'll consider the idea at least."

He closed his eyes and stroked his mustache, letting her squirm. She had at least tried.

Finally, he let out a long slow breath. "Go ahead. Make a fool of yourself. And if you do, then you won't have to worry about being the next star designer. You'll have to worry about finding a new job."

Her spine tingled with a million tiny pinpricks. "I'll do my best. That I promise."

She turned to leave when he called her back in. "You were wrong about one thing. When I promoted you to designer, you told me I wouldn't regret it. I already do."

Nell bit her lip and went to the conference room. He had agreed to let her narrate her part of the show. She should be dancing on air, but every fiber in her body was terrified.

She lifted the telephone receiver to call Soren with the news.

CHAPTER 30

The following week, a letter from her grandmother came, written in Jane Alistair's beautiful script.

Dearest Nell,

I'm writing on behalf of Lady Mira whose hand trembles too much to hold a pen these days. I trust your mother has given you the news of your grandmother's heart condition. I'm happy to report she has rallied somewhat and has started enjoying tea in the garden again. Although her heart seems stronger, her thoughts ramble more each day. She was pleased with your drawing of the nightingale and wanted me to tell you that their song is as lovely as ever.

We were going through some of her things a few days ago and came across this snippet. She thought you would like it. We both send our love.

Fondly,
Jane Alistair

The newspaper clipping was yellowed and cracked along the fold. Nell could scarcely make out the faded print for the moistness in her eyes.

Christmas is coming, the geese are getting fat.
Please do put a penny in the old man's hat.
If you haven't got a penny, a ha'penny will do.
If you haven't got a ha'penny, then God bless you!

Once upon a time, Nell had recited this in front of the whole church. Without stammering. Was a runway show any different? She laughed. Yes. Her neck and her job were on the line.

Soren hadn't gotten back to her to write the script yet, so as she spent long hours working on the hats, Nell formed the description in her mind for each of them. The words flowed like lengths of silk in her thoughts while doubts gnawed at the lining of her stomach.

She wrote her grandmother on Saturday and thanked her for the poem, then sealed the letter and took it to the letter box on the corner.

"Hey, Nellie March!" The shout came from up the street a ways, but only one person called her that. Nell turned and waved, then waited until Calvin caught up with her, Jeanette in tow. "I haven't seen you around. I guess Oscar's keeping you busy."

"No more than usual. So what have you two been up to?"

Jeanette said, "I took Calvin to the dance studio to watch the ten-year-olds rehearse. I had to remind him to behave in front of the little girls. We don't want to be putting ideas in their heads." She had a glow about her that Nell was sure came from being in love.

Calvin pulled Jeanette into the crook of his arm and kissed her lightly on the temple. "We're not in the studio now."

Nell fell in stride with them as Jeanette prattled on about the newest dance steps her students had mastered and their upcoming recital. "You two should try and come. Two weeks from today. On the twenty-first."

"I'd love to, but I have another engagement that day."

Jeanette's eyebrows shot up. "Get out. You have a date?"

Nell glared at her. "Would that be such a shock?"

"High time, that's what I think. Calvin and I were just thinking about who we could fix you up with."

"I can find my own suitors."

"Then who is it?"

"No one you know."

Calvin narrowed his eyes. "You don't have to play coy with us. Smooth of Soren Michaels to move his show up the week ahead of ours."

Nell elbowed him. "You promised. No talk about the salons."

"What? You want I should just pretend I'm deaf and dumb? The adverts are out. Invitations in the mail. Should be quite the show."

Nell laughed. "You're right. I shouldn't be so prickly. There are a few surprises that you don't know about."

Calvin said he could hardly wait.

Jeanette glared at Calvin. "Does this mean you won't go to my studio's recital?"

"Guess not, cupcake, although it breaks my heart."

Jeanette stalked off toward the flat, then shot a remark over her shoulder. "I know where I rank."

Calvin hurried up to her and draped his arm over her shoulders. "You're the top, Jeanette, and just because I can't make this recital doesn't mean I won't have a dozen other chances." He pecked her on the cheek.

She turned her face to his, her lips poised for his.

Nell hung back, her heart warm at seeing them like this. A simple disagreement erased in a tick with a kiss. She sighed, remembering when things were that simple with Quentin.

A knot formed in her throat.

❦

Since Aunt Sarah, Iris, and Mittie were arriving on Friday morning, Nell had wired and asked them to meet her at the salon when they got settled. The show was a week away, and with each passing day, the tangle in Nell's stomach wound more tightly. She and Soren wrote the final copy for the presentation, then rewrote it when he added two gowns for the event he heralded as Golden Days and Velvet Nights.

The new designs were Soren's most adventurous yet; one was a dress that would appeal to the older clientele. It featured a slim silhouette with sheer sleeves and cascading petals of silk in warm honey, chestnut, and ending with a burnt-pumpkin color at the midcalf. To complete the ensemble, Nell kept with the basic cloche pattern that had become the staple for the show, but then added a heavily wired brim and covered it with gold bullion lamé that had a solid feel and would keep its shape. Because Hazel and Marcella were still stitching some of the embroidered designs, she added a single large velvet flower. The simplicity of it with the ornate hat fabric was perfect.

The other was a cream underdress with an overlay of the same color with random placement of gold-and-bronze beading and a slightly flared hemline that skimmed the knees. It was both flirty and pretentious and sure to be a hit with the girls who were clamoring for the flapper styles. The accompanying hat would have a gossamer effect with intricate beading and seed pearls that matched the dress, a design that would require long hours to finish in time.

Not counting the hours of practice with the script to ensure that she didn't embarrass Oscar and lose her job. But then, he wouldn't really fire her, would he? She thought of Nora Remming and how Nora's hats had been featured regularly in the front window when Nell had started at the salon. Look where Nora ended up two years later. With Oscar there were no guarantees.

By four on Friday afternoon, she still hadn't heard from Aunt

Sarah, so she went to the showroom, waited on a couple of customers, and rearranged a late summer display. At half past four, the door jangled and Iris and Mittie came breezing in with armloads of shopping bags. Hugs and hellos, questions and chatter erupted until Nell pulled them toward the back of the shop.

"You look wonderful, but where's Aunt Sarah? You've not worn her out already, I hope."

Mittie tried on one of the new floppy-brimmed hats made in an open lacy weave and looked in the mirror, her chocolate eyes dancing. "My darling cousin, we are on our own. Mother came down with a dreadful stomach ailment six hours before the train left, but we already had our tickets, so she relented and sent us on our way. Here we are."

Iris, cute as ever with a new curly bob of her own, said, "We had to promise not to do anything outrageous, so just in case your roommate tries to drag us off to one of those speakeasies—"

Nell held up her hand. "Jeanette doesn't frequent them anymore. She's found something better...or should I say someone better to occupy her time." Nell filled them in on Jeanette and Calvin, about Greta touring the country, and then asked who their latest loves were.

Iris shook her head. "It about broke Mother's heart that her plan for me to go through the season didn't bring the man of *her* dreams into my life."

"So no proposals or wedding bells?"

"Afraid not. Just college classes and a chic new wardrobe to take me there." She pointed to the bags. "We've got a good start."

"And you, Mittie? Off to college?"

"Not on your life. Although I'm planning to take a few classes in Louisville, but mostly I'll be helping out in the stables, doing some of the training for Daddy until I figure out what I want. Mother would prefer us to have suitors in the wings, but she's trying to be a good sport."

Mittie and Iris picked out two hats each, and while Bea boxed them up, Nell offered to show them around. The conference room was off-limits because of Oscar's rule about security, but she showed them the fabric and notions room, and when they got to the lift to go upstairs to the workroom, the doors opened and Mavis Benchley stepped out.

After the introductions, Mavis clucked her tongue and shook her head. "My goodness, Nell, but you and Iris favor one another."

They laughed and said in unison, "So we've heard."

Nell explained to her cousins Mrs. Benchley's role in making the Stottlemeir Club arrangements. She turned to the older woman. "I'm guessing you and Oscar have everything in order. Anything I can help with?"

"Not a thing. Actually, I dropped by to give dear Oscar directions to our house party in the country tomorrow. And wouldn't you know, he's decided at the last minute to decline, said he felt a head cold coming on. You ask me, he's just a wreck over the show next week."

"There's a lot riding on it." *The understatement of the hour.* "Have a good time. And tell your daughters I said hello."

Mrs. Benchley said she would, then stopped. "Why, heavenly days, I didn't even think to ask before—why don't you all come out to the party? We have worlds of food ordered, and some of Daphne's friends are going to provide the music. It will be the horror of horrors, I imagine, but the fresh air will be good for all of us."

Mittie was nodding her head before Mrs. Benchley finished. "Sounds divine! What say we go?"

Nell couldn't think of any reason not to. It would keep Mittie from pouting about missing the jazz clubs, and Nell had always wanted to see Mrs. Benchley's little place in the country, as Daphne had called it.

Mrs. Benchley dug in her handbag and handed Nell a slip of paper. "The directions I had for Oscar. Come any time after three o'clock. Casual dress."

Friday evening and Saturday's shopping flew by in a blur, and when they went back to the Algonquin, Mittie sunk onto the davenport and tucked her legs under her.

"You've been awfully quiet, Nell. I thought you'd be all bubbly with your promotion and the runway show coming up."

Nell swallowed the brick in her throat. "The ensembles are fabulous, but I've got the willies. Getting the promotion was nice, but Soren came up with an idea that may be my undoing." She told them about narrating the millinery portion onstage. "I'm afraid I'll freeze and won't remember the lines or start stammering and ruin everything."

Iris told her she'd be fine. Sweet Iris. Always the cheerleader.

Mittie, though, said, "I'd be scared out of my wits." She swung her legs down. "Hey, why don't you practice on us? Stand over there by the lamp. Iris, go get your hairbrush for the mic."

While Nell protested, Iris ran in to bedroom and came back with a brush; then her cousins lined up and Mittie said, "And now, ladies and gentlemen, the star of our show." She made a swooping motion with her hand toward Nell.

Nell knew the script by heart. She took a deep breath, held the fake mic, and started at the top. "The silk cloche with an o-overlay of gold metallic lace features a...a flared b-brim and...and is accented with a ribbon. No, wait...a black velvet r-r-ribbon." Her hand fell to her side, her face flaming.

Iris said, "Not bad. Just a couple of stumbles. I'm sure we make you nervous. Want to try again?"

Nell shook her head. Oscar was right. She would make a fool of herself and worse...him. If she couldn't even keep her wits with the twins, what would she do in front of a crowd? She wanted to crawl into a hole.

Mittie saved the day by saying it was time to go to the party, and shortly afterward, Nell gave their cabdriver directions to Mrs. Benchley's house on the North Shore of Long Island.

Mrs. Benchley's *little house* wasn't like that of the Vanderbilts or J. P. Morgan or the Roosevelts that the cabbie mentioned on the drive, but it was a stately Federal design set back from the highway and accessed through iron gates. Seagulls swooped over the water of Long Island Sound, its pearly beaches like a ribbon streaming all the way to the Atlantic.

A butler opened the door for them and a passing guest thumbed over his shoulder toward the rear of the house. "Whole blamed mess of people out back. You can't miss it for the racket."

They stepped through French doors onto a wide expanse of lawn. Dozens of people milled about, laughing, dressed like they were going to the Kentucky Derby with their summer dresses and hats. Casual by city standards, perhaps, but still smart. Seersucker suits and boater hats on the gentlemen. Black-and-white patent spats.

Claudia Benchley saw them first and came bustling over. "Mother said you might come. Oh, isn't it just divine out here in the country?" She leaned back, her face to the sun. "You can actually see the sky here. And the stars at night. Come on, I'll introduce you."

She linked arms with Nell and Iris and told Mittie to follow along.

"I didn't expect such a crowd. Are these your neighbors or friends from the city?" Nell asked.

"Some of both. We used to spend the summer months out here. Mother grew up here so she knows hoards of people." She waved at a stylish woman around Mrs. Benchley's age dangling a long cigarette holder. "Mrs. Vandercleeve. Her husband's in the publishing business. Sweet folks, but watch what you say or you'll end up in the newspapers."

Claudia certainly seemed in her element and not the shy, retiring girl Nell had met nine months ago. Or maybe she was just maturing.

"Hey, Claudia, who do we have here?" A guy with a shock of blond hair and a dark caramel tan waved them over. He scurried around dragging up more chairs so they could join the group and said his name was Steve.

"So why is it we've never met you dolls before?" he asked when Claudia introduced them. A waiter brought a tray loaded with glasses of frosty, sweet lemonade, and as they sipped the drinks, the discussion bounced from tennis to the latest Jack Dempsey boxing match to Lillian Gish's new movie. Nell's thoughts drifted to her script as she silently rehearsed her lines. She blinked when she heard Kentucky Derby and realized the group was asking where Mittie and Iris got their Southern accents. *Relax. Enjoy the party and forget about the show.* If only she could.

"You dolls up for the whole weekend?" Steve asked. "We've got a sailing party set for in the morning. You'd be welcome to join us."

"Just here for the evening," Nell told him, trying to add a little sass to her voice.

A trio of girls came from the refreshment tables and said the pie-eating contest was about to begin, which drew several of the guys away from the table, and Claudia said there was oodles of food if they wanted to eat. Mittie jumped up, saying she was starving, and disappeared into the crush of people.

Claudia went to watch the pie eating, so Nell asked Iris about college and what she wanted to study.

"Fundamentals at first. Maybe go for a degree in education. Or music. How about you? You've not said much about your trip to England. What was it like going back?"

"Highs and lows. We were frightfully busy in London. Seeing my grandmother was probably the best part."

"What about that friend of yours you used to write? Did you see him?"

Her stomach lurched. "Quentin? I did see him. He's en-en-engaged."

Iris patted her hand. "Oh no. I always thought you had a soft spot for him."

Emotion bubbled up. "You know, I did. And I guess I still do, even though I know I should be happy for him." Her lips trembled as Iris kept patting her hand and changed the subject.

"You know everyone in Louisville is just as proud as punch of you. Getting to go to England and all. You've done us up proud."

Nell blinked to keep the tears at bay, but then Mittie's laugh rose above the hum of voices. Iris pointed at her twin in the middle of a group of people, her long hair floating in the ocean breeze. "Looks like someone is having a good time."

Iris said, "You know, I am getting hungry. Let's see what they're serving."

They loaded their plates with chunks of fresh lobster, skewered pork, and several kinds of salad and were looking for a new place to sit when Mrs. Benchley called to them.

"Oh, girls, Claudia said you were here." She glided across the lawn and gave Nell a peck on the cheek. "I saw your other cousin earlier, talking with Daphne and her pals. So glad she's jumped right in." She leaned in close. "I've been telling some of the women about the stunning creations you're making for the girls and me for next Saturday for the big show."

Nell smiled and groaned inwardly. They still weren't finished, but they would be. "They're turning out lovely. Would next Thursday work for you to pick them up?"

"That will be perfect."

Nell thanked her for inviting them and told her how much she liked her house. "Is your husband here? I'd like to thank him for his part in all of this."

"Porter? Heavens, no. The man has an aversion to fresh air and mosquitoes and the country in general. You girls have fun." She tottered off to greet someone at the next table.

While they ate, Iris looked around and asked if Nell had seen Mittie.

"Not in a while."

"Drama always follows her around. I hope she's all right."

"I'm sure she is."

Steve came back and sat with them, playing twenty questions it seemed. And when the sun dipped in the west, casting golden shadows across the lawn, a few people started dancing. Iris accepted Steve's invitation to have a whirl at the fox-trot, and one of his friends asked Nell to dance. Nell laughed and tried to keep her eyes on her dance partner, but she kept thinking about Mittie and found herself looking through the crowd with every turn.

Nell nearly bumped into Iris who said she, too, was getting worried. They went in opposite directions to look for Mittie. Nell found Claudia and asked if she'd seen her.

"Probably over there with Daphne and her friends. Last I looked, they were playing charades and howling over how clever they were."

Nell found Daphne who said, "Hey, come on, join in the fun."

"I'd love to, just not now, I'm looking for my cousin. Tall. Long, dark hair. She's wearing an emerald dress and several long strands of pearls. Southern accent."

"Darling girl. She was here a while ago. Talking to some guy I didn't know, but I thought they were old friends the way they were chatting. Sure you don't want to play charades?"

Nell shook her head and hurried off, the food in her stomach now churning. It would be dark in another hour or so and impossible to find her. They should have stuck together. She searched for Iris, and as she looked across the lawn, a roar from overhead filled her ears. Everyone stopped and looked up as an airplane approached, flying low.

Shouts went up, "Look at that! Holy smithereens, that's one way to arrive at a party."

It flew so low it looked as if Nell could reach up and touch the wings, and like everyone else, she watched until it passed before she and Iris went back to looking for Mittie.

The roar came again, as if the plane had circled back, even lower this time, and one of the goggled people, with hair streaming behind a leather helmet, waved furiously from the open cockpit. Nell's heart went to her throat.

Mittie.

CHAPTER 31

"Mittie Humphreys, what were you doing? Do you know how dangerous that was? Of all the stupid things." Nell's voice shook, but her body shook even harder at the relief of seeing Mittie loping across Mrs. Benchley's lawn. It had been more than an hour since the airplane flew over, and both Iris and Nell were convinced it had dived into Long Island Sound and sunk. Then there Mittie was, her hair a rumpled mess, her face beaming in the light from the Japanese lanterns strung across the yard.

Iris glared at her twin sister. "How could you?"

"How could I not? I mean, goodness gracious, my heart is still dancing at the thrill. It's the most freeing thing you can ever imagine." She held out her arms like she was floating.

"It's the most outrageous thing I can imagine. Mother and Daddy will be livid when then find out, and you can be sure I'll tell them."

"You don't have to. I'm telling them myself. And I'm going to fly again. Again and again."

Iris yanked Mittie's arm. "We're leaving. I'm just glad the airplane didn't crash into the party."

The rest of the night and all the next day, Mittie talked of nothing else. The freedom she felt and how she gave her phone number to the guy who'd convinced her to soar with him. Ames Dewberry.

"Sometimes you just have to take a chance." Mittie's dreamy-eyed look sent rivulets of apprehension through Nell. Those were the very words Nell had used to convince her mother that coming to New York was a good idea. That if she didn't take a chance, she'd never know if she could become a successful hat designer. With the show in less than a week, success still dangled like a hypnotist's bauble. Swinging. Swinging. Back and forth. Success on one side, losing everything she'd worked for on the other.

❦

When Oscar strolled through the conference room on Monday, Nell asked if he was feeling better.

"Whatever gave you the impression I was ill?"

"Just something Mrs. Benchley said, the reason you couldn't go to her party last Saturday."

He snorted. "That. Matter of fact, I've recovered quite nicely. With this show breathing down our necks, I had to work out a few details."

Nell braced herself, determined to let his comment roll past her. "If you needed help, you should have asked."

"What, and disturb your little reunion with your Kentucky kin? Quite the show one of them put on from the sounds of it."

"They did have fun trying on the hats downstairs. I hope none of the customers complained."

"Don't be daft. I'm talking about the exhibition at Mavis's party. Going off on an airplane ride with a stranger."

Nell wondered how he had found out so fast, but told him not to worry, they would be on their way back to Kentucky tomorrow.

"Going out again tonight?"

"No, I told them my place was here. Working."

It was nearly midnight when Nell got home from work. She had finished the hats for Mrs. Benchley and practiced her presentation. It was better, but not perfect. She was so tired she thought of crawling into bed with her clothes on, but changed into her nightgown anyway. When she reached to click off the lamp she saw the letter propped against it.

Quentin. She scrambled out of bed and got the letter opener from her desk, then slid under the covers and slipped the letter from the envelope. Two pages.

Dearest Nell,

Thank you for letting me know you arrived home safely, and please forgive me for not writing sooner. I've wrestled with how to tell you my news. I had, in fact, hoped to discuss it with you when you came to London. The time never seemed right, especially when I saw the glow of happiness that graced your beautiful face.

Nell held her breath, hoping…praying…that he was going to tell her he was no longer engaged, that he'd made a mistake. She held her breath and continued reading.

What I mean to say is that I wasn't completely honest with you. While I do have an interesting job and seem to have hit it off with my colleagues, I've known for quite some time that banking is not the profession the Lord has for me. I've ignored the signs for entirely too long, but am coming to grips with the reality that unless you walk in the light of his will you will never find true happiness.

When I asked if you were happy, I saw in your eyes and heard in your voice the utter satisfaction you have in your work as a milliner. You are destined for great things, and nothing gives me more peace

than knowing you are doing what you were meant to do. It also gave
me courage to face my own longings.

My plans are still uncertain at the moment, but I feel God has
called me into the ministry. I guess the apple never falls far from the
tree, and my parents have received the news joyfully. Now that I've
settled it in my heart, there is a quietness in my spirit. I will wait
upon God's leading for the next steps.

As I mentioned earlier, this was one of the things I wanted to talk
to you about when you were in London. We've always shared each
other's hearts, and even though we've taken separate paths, I still trea-
sure your friendship.

Best wishes on the upcoming show. I'm sure your creations will be
the best ever. And that's what I wish for you. The best life has to offer.

With kindest regard,
Quentin

Nell stared at the pages, her limbs numb, her heart as well. Like a
puzzle, a few of the pieces fell into place. Quentin's reluctance to
talk about his job, his lack of enthusiasm over it. He'd always had a
tender spirit toward others, those he somehow sensed were in need
of a gentle touch. A friend to lean on.

Even on that day when he'd rescued her from Simone and
the boys in the confirmation class, Quentin had a pastoral quality.
Strength of character. Kind, uncondemning words. And with others, too. Taking Simone to the theater as a favor. His faithfulness to
visit her grandmother.

She read the letter again. Then yet again, all hope of sleep
for the night gone. Quentin had seen in her eyes and heard in
her voice what he regarded as happiness. Had she been honest
with him? With herself? All she'd thought of in London was
how pushing herself to succeed and bowing to Oscar's demands

would gain her recognition as a top designer. Would that bring her happiness?

The answer pierced her.

Making women look and feel beautiful did make her happy. Learning new techniques and perfecting her craft still thrilled her. Catching a whiff of inspiration made her float for days. Did she view all of those things only as a means to the end—making a name for herself?

She switched off the lamp and watched the shadows of the night. The curtains riffled through her open window, shifting the faint light from outside. A familiar knot filled her chest, her arms prickly. Not all of the puzzle pieces fit. Some were missing.

Did her need for success overshadow the true desires of her heart and the life God had designed for her?

A thought niggled. In her selfishness, Nell hadn't seen her mother's need to start a new life in the States. When Oscar Fields appeared that day at the derby, he'd been utterly charming, luring Nell away, feeding her insatiable appetite to make something of herself. A bitter taste came in her mouth.

While she chased a flimsy dream, she hadn't even given Quentin a chance to open up to her. How could he be frank with her when she babbled on about herself and the time constraints Oscar put on her. *Oscar.* He'd played her like a kite string, giving her a taste of success, then reeling her back in. A spidery feeling crawled up her arms. He'd even tried to lure her grandmother into his web. Hazel had a point—Oscar had a decent salon, but how many others had paid a price? She owed Quentin the same honesty he'd given her.

She went to her desk and retrieved her stationery supplies, took them back to her bed, and began writing. She told Quentin about Mr. Fields, his unkept promises from the very beginning, his controlling nature, which only increased her own lust to succeed. Her fingers cramped from clenching the fountain pen, her breaths labored. She thought of ripping the letter to shreds, but continued writing.

You will, no doubt, think I've become a candidate for an asylum, and it's something I've wondered myself. The one true thing I know is that I do love making hats, seeing the glow on women's faces when they look in the mirror. I've considered making a change in my career, but like you, I must wait for God's direction. I thank you for reminding me of that truth.

May you and Colleen find much happiness on the road ahead. The invitation for a tour of New York still stands should you decide to honeymoon here. I will pray for you and ask the same of you. You've always been a pillar for me, and I still consider you the truest friend I've ever had.

Your friend,
Nell

She read over what she'd written, put it in an envelope, and sealed it. She sighed as the first light of the dawn peeked through the window.

CHAPTER 32

On Thursday, Mrs. Benchley called and said she wouldn't be in until right before closing time, so Nell spent the bulk of the day tidying the conference room and running supplies back to the notions room. At half past four, she went to the showroom to wait on Mrs. Benchley.

She bustled in at straight-up five and leaned on the counter to catch her breath. "Oh, sweetie, what a day this has been. I have been running myself ragged all over the city. Do you have the hats?"

"In the consultation room. I thought you might want to try yours on in private."

"I'm sure it's fine. Just leave them on the counter, and I'll pick them up after I deliver this envelope to Oscar. Soren asked me to drop it off. Poor man's prancing around like his pants are on fire, fretting about the show."

"I know what you mean. I saw him yesterday. If you'd like, I can take the envelope to Oscar, and you can be on your way."

"Sweet of you to offer, but I'll take it up. Oscar is expecting me."

Nell joined her in the lift, and when they got to Oscar's office, Harjo waved them in, saying he was just leaving.

Oscar greeted Mrs. Benchley with a kiss on the cheek. "Ah, here you are. Soren said you have the seating arrangements."

Mrs. Benchley handed them over as Nell backed toward the door. "If you don't need me, I'll be going."

Oscar said, "Splendid. And you can knock off early tonight. You deserve a little time to relax after the month we've had."

"Thank you. I appreciate that. I'll see you on Saturday, Mrs. Benchley."

Nell slipped into the conference room and gathered up another armload of ribbon and lace for the notions' bins, and after putting them away, she stopped off at the second-floor workroom to return a pair of Hazel's scissors and thank her for her hard work.

Hazel said, "At least someone appreciates us."

"I'm sure Mr. Fields does, too. Men just have a different way of showing it. I believe there will be a rise in your paychecks tomorrow."

"Certainly do hope so. Have a seat while I finish up here."

Nell sat and chatted with Hazel, marveling at the skill with which her fingers worked the hat rim, caressing it into shape until at last she was satisfied. "Another one done. Six to go."

"Not tonight, I hope."

"No, just calculating out loud. Here, I'll get my pocketbook and walk out with you if you're leaving."

"I've still got a couple of loose ends to tie up. See you tomorrow."

The lights were off in the hall outside the conference room, no sounds of Oscar and Mrs. Benchley behind her boss's office door. Nell made a final inspection of the hats for the show, praying she hadn't forgotten anything. She would box them up in the morning for the courier to deliver to Soren. She sighed and looked around. Done. She'd done it. With a lot of good help. Now if she could just get through the speaking part at the show, she would be at peace and decide where to go from here. And this time, she would seek God's counsel and wait on him.

She picked up a counter mannequin to return to the consulting salon on her way out. There was a certain calm she'd learned to enjoy in the evenings when she worked late, and she walked softly, without hurrying. Still, her heels echoed like the tick of a clock. She set the mannequin on the floor and inserted the key for the consulting salon, reached around the corner, and flipped the light switch. Then bobbling the head form she stepped into the room.

Her mouth gaped open, her heart instantly in her throat. The mannequin tumbled from her arms as Oscar Fields bolted from the davenport, his shirttail flapping against his bare legs.

Reclining in an equal state of undress on the brocade was Mavis Benchley.

Nell froze as heat rushed to her cheeks. Without a word, she turned, pulled the door shut with force, and fled the salon.

❦

Why can't I stop shaking?

She tried to bleat out the question, but it was no use, and as Jeanette and Calvin hovered over her, she explained again, in halting words, what had happened.

Jeanette's face glowered. "I'm not surprised at anything that man does."

Nell raised her hand. "Yes, but…what Oscar…does is none of my b-business."

"It could have been you."

"Not without my consent, and I would n-n-never." A harsh laugh screeched against her vocal cords. "And Mavis Benchley wasn't being f-f-forced." It infuriated her that she couldn't spit out the words. Mrs. Benchley? She was Nell's friend. Her mentor. Oscar's lover?

Calvin crossed his arms and sat on the settee, his eyes looking about the flat. He ran his tongue over his lips as if he wanted to say something, then thought better of it and fiddled with the fringe on the throw pillow.

Jeanette sidled up to him. "What's your opinion of this?"

"Hey, I'm not going to get caught in the crosshairs of this. I work for the competition and am sorry I have knowledge of anything."

Nell scowled. "I'm sorry. I shouldn't have dragged you into it. What I do know is that it took courage for you to leave Oscar's salon. A courage I wish I had."

Jeanette ran her finger along Calvin's forearm, but she looked at Nell, her eyes drooping at the corners. "So, what will you do?"

"The only thing I can do—pretend I didn't see anything. Go through with the show. I owe that much at least to Soren."

Jeanette cringed. "That will be awkward. Gee, I wish I didn't have that recital after all on Saturday. There's no telling what kind of fireworks I'm going to miss at the runway show."

Nell assured her she'd be missing nothing. "Except watching me stumble over the script." Her hand went to her mouth. "That was supposed to be a surprise, Calvin. But now, with all this tension in the air, it's likely to be a mess."

At least having Jeanette and Calvin to lean on had helped Nell through the shock. Having a double helping of Angelo's gnocchi later that evening helped even more. But when she rolled over to go to sleep that night, all she could think of was facing Oscar and Mrs. Benchley.

⚜

The courier loaded the last hatboxes onto his dolly and presented the invoice to Nell to sign. Oscar, who'd been holed up in his office all morning, stepped up and said, "I'll sign for them."

Silence hung in the air when the courier left—Nell on one side of the conference table, Oscar on the other.

Nell spoke first. "I've c-cleared everything out, so if it's all r-right with you, I...I'll go back to the studio."

"Not so fast." In a half-dozen strides, Oscar was next to her. "About yesterday..."

"Wh-what about yesterday?"

"Don't play dumb with me. You know what I'm talking about." His eyebrows bristled over smoldering eyes. "It's not what you think."

Nell took a step back, a wedge in her throat that allowed only a whisper. "I know what I saw."

His jaw tensed, his muscled hand grabbing her wrist. "You saw nothing. You hear me? Nothing."

Nell gasped, the whiskey on his breath like plumes of fire, the grasp on her wrist a steel trap. "Stop. You're hurting me."

"I'll do more than hurt you if you breathe a word to anyone. Anyone. You hear me?"

Nell massaged her wrist, remembering how the vile man at the Emerald Jungle had threatened her and the man at the bus stop had grabbed her, innocently trying to help her. *Grandfather.*

Nell stumbled back and collapsed into the nearest chair, her insides a mass of jelly. Oscar was nothing more than a shop owner's version of her grandfather. Pushing to get whatever he wanted. Berating anyone who stood in his path. Shaking an iron fist at the upstart who dared disagree with him. The only difference was that Oscar hadn't committed murder. Yet.

She lifted her chin. "I heard you. And I know what I saw."

"There's an explanation, if you can bring yourself out of that stupor you seem to be in and hear it."

"I'm listening."

His voice was distant, and it took every ounce of concentration she could muster to follow what he was saying. "As you know, our fortunes have been less than stellar for quite some time, and Mavis is a woman of considerable means in her own right."

"Mavis?"

"Yes, Mavis. Mavis Benchley. Are you sure you're all right?"

"Mrs. Benchley must be ten years older than you."

"Not quite. And age has nothing to do with attraction and desires. I won't disgrace Mavis by divulging details of her personal life, but you may rest assured our arrangement is mutually beneficial."

He had Nell's full attention, but she hadn't quite connected what Mrs. Benchley had to do with anything. "Arrangement?"

"I provide her with something she's in need of, and she's been most supportive of the salon. A quite suitable collaboration, which ensures not only the fiscal soundness of Oscar Fields Millinery, but also ensures your future here, my dear."

Her future here? He had to be joking if he thought she meant to stay under the current circumstances.

Strength and honor are her clothing.

Oscar stared at her, expecting her to grovel. Or cower.

"I wasn't aware that bedding preferred customers was a business tactic."

"You know nothing of business, and obviously know even less about discretion. May I count on your silence?"

"The only thing I can offer you now is that I will take it under consideration."

An hour later, Nell had collected her wits and called Dr. Underwood. "I'd like to make an appointment for this afternoon, please."

The receptionist told her the first available appointment was next Thursday.

"Please tell Dr. Underwood it's for Nell Marchwold. An emergency."

CHAPTER 33

Soren Michaels, his hair sleek with pomade, flitted from model to model, giving last-minute instructions and exclaiming how wonderful they all looked. He smelled of shower soap and tooth powder when he draped an arm around Nell's shoulders and asked if she was ready.

"As ready as I'll ever be." She held up the script she knew by heart.

A murmur from the back of the dressing room drew her attention to a man in a tuxedo with a carrot-colored cummerbund and matching bow tie. Nell stepped away from Soren and greeted Dr. Underwood.

She smiled at Mrs. Benchley, whose stern look accented the crow's-feet that had deepened in the two days since Nell had last seen her.

"Mrs. Benchley, have you met Dr. Underwood? He's the speech therapist you so kindly recommended." Something akin to alarm flashed in Mrs. Benchley's eyes. "He's done me a world of good, getting to the root of my stammering."

"One of my most difficult cases, I must admit." Dr. Underwood winked at her. "But such remarkable progress." He extended a hand to Nell. "I only wanted to let you know I was here. I've a feeling you're going to be just fine."

Nell thought she would be, too. Her appointment with him had given her perspective and a bit of closure. Dr. Underwood had agreed that allowing herself to be intimidated by Oscar was likely a result of her encounter with her murderous grandfather and the later taunting from classmates who made her feel helpless. He also agreed that going forward with the public speaking would be a good test of the inner strength she'd gained in the process. His arrival and show of support buoyed her spirit.

Oscar came through the stage door as Dr. Underwood left. He sauntered up to Nell. "Who was that man? He was too well dressed to be a reporter."

Nell braced herself. "My speech therapist. The one to whom I confide my secrets."

Oscar leaned in and brushed his lips across her cheek and whispered, "Not all of them, I trust."

Nell felt a perverse pleasure when she said, "Only the ones that are true. Say, doesn't Mrs. Benchley look lovely? Soren certainly outdid himself on her gown." It was weak, she knew, but for once it felt good not to be the one squirming. Oscar didn't know she'd kept Mrs. Benchley's name out of her confession to Dr. Underwood, but it seemed irrelevant. Irrelevant because Nell had finally come to the decision that she would fulfill her obligation to Oscar and Soren and then turn in her resignation on Monday morning.

Strength and honor. It was a cloak she wanted. How and where she would find it, she didn't know. She only knew it was honorable to keep her word in doing the show, but it would be dishonorable to continue her association with a firm whose owner she'd didn't respect.

Soren shushed everyone and announced, "Places. It's time to begin."

Oscar pulled Nell aside. "You look ravishing, dear. This is going to be a night to remember, one we can look back on and mark as the turning point for the salon. And for us." He kissed her on the cheek, his lips curved into a smile that made Nell's stomach curdle.

A hush fell across the crowd when Mrs. Benchley stepped to the microphone and gave the welcome. She fit the part, but Nell saw her in a new light—a woman who had money and a place in society, but also one with a hole in her life that none of those things could fill. Perhaps she, too, was chasing an illusion by thinking a younger man could replace the missing pieces.

"And now, ladies and gentlemen, please welcome Soren Michaels and Nell Marchwold for an evening of Golden Days and Velvet Nights."

Nell smoothed the butterscotch brocade of her gown and took a deep breath, waiting in the shadows for the spotlight to fall on her. She chewed her bottom lip and whispered a prayer as the mannequin stopped center stage and turned, the rich timbre of Soren's voice filling the room.

"Completing the ensemble is a hat from Nell Marchwold."

On cue, Nell stepped to the microphone on her side of the stage and swallowed the knot in her throat. She focused on an imaginary spot at the back of the ballroom, then spoke in a clear, calm voice. "The silk cloche with an overlay of gold metallic lace features a flared brim and is accented with a black velvet ribbon." *Steady. Inhale.* "Black bugle beads and rhinestones echo the gown's bodice."

The applause was enthusiastic, but not thunderous like Nell's heartbeat. She wanted to throw her own velvet cloche in the air in the small victory of getting through the first segment. Only fifteen more to go.

By the halfway point, Nell's T-strapped shoes with gold spooled heels cramped her toes, and she longed for a sip of water. She ran her tongue over her teeth to moisten them and waited for her turn again. Her eyes barely had time to adjust to the change from standing in darkness to the sudden glare of the spotlight, but near the end of the show, she chanced a look into the audience. In a table in the center of the room, Calvin sat with a group of men she didn't know. Murdoch's designers, she assumed. His eyes met hers, and she thought she caught a wink. Then the spotlight fell on her again.

"Red sequins cover the puff cloche that hugs the head, but you will hardly notice you're wearing it because of the breathable cotton base and cushioned comfort band that secures it. An added accent is a matching rosette made of tulle with a diamond cluster pin in the center."

The mannequin tilted her head and raised elegant fingers to demonstrate. This time the applause was deafening as the girl made a final flirty walk down the center aisle and struck a pose with one heel lifted behind her, the fringe at the hem shimmering.

A trio of formal evening gowns completed the show, and then Soren waved her over to his side and invited Oscar to join them.

"It is with distinct pleasure that I give you the fall collection from the Soren Michaels and Oscar Fields salons. Oscar, would you please say a few words?"

Oscar draped his arm around Nell's shoulders and drew her with him to the microphone. "It is indeed my pleasure and honor to present you with this fine assortment of designs. I'm humbled to work with some of the most talented people in New York City…in all the world, if you must know."

He paused as applause rippled across the crowd. He pulled Nell closer and gave her a kiss on the cheek, but then spoke toward the audience. "What a fine night this is, a night of celebration, and one that I've anticipated with glee. I've saved an extraordinarily special announcement for this very moment."

Murmurs rippled like an undertow, Nell's attention now riveted on Oscar.

With a dramatic pause, Oscar continued. "Ladies and gentlemen, tonight is the unveiling of a new label for Oscar Fields Millinery— my protégé and colleague Nell Marchwold's designs will now be known as the Nellie March collection."

Nell heard a gasp and realized it was from her own throat. *What nerve.* Applause and powder flashes from cameras deafened and blinded her. She wanted to crawl out of her skin and disappear. Oscar's gall in making such a grandstand announcement was matched only by his stupidity in believing that Nell's loyalty and silence were for sale. That the Nellie March label would erase the memory of him and Mrs. Benchley and all the times she'd been intimidated by him.

His arm around her waist pulled her closer to him, so close she could feel the dampness of his underarms. She rose on tiptoes and whispered to him, "I quit."

He blinked and smiled, his face to the audience, his grip around her tighter as he made a bowing gesture and then exited into the wings, Soren behind them.

"You rascal, Fields, keeping that announcement under wraps, ending the show on such a feverish pitch." Soren opened his arms to Nell. "Congratulations, my dear. This honor couldn't happen to a more deserving nor lovelier lady."

Nell swallowed the bile that rose in her throat. "You are too kind, Soren." She gave a sidelong glance toward Oscar, their eyes locked in a war of wills, but she didn't budge. She couldn't now. Finally, she broke the gaze and turned to Soren.

"I had intended to make my own announcement on Monday, but Mr. Fields has given me no choice but to go ahead and tell you the news now. I no longer work for Oscar Fields Millinery. Oscar's ploy was a desperate attempt to exert his control over me...I'll let him fill you in on the details. Whether the Nellie March label appears on this evening's designs or not is up to the two of you."

Oscar cocked his head. "I do believe you've come down with a fever, sweetheart. You're talking nonsense when I thought you would be thrilled, and I wanted to surprise you. Think of your future...our future."

"I have. Good-bye, Mr. Fields. Good-bye, Soren." She turned to go, but Oscar grabbed her arm and spun her around.

"Don't you dare walk away. Leaving me now would sabotage your career."

She planted the heel of her pump on top of his shoe and put all of her weight on it, grinding the heel as she did so. He let go, and she hurried through the exit, found the stairs and raced down them, ran across the lobby and into the night air.

Tears blurred her vision as she ran, desperate to put distance between herself and the Stottlemeir Club.

Another two blocks and she slowed down. She should get a cab and go home. How? Her evening bag with her coin purse was backstage at the Stottlemeir ballroom. She had no money, not even a nickel for a phone call nor the fare for a motor bus should she stumble upon a stop.

Lights flickered outside of unfamiliar eateries as she passed by streets she'd never heard of. Blisters burned her feet from beautiful, ill-fitting shoes. She took off the shoes and tossed them into a rubbish bin and kept walking in what she hoped was the right direction. The more blocks that passed, the lighter she felt, and after a while, she saw the lights of Times Square.

At an intersection, she spotted a bench for waiting motor bus passengers and welcomed the rough wooden seat. She rubbed the fresh blisters on the bottoms of her feet and those already on her toes through her shredded silk stockings and leaned back, too tired to think, but knowing if she dozed off, something terrible could happen. A mugger or ruffian might take advantage of a nicely dressed woman alone. She almost laughed. Her dress had mud staining the hem where she'd steeped in a puddle, and she was barefoot. She was the one who looked like a ruffian.

She removed her hat, a velvet cloche with a satin lining, and held it to her face and sobbed.

"Hey, lady, off the streets." A policeman twirled his nightstick in front of her face.

Nell blinked, the haze of city lights reflecting back from the inky sky. "Excuse me, sir. Could you tell me where I am?"

"Dames like you generally know the territory where you conduct your business. Come on. Get up." He thumbed over his shoulder. "And out. Off my beat, or I'll have to take you in to the station."

"Would they give me a phone call?"

"Don't get fresh with me. Whazza matter? Your fancy man leave you without any money."

Nell straightened, fresh energy surging through her. "I'm not what you think. I've just had an unfortunate night and have lost my handbag. I need to find a phone box to call someone to fetch me. And if it's not too much trouble, I'd like to know the address of where I am."

"You sure don't talk like the usual dolls around here. Gotcha some kind of accent. Takes all kinds, I guess."

The officer gave her a second look. "Finer dress than most of them, too."

An idea formed. "Are you married, sir?"

"For eighteen years and three months."

"I bet your wife would love a new hat. Maybe for her birthday or something special?" She held out her velvet cloche, her fingers caressing the silk flower in the dim night. "One of my creations. You can have it if you'll give me the money for a phone call."

"You any idea what you get for bribery? Thirty-day vacation downtown in the city jail."

"Not a bribe. I'm selling it to you. How about one dollar?"

He dug in his pocket and produced three quarters. "All I got, ma'am."

"It's a deal. And don't forget to mention that it's an original."

He took the hat and stuffed it inside his shirt, then jerked his head to the right. "Get on your way, lady."

She hurried off. Forget the address. She would read the next street sign, look for a payphone station, and when she got hold of Jeanette, she would have her come in a cab and take her home where she could curl up and sleep for a solid week.

Jeanette answered on the first ring. "Nell! Where are you? Calvin called and is worried sick. Said you disappeared and he's afraid something's happened to you. Now Oscar's on the street below. He banged on the door and shouted while I was talking to Calvin, and Calvin told me not to answer."

"It's a long story. Can you call a cab and come get me?"

"I don't think that's a good idea with Oscar down there. Did he do something to you?"

"Not yet." Nell gave her the street name.

"I'll send Calvin."

Half an hour passed before Calvin arrived and gave the taxi driver the address of his parents' house, telling her Jeanette didn't think it safe to come home. "What in the world happened? Everyone was thrilled at Oscar's announcement."

"It was a desperate move on Oscar's part."

"I wondered after the incident with Mrs. Benchley."

"It's not even that. I couldn't tolerate his empty promises and intimidation any longer so I resigned. I finally came to my senses and drummed up some of your courage." She leaned forward and told the cabbie she'd changed her mind about where to take them and gave the address for her flat.

Calvin scowled. "Jeanette says he's in a foul mood, keeps banging on her door."

"I'd just as soon face him tonight as tomorrow. Besides, I need your moral support."

"You've always had that."

Nell knew she looked awful when they stepped from the cab. It was to her advantage, she thought, that she look defeated and vulnerable when facing Oscar. He didn't look much better sitting on the steps of Sal's Diner.

Mr. Fields's eyes narrowed when he saw her, then looked at Calvin. "Guess I should have expected as much. Two no-counts together." He reached for Nell, but Calvin stepped between them.

"You'll not lay a hand on her."

Oscar sneered. "Stay out of this. I've only had a misunderstanding with Nell. Nothing that concerns you."

Nell glared at him. "I meant what I said. It's over, Oscar. I no longer work for you. And unless I receive every penny you owe me, including a bonus for the Soren Michaels's show, plus an additional month's salary, I will go to the newspaper and tell them you assaulted me in your office."

"I didn't assault you."

"I have a bruise on my arm to show that you did."

"You wouldn't dare."

"Try me."

"They will never believe you over me. I have a stellar reputation. You're a nobody."

"I guess it's a risk you have to take. Think about it, Oscar. Once it's in print, people remember what they first read."

He lunged forward, his face inches from hers. "I will not stand by and let you ruin me."

"You've ruined yourself."

"You'll never get a recommendation from me, and in case you've forgotten, I own every one of your designs."

"I've not forgotten a thing. You've reminded me often enough.

And your recommendation wouldn't be worth the paper it's written on. I am sorry for you. Sorry that—"

"Save it for the funny papers." He reached for her, but Felice stepped out of the diner door at that moment.

"Nell? Are you in trouble?" Over her shoulder she called back into the diner for Angelo to call the police.

Nell said the police wouldn't be necessary, that Oscar was leaving. The cab still stood at the curb and Nell motioned for the driver. "I believe someone needs a ride."

She hooked her hand in the crook of Calvin's arm and ducked into the diner with Felice, where Jeanette sat at a table waiting.

"So what will you do now?" Jeanette asked.

"I'm going home. Home to Kentucky for now. I need time with my family. Then I'm going to pray for God's leading for the next step. Something I should have done a long time ago."

Felice said, "You're not going anywhere without a party. Tomorrow night, is that okay? We will have big time to eat and laugh and cry." She nodded to Jeanette. "You invite the people. Angelo will make the gnocchi."

No one argued with Felice Salvatore.

CHAPTER 34

On Monday, Nell called Mrs. Benchley and asked to see her. She'd heard Oscar's version of their relationship and was curious to hear Mrs. Benchley's.

They met in the dining room of the Algonquin Hotel for a late afternoon tea, and when Mrs. Benchley arrived, she kissed Nell on the cheek as she so often did.

Nell thanked her for coming as they took their places.

Mrs. Benchley let out a long sigh and pulled off her gloves. "You must think I'm horrid. And I can't blame you."

"We all make bad judgments, and it's probably none of my affair to ask about your arrangement with Oscar."

"Is that what he called it? An arrangement?" A gray pallor marked the older woman's sagging cheeks.

Nell nodded, not wanting to push, but after they'd ordered finger sandwiches and tea, Mrs. Benchley folded her hands and spoke. "When I was your age, I never dreamed I would do such a thing, lower myself in such a manner. It all started innocently enough. A friend of my mother's told me her son was employed at a millinery salon and I might find something suitable for a fancy dress party my husband Porter and I were invited to."

"Oscar's mother knew your mother?"

"No, Harjo Pritchard's mother. She was quite anxious that her son do well in the new venture they had financed for him."

"As a secretary?"

"That, too. The Pritchards were quite flush with money and heard about the salon, that it was near financial ruin but in a prime location. Oscar had just inherited the failing business from his father and jumped at the chance to have a partner who could get him and the shop back on its feet. Harjo is half owner—a silent partner, at least in the public eye. Being Oscar's secretary allows him ready access to everything Oscar says and does. I didn't know all of this, of course, until later. By then, I'd visited the shop and found Oscar to be quite charming and accommodating. I made several purchases, and one day, Oscar asked if I would go to lunch.

"Porter was gone from home frequently, and when he was home, he spent all his time working and building his empire. Oscar became my diversion. Like I said, it wasn't something I ever set out to do. Then one day, he confided in me that Harjo was putting pressure on him to marry Anna. She was their best designer and was looking for work elsewhere. All he's ever wanted was to preserve his dad's good name, and they needed Anna's talent to keep the company afloat."

Nell let out a long breath, not knowing whether Mrs. Benchley was trying to make Oscar look good to excuse her own actions or if she was telling the truth.

"Did he love Anna?"

"On some level I think he did. I tried to back away from the situation and let him find happiness with her—she was his wife and deserved that much at least—but he came to me one day and asked for a loan, said his income had been cut during the wartime slump and he couldn't pay the rent on his and Anna's flat. Foolishly I gave it to him, and it set a precedent that I regret. Then Anna died, and, well..."

Nell's skin prickled with disgust for Oscar while her chest ached with pity for him at the same time. A lot of what Mrs. Benchley said made sense. How Harjo kept tabs on her, following her in London and then when she and Oscar returned. But Oscar's actions were inexcusable, and Nell couldn't justify either his or Mrs. Benchley's behavior.

One question burned within, though. "What about your daughters? Your husband? Are they aware?"

"I've not told them, although I'm sure they have suspicions. And the girls will have questions about why you left. They love your hats and will miss you terribly. Claudia blossomed under your loving touch, you know."

"She was a beauty all the time. I just helped her find it."

"I'm grateful for that, and I'm toying with telling them about Oscar, about our arrangement—" She took a sip of tea and cocked her head. "Is that really what he called it?"

"It sounds better than affair."

Her voice caught. "Neither conjures up an image I'm proud of."

"Do you have feelings for him?"

Mrs. Benchley's eyes widened. "Not in a romantic sense, no. While he's young and dapper, he's also cunning and has made idle remarks on occasion of how he would sully my name if I didn't help him out." She sighed. "It's hard to explain—with Oscar, I always felt special..."

Images of the gowns and beautiful coats Oscar had given Nell drifted in and out. His compliments and attempts at chivalry. Yes, Oscar could be quite agreeable if it suited him. "I'm in no position to judge you, but after my own experience and hearing you today, it seems that Oscar used you for his own vanity and personal gain. Perhaps not in the same way he did Anna and me, but without regard for your personal worth."

Mrs. Benchley blotted the corner of her eye, her words thick when she said, "You've no idea how my stomach turns with knowledge that I've traded fleeting moments of feeling lovely in Oscar's arms with the glaring truth of my own wanton actions."

"But you are lovely—one of the most beautiful women I know. And no matter what you think, it's never too late for a fresh start."

Mrs. Benchley worked the linen napkin in her fingers, her eyes downcast. When she looked up, the merest of smiles graced her lips. "I can only try."

"I'll pray for you. And thank you for being frank with me. You've been a wonderful friend."

"As have you." Mrs. Benchley sat up taller, her face not so sallow. "Do you need a recommendation for another position?"

Nell shook her head. "I'm going home to Kentucky." *Home.* It had a warm biscuits and honey sound.

"I've always wanted to go to the Kentucky Derby."

"You're welcome anytime. The derby's always the first Saturday in May."

They walked out of the Algonquin and went their separate ways, each of them with an uncertain future, but the air cleared between them. Nell's steps were light as she raced toward the cheerful clang of the trolley.

CHAPTER 35

Nell and her mother strolled arm in arm through the rose garden, Mama stooping now and then to pick off a blighted leaf. They talked as they'd done every day for two weeks about what had happened at Greystone Hall, the complicated joys and regrets with Oscar Fields, and Mrs. Benchley's confession. At times it all felt unreal, as if the three years in New York were one long dream with the occasional nightmare. Her decision to move permanently back to Kentucky was the right one, Nell was certain of that. And she was even able to finally tell her mother about Quentin, the wonder of seeing him again in London, the knife that sliced through her when she'd found out he was engaged.

"You never forget your first love. Your father was mine, and even though I love Granville with all my being, Richard Marchwold will never be more than a moment's thought away."

"I know how you grieved."

"The Lord blessed me with Caroline. She's so much like your father. Her laugh. Her insatiable love of the water. She's already drawing pictures of sailboats and loves to go down to the Ohio River and watched them raise the bridge when the boats pass under."

"I know. I heard her pestering Granville last night, asking him to take her."

"You'll be blessed with love one day, my dear. Trust me."

Nell didn't answer. She wasn't sure she could ever give her heart fully to someone and risk breaking it again. She was listening for God's voice, though, and willing now to heed his answer.

When they stopped and rested on a garden bench, Mama said, "Do you miss it?"

"New York? Sometimes. I miss Jeanette and regret that I didn't get to say good-bye to Greta. I keep hoping her vaudeville show will stop in Louisville. And I miss Felice. In fact, I've developed the most horrid craving for Angelo's gnocchi."

"That's not what I meant."

Nell knew what her mother meant. The hats. She sighed.

"I've always had my roses, wherever I went. It's what I dream of at night and what has pulled me through many dark days. Some things we're meant to do."

"I've had an idea. Mittie's coming by in her new roadster, and we're going to see if the room over on Bardstown where I made the derby hats is still available. I'll start small, take it slow, and see what happens."

"I know the man who owns the building. You want me to give him a call?"

"No, this is something I have to do on my own."

Orianna, the housekeeper, stepped out from the veranda. "Say Miz Evangeline, telegram just came." She waved the tan envelope, and Nell's mother met her halfway across the garden. Mama read it with a frown, putting her fist to her mouth, then rushed to Nell.

"Lady Mira. She's gone."

Jane Alistair had wired that Lady Mira passed peacefully from this earth in her sleep and would be laid to rest beside her beloved Nigel.

But a sentence at the end left Nell and her mother looking at one another in puzzlement.

```
Solicitor will be in touch with details of estate
STOP Prunella and Caroline named beneficiaries
```

The official word came a week later. Unknown to any of them, Lady Mira had modest holdings from her parents before her, most of which had been converted into cash and held by a solicitor in York, which was now bequeathed to Nell and her sister Caroline. Her house in Heathdown reverted to Preston, the possessions to be divided among Lady's Mira's four grandchildren, and a onetime benevolence given to each of her three faithful servants: Jane Alistair, Davenport, and Zilla Hatch.

It was recommended that an American solicitor handle the details of transfer, a process that could take sixty to ninety days.

It was a windfall Nell didn't expect, at a price that weighed heavily on her heart. She would never look into her grandmother's clear blue eyes again or touch her soft cheeks, but as she strolled in the garden a few days later, she felt her grandmother's presence. As clear as if they were in the same room, Nell thought she could hear the laughter of two childhood friends—Mira and Josie—together at last on the heavenly shore.

Nell signed a lease on the building in Louisville where she first made hats and took out a small loan to carry her until her grandmother's inheritance arrived.

On a bright, sunny day in late August, Nell sat by the window and worked the flexible buckram over the block, already envisioning the sky-blue felt she would apply over the foundation. A sketch of a nightingale was propped up against the bottle of sizing, and her fingers itched to embroider the tiny bird that would grace the hat.

Outside the window, a pair of workmen were hanging the new sign on wrought iron brackets. One of them stuck his head in the door. "Miss Marchwold. Can you come and have a look?"

She stood on the sidewalk and craned her neck, excitement skimming along her bones.

The Nightingale's Song Hat Shoppe.
Est. 1923.

"It's perfect," she hollered to the one on the ladder.

"I couldn't agree more." The voice came from behind her, and Nell thought for a moment she'd imagined it. She whirled around and came face-to-face with Quentin Bledsoe, a wide grin parting his lips.

"Quentin? What—? How did you find me? What are you doing here?"

"Which question do you want me to answer first?"

"Both, but you scared me half out of my wits. And you didn't tell me you were coming."

"It was a little difficult to find out exactly where you were, if you must know. Your friends in New York said you'd gone home to Kentucky. The only address I had was for your aunt's farm. I hired a driver to take me there when I arrived in Louisville, only to discover that you were back here all along."

He opened his arms and drew Nell into them, kissing the top of her head.

"Excuse me." One of the sign hangers tapped her on the shoulder. "I don't mean to interrupt, ma'am, but we're done here."

Nell's face flushed. "Yes. Okay. It's perfect, like I said. Shall I write you a check?"

"No, ma'am. We'll send you a bill. Thanks for the business."

"Thank you."

She turned back to Quentin. "Where were we?" Her heart pounded with a thousand questions, but the one foremost she blurted out. "You've come this far on your honeymoon? Where's Colleen?"

Quentin's shoulders sagged. "I have a lot to tell you."

"Then come inside, and I'll put the kettle on. Unless you'd like a lemonade. For that you'll have to wait while I run two doors down to the drugstore and get you one from the soda fountain."

"Tea's fine. Or nothing. Just seeing you is all I need right now."

Nell drank in the blue of his eyes, the freckles she'd memorized a lifetime ago, the fullness of his lips and waited to hear what he had to say.

"My soul-searching led me to the realization that I'd been premature in my commitment to Colleen, and when I gathered the nerve to break it off with her, she was relieved. She wasn't keen on being married to a clergyman."

"And now?" She chewed her bottom lip and closed her eyes, hoping for the answer she didn't believe she would ever hear, afraid her heart would crack if it wasn't.

"It was you I wanted all along. Like my choice of career, I was just too stubborn to hear God's voice. I know it's sudden and we'll need time, but I really want to make a fresh start and see where it leads."

"Yes" was the only syllable she could manage.

That grin again. The one that had stolen her twelve-year-old heart. Her stomach did a strange fox-trot. *Wherever you lead, I'll go.* She held her breath, afraid of breaking Mama's heart all over again if Quentin asked her to move to London. "How? Where?"

He moved closer and drew her into his arms, gently cupping her chin in his fingers. "I'm looking for a divinity school in America. I'm not sure how long it will take, but I know without a doubt that

I'm to be here. In the States. With you." His lips found hers, caressing them with tenderness.

Her heart rose to her throat as she kissed him back and whispered, "I love you, Quentin Bledsoe. I always have."

It was the song of her heart.

Reading Group Guide

1. The Roaring Twenties were a time of turmoil and extrava-
gance, Prohibition and gangsters, jazz music and fashions that
reflected the change from more gentle times. What are some of
the parallels of that to today? What uncertainties about today's
world concern you?

2. What are some of the fun things that you enjoyed reading about
this era? Is there a particular era that is your favorite to learn
and read about?

3. Nell, her mother, and younger sister lived in relative luxury
while in England. When they were displaced and came to
America, what challenges do you think they faced both living in
a different culture and on limited income? In what ways might
this have influenced Nell to succeed?

4. Nell was only nineteen when she moved to New York with
naive dreams of making a name for herself immediately. Were
her expectations realistic? How can you relate her struggles to
your own early dreams of what life would be like in the grown-
up world? What challenges have you faced in pursuing your
dreams?

5. Nell's grandmother gave her a sampler with the verse, "Strength

and honor are her clothing" (Proverbs 31:25), which became her compass to live by. What scriptures or quotes have helped you in making decisions or navigating difficult times in your life?

6. Quentin was Nell's first love. Do you think it's possible for young love to be the real thing? What experiences bound them? Were you surprised and/or pleased with the way their relationship turned out?

7. Oscar Fields was a difficult man to work for. In what ways did his intimidation of Nell make her stronger? What do you think his true feelings were about her talent? What motivated him to act the way he did?

8. Stammering usually has an organic basis, although it can stem from a trauma as Nell's did. How did her stammering affect her self-image and/or limit her? What childhood experiences or embarrassing moments have challenged your belief in yourself or been a stumbling block?

9. Nell was bullied as a child and again by Oscar Fields. Do you see bullying as a problem in today's world? Have you or has someone close to you ever been a victim of bullying, and if so, how did you handle it?

10. Nell used her talent to bring out the inner beauty of her clients. In what ways do you think this stemmed from her own need to feel worthy? Do you struggle with imperfections that affect your self-image? Name three positive qualities that you have.

If you liked *The Hatmaker's Heart*, don't miss Carla Stewart's
next 1920s novel,

A Flying Affair

High-spirited Mittie Humphreys has a passion for the exhilarating
thrill of the skies thanks to a young pilot named Ames. When her
parents agree to let her take flying lessons from an ace British pilot named Bobby, Mittie soon finds her affections torn between
the two aviators. As she competes in barnstorming events and an
all-woman cross-country competition, where Amelia Earhart is one
of the pilots, she discovers a secret that threatens her career, the romance she's embraced, and her family.

**Available from FaithWords in summer 2015 wherever books are
sold.**

More timeless fiction from Carla Stewart

Sweet Dreams

"*Sweet Dreams* is an inspiring novel and one that is heartfelt. Readers are sure to savor every page of this wonderful story."
—Michael Morris, author of *A Place Called Wiregrass*

In 1962, Dusty Fairchild and her cousin Paisley attend Miss Fontaine's, a finishing school in East Texas. Although their loyalty to each other binds them, when they fall in love with the same handsome young man, their relationship teeters on shaky ground.

Stardust

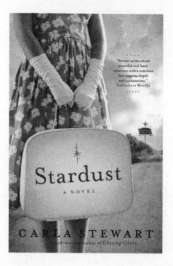

"*Stardust* is a smooth, inviting, well told story that will stick with you long after you read the last line and close the book. A worthy read."

—Rachel Hauck, award-winning author of *Dining with Joy*

When Georgia Peyton is suddenly widowed in 1952 with two young daughters, she tries to make a new life by taking over the run-down Stardust motel. But through her acquaintance with an unusual group of guests, she uncovers disturbing links to her past.

Broken Wings

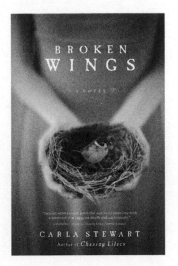

"*Broken Wings* is a captivating intergenerational tale of friendship, love, and music that surpasses the boundaries of age and time."
— Tina Ann Forkner, author of *Ruby Among Us* and *Rose House*

As a singing duo, Mitzi and Gabe Steiger captured America's heart for over two decades. Now, with Gabe slipping into the tangles of Alzheimer's, Mitzi ponders her future alone as a volunteer at the local hospital, where she meets a troubled young woman who needs her help.

Chasing Lilacs

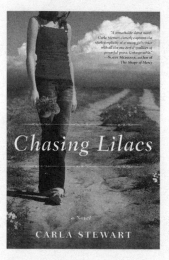

Winner of the 2011 Oklahoma Writers Federation, Inc.
Fiction Book of the Year

"Coming-of-age stories are a fiction staple, but well-done ones much rarer. This emotionally acute novel is one of the rare ones."
—*Publishers Weekly*, starred review

The summer of 1958 should be carefree for Sammie Tucker, but she has plenty of questions—about her mother's "nerve" problems, shock treatments, and whether her mother truly loves her. Soon Sammie must choose whom to trust with her deepest fears and learn to face the truth, which may be the hardest thing she's ever done.

Available from FaithWords wherever books are sold.